FRANCIS VIVIAN

THE SINGING MASONS

With an introduction by Curtis Evans

DEAN STREET PRESS

INTRODUCTION

SHORTLY BEFORE his death in 1951, American agriculturalist and scholar Everett Franklin Phillips, then Professor Emeritus of Apiculture (beekeeping) at Cornell University, wrote British newspaperman Arthur Ernest Ashley (1906-1979), author of detective novels under the pseudonym Francis Vivian, requesting a copy of his beekeeping mystery *The Singing Masons*, the sixth Inspector Gordon Knollis investigation, which had been published the previous year in the United Kingdom. The eminent professor wanted the book for Cornell's Everett F. Phillips Beekeeping Collection, "one of the largest and most complete apiculture libraries in the world" (currently in the process of digitization at Cornell's The Hive and the Honeybee website). Sixteen years later Ernest Ashely, or Francis Vivian as I shall henceforward name him, to an American fan requesting an autograph ("Why anyone in the United States, where I am not known," he self-deprecatingly observed, "should want my autograph I cannot imagine, but I am flattered by your request and return your card, duly signed.") declared that fulfilling Professor Phillip's donation request was his "greatest satisfaction as a writer." With ghoulish relish he added, "I believe there was some objection by the Librarian, but the good doctor insisted, and so in it went! It was probably destroyed after Dr. Phillips died. Stung to death."

After investigation I have found no indication that the August 1951 death of Professor Phillips, who was 73 years old at the time, was due to anything other than natural causes. One assumes that what would have been the painfully ironic demise of the American nation's most distinguished apiculturist from bee stings would have merited some mention in his death notices. Yet Francis Vivian's fabulistic claim otherwise provides us with a glimpse of that mordant sense of humor and storytelling relish which glint throughout the eighteen mystery novels Vivian published between 1937 and 1959.

Ten of these mysteries were tales of the ingenious sleuthing exploits of series detective Inspector Gordon Knollis, head of the Burnham C.I.D. in the first novel in the series and a Scotland Yard detective in the rest. (Knollis returns to Burnham in later novels.) The debut Inspector Knollis mystery, *The Death of Mr. Lomas*, which was published in 1941, is actually the seventh Francis Vivian detective novel. However, after the Second World War, when the author belatedly returned to his vocation of mystery writing, all of the remaining detective novels he published, with two exceptions, chronicle the criminal cases of the keen and clever Knollis. These other Inspector Knollis tales are: *Sable Messenger* (1947), *The Threefold Cord* (1947), *The Ninth Enemy* (1948), *The Laughing Dog* (1949), *The Singing Masons* (1950), *The Elusive Bowman* (1951), *The Sleeping Island* (1951), *The Ladies of Locksley* (1953) and *Darkling Death* (1956). (Inspector Knollis also is passingly mentioned in Francis Vivian's final mystery, published in 1959, *Dead Opposite the Church*.) By the late Forties and early Fifties, when Hodder & Stoughton, one of England's most important purveyors of crime and mystery fiction, was publishing the Francis Vivian novels, the Inspector Knollis mysteries had achieved wide popularity in the UK, where "according to the booksellers and librarians," the author's newspaper colleague John Hall later recalled in the *Guardian* (possibly with some exaggeration), "Francis Vivian was neck and neck with Ngaio Marsh in second place after Agatha Christie." (Hardcover sales and penny library rentals must be meant here, as with one exception--a paperback original--Francis Vivian, in great contrast with Crime Queens Marsh and Christie, both mainstays of Penguin Books in the UK, was never published in softcover.)

John Hall asserted that in Francis Vivian's native coal and iron county of Nottinghamshire, where Vivian from the 1940s through the 1960s was an assistant editor and "colour man" (writer of local color stories) on the Nottingham, or Notts, *Free Press*, the detective novelist "through a large stretch of the coalfield is reckoned the best local author after Byron and D. H. Lawrence." Hall added that "People who wouldn't know Alan

Sillitoe from George Eliot will stop Ernest in the street and tell him they solved his last detective story." Somewhat ironically, given this assertion, Vivian in his capacity as a founding member of the Nottingham Writers Club awarded first prize in a 1950 Nottingham writing competition to no other than 22-year-old local aspirant Alan Sillitoe, future "angry young man" author of *Saturday Night and Sunday Morning* (1958) and *The Loneliness of the Long Distance Runner* (1959). In his 1995 autobiography Sillitoe recollected that Vivian, "a crime novelist who earned his living by writing . . . gave [my story] first prize, telling me it was so well written and original that nothing further need be done, and that I should try to get it published." This was "The General's Dilemma," which Sillitoe later expanded into his second novel, *The General* (1960).

While never himself an angry young man (he was, rather, a "ragged-trousered" philosopher), Francis Vivian came from fairly humble origins in life and well knew how to wield both the hammer and the pen. Born on March 23, 1906, Vivian was one of two children of Arthur Ernest Ashley, Sr., a photographer and picture framer in East Retford, Nottinghamshire, and Elizabeth Hallam. His elder brother, Hallam Ashley (1900-1987), moved to Norwich and became a freelance photographer. Today he is known for his photographs, taken from the 1940s through the 1960s, chronicling rural labor in East Anglia (many of which were collected in the 2010 book *Traditional Crafts and Industries in East Anglia: The Photographs of Hallam Ashley*). For his part, Francis Vivian started working at age 15 as a gas meter emptier, then labored for 11 years as a housepainter and decorator before successfully establishing himself in 1932 as a writer of short fiction for newspapers and general magazines. In 1937, he published his first detective novel, *Death at the Salutation*. Three years later, he wed schoolteacher Dorothy Wallwork, with whom he had one daughter.

After the Second World War Francis Vivian's work with the Notts *Free Press* consumed much of his time, yet he was still able for the next half-dozen years to publish annually a detective novel (or two), as well as to give popular lectures on a plethora of intriguing subjects, including, naturally enough, crime, but also fiction writing (he published two guidebooks on that subject), psychic forces (he believed himself to be psychic), black magic, Greek civilization, drama, psychology and beekeeping. The latter occupation he himself took up as a hobby, following in the path of Sherlock Holmes. Vivian's fascination with such esoterica invariably found its way into his detective novels, much to the delight of his loyal readership.

As a detective novelist, John Hall recalled, Francis Vivian "took great pride in the fact that the reader could always arrive at a correct solution from the given data. His Inspector never picked up an undisclosed clue which, it was later revealed, held the solution to the mystery all along." Vivian died on April 2, 1979, at the respectable if not quite venerable age of 73, just like Professor Everett Franklin Phillips. To my knowledge the late mystery writer had not been stung to death by bees.

Curtis Evans

For so work the honey-bees;
Creatures that, by a rule in nature, teach
The act of order to a peopled kingdom.
They have a king, and officers of sorts:
Where some, like magistrates, correct at home;
Others, like merchants, venture trade abroad;
Others, like soldiers, armed in their stings,
Make boot upon the summer's velvet buds;
Which pillage they with merry march bring home
To the tent-royal of their emperor:
Who, busied in his majesty, surveys
The singing masons building roofs of gold;
The civil citizens kneading up the honey;
The poor mechanic porters crowding in
Their heavy burdens at his narrow gate;
The sad-ey'd justice, with his surly hum
Delivering o'er to executors pale
The lazy yawning drone."

Henry V, Act I, Scene ii.

WITH THANKS TO ALL THE EXPERTS
WHO HAVE ASSISTED ME,
NOT FORGETTING
JJL
AND
THE SINGING MASONS

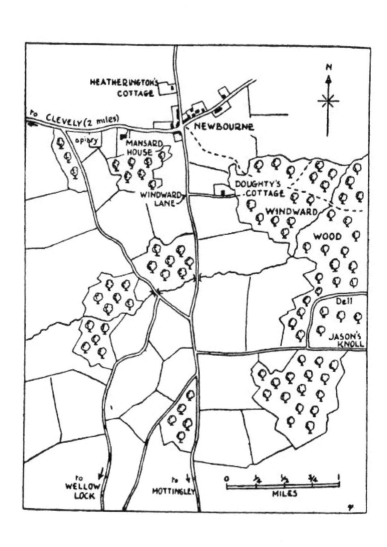

HEATHERINGTON'S COTTAGE

N

To CLEVELY (2 miles)

NEWBOURNE

apiary

MANSARD HOUSE

DOUGHTY'S COTTAGE

WINDWARD LANE

WINDWARD

WOOD

Dell

JASON'S KNOLL

to WELLOW LOCK

to MOTTINGLEY

0   ¼   ½   ¾   1
MILES

Chapter I
THE TESTIMONY OF THE MASONS

THERE IS NO such thing as chance, said Voltaire; we have invented this word to express the known effect of every unknown cause.

Detective Inspector Gordon Knollis, after twenty-five years of police work, heartily agreed with him, although at first he looked down his long thin nose and was hard put to it to explain the peculiar workings of circumstance that led Old Heatherington from his home garden in Newbourne to the cottage of the late Mrs. Roxana Doughty in Windward Lane, half a mile outside the village, on a warm July morning.

Samuel Heatherington was a retired carpenter and wheelwright, seventy-two years of age, grey-haired, straight-backed, kindly eyed, and a bee-master of the old school. He'd helped with bees since he was twelve, and kept them himself since he was eighteen, and what he didn't know about them and their ways wasn't worth knowing; reputed experts often made their way to his door, to sit and sip the nectar of experience.

Telling his story later that day to Inspector Wilson of the Borough of Clevely C.I.D., he said, with what to Wilson seemed an unnecessary wealth of detail, that at half-past ten on this morning of the seventh of July he'd pulled on his white linen jacket, not so clean as it used to be in the days when his wife was alive, and walked to the bottom of the garden, there to relax on the rustic bench he'd made long years before, to smoke the twist tobacco which he favoured, and watch the busy alighting-boards of his twelve beehives.

There was unusual activity on the board of the third hive on the front row, an activity that told him his eyes were indeed failing, that he'd missed a queen cell when going through the hive, and that the stock were about to swarm.

The bees reminded him of a group of village women preparing for an annual outing from the chapel. Some trotted from the interior of the hive, seemed to chat with other bees, and hurried back indoors as if they'd forgotten something, or had a message to leave. Others wiped their faces as if dabbing a final touch of powder on a shiny spot. Others took off to circumnavigate the hive and land again with weather reports. All were waiting for the signal to leave their home and go out into the world to found a new colony, obeying the primal order that all living things shall endure, shall multiply, and endeavour to cover the earth.

He had expected this stock to swarm, although he had tried to prevent them. They were strong and healthy, with a last year's queen rich in fecundity. Normally, he cut out the queen cells as they appeared, but he had missed one this time, and now a new queen had emerged and was prepared to take over the duties of the old queen, releasing her to lead out a balanced proportion of young bees to produce wax and build comb, old bees to search the fields and meadows for nectar and pollen with which to feed the egg and larvae, and drones taken along in case the old queen failed the hive, when a new queen would be raised from one of her eggs to be fertilized by the fastest and strongest drone in her nuptial flight high above the earth.

He waited with a patience born of the years. Above him and around him sounded the music of the bees, Shakespeare's singing masons. Bees going out to forage, bees returning with their honey-stomachs filled with the early morning nectar, bees with their pollen baskets piled high with white, green, or golden bee-flour, to be made into bee-bread; a constant hum, lulling and soothing.

The roar within the hive increased in volume. Bees poured out on the alighting-board, paused a moment to fill their bodies with air, and launched themselves into space. By the thousand they poured out, and within a few minutes the air was thick with circling bees, a dark whirling mass of excitement.

Old Heatherington watched them closely. A thin stream, not unlike the tail of a dark comet, began to detach itself from the nebula, and slowly reached out to the highest branch of an apple tree ten yards away.

He went to his workshop for an extension ladder, and when he returned the mass of bees were hanging from the branch in a great cluster. A few bees darted off in all directions, seeking a new home. They returned to the swarm to run busily over the backs of their clinging sisters as if passing on glad news.

The old man slowly and cautiously manoeuvred the head of the ladder through the branches until it found a safe resting-place. Satisfied that both head and foot were secure, he went to the honey-house for a straw skep and a smoker. He looked up at the swarm, nodded his head, and laid the smoker aside; he could take 'em without it. He tested the first rung of the ladder, and began to climb, easing the branches as he went, and taking care not to shake the tree and disturb the swarm.

It was then he danged the bees, although without malice, for, as he tried to wedge the skep in the fork of two branches, the swarm decided it was time to move; returning scouts had brought news of a suitable home found and ready for occupation.

He wasted no more time. He dropped the skep to the ground and came down the ladder. He picked up the skep and the smoker, and walked through the garden and round the cottage to the front gate, from where he watched the direction being taken by the colonists. He grunted, and danged them a second time; they were making across the meadows to the woods down Windward Lane.

He spotted a lad cycling down the street and hailed him. Was he doing anything in particular? The lad wasn't. Would he cycle after the swarm and try to find where they settled—it was worth five bob! The lad was willing to earn five bob, and set off up the Mottingley Road as if racing for a trophy at Herne Hill.

Old Heatherington followed slowly on foot, jog-trotting up the road with the skep and the smoker, and the veil which he always carried in an inside pocket. Half a mile out of the village he came to the entrance to Windward Lane, an old track leading to nowhere in particular unless it was to the five-barred gate giving on to Windward Wood half a mile on.

Peering along the lane, he saw the lad, leaning on the saddle of his cycle and pointing over the hedge. He shouted something indistinguishable. Old Heatherington waved back and ambled down the lane, his feet well spread out and his long legs taking strides which covered a deceptive length of ground.

"They've gone somewhere up the old lady's garden," said the lad. "I dussn't go no farther. They sting."

"That's all right," said Old Heatherington. "You wait here in case I need anything fetching from home. That all right, lad?"

It was, for the lad still hadn't got his five bob. The old man pushed open the white-painted gate, and marched up the path to the white-walled and thatched cottage. The idea of calling it a cottage amused him, as he pointed out to the impatient Inspector Wilson; it was bigger than three like his own, but then the late owner, who'd died early in the year, had been a wealthy woman and could afford to add bits here and there, and knock an old dairy into the house; a writer woman she was, who wrote love novels and seemingly made money with them. She'd a nephew in Clevely, the market town three miles away, and it was said he stood fair to come into everything she left, if only they could find him. He'd taken off somewhere about a month back, and the lawyers were still trying to find him to tell him about his luck. All these things went through his mind as he walked up the path, he said, and Wilson sat back and sighed, realizing the old man would have to tell the story his own way or not at all.

The cottage was unoccupied, so Old Heatherington had no need to knock on the door and inquire if it was all right for him to collect his bees. He followed the flagged path round the western end of the house, and walked across the wide lawn, through the rosery and the kitchen garden, and then paused and stared.

At the far end of the orchard was a hive, and that was queer, because old Mrs. Doughty hadn't liked bees, and although he'd tried to convert her more than once she stuck to her opinion that bees were nasty stinging insects and she wouldn't have them on the place.

The bees were there all right. Some had already gone in the hive, and the rest, as was their fashion, were playing round on the alighting-board. Perhaps a dozen or more were standing in the entrance, their heads down, their behinds in the air, their wings rotating at a fantastic rate as they ejected the scent from an abdominal gland to notify stragglers of the site of their new home.

He watched them for a time, and then decided to lift the roof and see what was happening inside. It was all right if the hive was fitted with a brood box and frames of comb; the bees could go to work in an orderly fashion as required by the bee-keeper, but if it was an empty shell they would build comb all over the place, wasting time and wax. He gently raised the roof. The hive was empty of everything but bees, and it was one of the strongest swarms he had seen for many a long year.

He went back to the lad in the lane. "You can use a telephone? Then here's your five bob, and twopence for a call. Hurry to the box outside the post office and ring up Mr. Maynard at Mansard House—Clevely 732. Got that? Tell him I've a prime swarm for him—that's the first swarm from a hive, and he's to come and fetch it straight away. Now don't forget to tell him where I am, will you? Tell him to bring his own tackle."

He returned to the hive, and it was then, as he told the impatiently listening Wilson, that he began to ponder on the queer thing of the hive being here at all. Mrs. Doughty had been very definite about not keeping bees, although he'd pointed out that a nicely painted W.B.C. hive, so called after a Mr. William Broughton Carr who invented it, was a decoration in a garden, and apart from that there was the pollination value, and the honey harvest.

Mrs. Doughty told him very firmly that she didn't want bees, had no intention of having a nice hive, empty or full, painted or not, in or near or around any garden belonging to her. If she saw a bee in the house she would swat it as she did flies and wasps, and what was more she intended from now on to spray all her fruit trees with D.D.T., which she understood was fatal to honey-bees. "So don't keep on at me, you—you bee-keeper!"

All of which proved that it couldn't have been put there by Mrs. Roxana Doughty, late of this parish!

So where had it come from, sir?

It was standing on two flagstones, which looked as if they'd been taken up from the path, and from just outside the doors of the two disused outhouses. The stones were standing on red bricks, around the edges of which green moss was growing. That was no place to stand a hive! Bees can stand cold, they can stand heat, but damp is fatal to them. Which made it all the queerer!

Still, his bees wouldn't have to live on this damp spot. The Maynards, Phil and Georgie, could have this swarm, and for nothing. He felt sorry for them. They'd had some awful danged luck since they got married. First Phil went into the Army, got out to Burma, was taken ill and shipped home. He spent two years in Rossall Sanatorium, getting rid of the tuberculosis trouble in his left lung. Then, when he got out he and his wife sank all their savings, such as they were, in trying to make a go of small-holding at Mansard House, half a mile out of Newbourne, on the Clevely Road.

Nothing went right for them. They got virus in the soft fruit and it had to be destroyed. The apple and pear trees took on some queer disease and failed. To top it up, foul brood—the foot-and-mouth disease of bee-keeping somehow got into the apiary and they had to kill off and burn all their stocks, and that nearly finished them.

As if that wasn't enough, they'd planned to open up out-apiaries at Farndon Howe and Wellow Lock, and the honey-house at Wellow went up in flames, and nigh on a hundred pounds' worth of equipment was lost.

It made you wonder about Mrs. Doughty and all her money. Georgie was her niece, of course, but the old girl refused to help them with a single shilling, saying she'd fought her own way through difficulties and it was character-forming; if she helped them it would rob them of their independence and their will to fight, and she wasn't going to be responsible for such a thing. Solid enough as talk, but hardly human. She'd been a hard-souled old girl if ever there was one! He only hoped she'd left them a bit of something in her will, and not left it all to the missing scapegoat nephew—Georgie's cousin—who did nothing but chase young girls and try to run away with married women.

The noise of a car engine joined the hum of the bees, and died away at the gate. Philip and Georgie Maynard joined him, carrying the travelling box in which they'd take away the bees.

Phil Maynard was a pale, lank young fellow of thirty-two, with pale grey eyes, and straight brown hair that had no stiffening in it and just hung over his well-shaped head like wet hay. He seemed a negative individual until you got to know him, and then you discovered he was as tough as willow-wood—he could bend without breaking, which was perhaps as well considering what he'd gone through one way or another.

Georgie, now Georgie was all life and energy, an eager little person, only an inch or so above five feet. She was comfortably plump, with a rosy-cheeked round face, and big blue eyes always shining with interest in the life going on around her. Her hair was jet black and glossy, twisted into tight coils over her ears. She'd a nice mouth, too; her lower lip a perfect crescent, and her upper one a perfect bow, and all without the help of chemists' stuff.

A lovable little person was Georgie, and Old Heatherington smiled happily at her as she stood beside him, not coming up to his shoulder, in lightish-brown slacks, a champagne-coloured blouse, and a brown waistcoat which she'd told him was really called a bolero—although it still looked like a waistcoat to him.

A gallant little lass, and, without her, Phil, for all his willow-toughness, would have been like a drifting ship; no engine, no steering, no anchor, and no harbour—simply because without her there would have been no incentive to continue the struggle.

She had her own bit of bad luck this year, the night of the fire. That was only a month ago, as he reminded Inspector Wilson. She had to be rushed to a nursing home when they got back from the ruins at Wellow Lock. Baby trouble it was. She'd gone straight on the operation-table, and when she came off she'd lost her baby. What was more, she couldn't have another. So now she and Phil were everything to each other, with Old Heatherington, alone in the world himself, standing over their bee-keeping and gardening endeavours like a benevolent guardian angel.

"The story, man, the story!" moaned Wilson.

Aye, well, the old man had his own way of setting about jobs, and he lowered frames of comb into the empty hive and coaxed the bees to climb on them. He looked anxiously for the queen, and once he saw her clinging there with her sisters he relaxed, because he knew when she was in the travelling-box the others would soon follow. In an hour or so the ventilated lid of the box was fastened down by four thumb-screws.

It was then he'd pointed out the dampness of the ground to Phil and Georgie, warning them to avoid any such sites in their own bee-keeping.

"Is there a brook in the vicinity?" Phil wondered.

The old man snapped his fingers. "There's a spring in the middle of the field beyond the wood—y'know, behind the tongue of wood that stretches out. It must run this way."

It was Georgie who suggested there might be a well under the flagstones.

"Might be!" Old Heatherington agreed.

"A well!" enthused Georgie. "I love wells—they're so romantic. I wish we had one in the garden. You know, with a red-tiled roof standing on red brick pillars, and a roller and a handle so you could wind up the bucket. It's grand fun!"

"Until you have to get your house-water from one," grunted the practical Philip.

"Let's see if it really is a well!" Georgie pleaded.

"Let's get home with the swarm," said Philip.

"The well," said Georgie.

Old Heatherington thought it might be a good idea. He hated leaving things without knowing what they were all about. "Let's humour her, Phil lad," he said.

They took the hive to pieces, laying the gabled roof, the lifts, and the floorboard under the lee of the hedge.

The old man got his fingers under the corner of one of the stones and tried to lift it. Phil joined him, and together they stood it on end. Warning Georgie to watch her toes, they threw the stone on its back.

"It really is a well!" Georgie enthused. "But what a queer smell!"

Phil and the old man knelt beside her and peered into the gloomy depths. Then Phil sat back on his heels and looked curiously at Old Heatherington.

"It's like the stuff we killed my bees with!"

"Cyanide," nodded the old man.

"There's something down here," said Phil, bending over the mouth of the well. "The sun's rays light up this side of the shaft. . . ."

"We need a torch."

"There's one in the car," said Georgie. "I'll fetch it for you. I wonder what's down there?"

Old Heatherington and Phil looked at each other with searching eyes as Georgie hurried away.

"I'd send her to the phone box," said the old man. "Get her out of the way."

"Who's she to phone?" asked Phil.

Old Heatherington didn't answer. When Georgie came back with the torch he shone it into the depths of the well. There was water at the foot of the shaft. Something dark and mis-shapen was huddled against the brickwork. He handed the torch to Phil and got to his feet.

"Georgie," he said, "will you take the swarm home and put it in a shady place until to-night. Then ring the Clevely police—I think Inspector Wilson's the man you want. Tell him to come straight out here, please."

"There's—there's something . . . ?" she whispered, nodding towards the well.

"Something horrible, Georgie," said the old man.

"Something nasty in the woodshed," she giggled. Then laughed nervously, and clasped her hands together.

Philip got up, looking sickly pale.

Georgie ran to him and grasped his arm. "What—what is it, Phil?"

Phil looked over her shoulder at the old man, and then down into her dark-blue eyes, wide with wonder.

"It's your cousin Jerry," he said.

* * *

"And that's how it all came about," said Old Heatherington.

"You were led to the body by a swarm of bees!"

"You can say that," said the old man. "Shakespeare knew the wisdom of the bees—*creatures by a rule in nature, teach the act of order to a peopled kingdom.* That's *Henry the Fifth*, act one—"

"Quite!" Inspector Wilson said impatiently. He turned to his sergeant, who was putting a reporter's note-book and a pen into his pocket. "Sergeant Coxon, will you please run Mr. Heatherington home in the car?"

Chapter II
OLD HEATHERINGTON
REPEATS HIMSELF

GORDON KNOLLIS was slightly above medium height, and slimly built. He had a long nose and keen grey eyes. His lips were thin and tight, although revealing signs of a sense of humour lurking behind the mask-like and expressionless face. There were two perpendicular wrinkles at the root of his nose, caused by his habit of frowning when in deep thought, which was during most of his waking life.

Inspector Osiah Wilson, waiting for him at nine o'clock the next morning, raised a doubtful eyebrow as he watched him step from the train. Dressed neatly in a grey lounge suit, the fellow walked with a back like a ramrod, and his chin just half an inch too high in the air, as if he was constantly under the impression that he was mixing with people inferior to himself.

Wilson groaned. The man might be the most uncomfortable companion. It looked as if he was accustomed to having his own way; there was something about the cut of his jib that denoted the lone worker and the perfect organizer—the fellow who sat in the middle of the web and told everybody else what to do, he acting as clearing-house and sole arbiter. He sighed. Even murder cases didn't last for ever, thank goodness!

He ran a hand over his fresh-complexioned face and was satisfied with its morning smoothness. He patted down his near-ginger hair, buttoned up his double-breasted jacket, and stepped forward to meet the man from the Yard.

"Inspector Knollis? I'm Wilson, Borough C.I.D. Thought I'd meet you myself."

Much to his surprise, the mask dissolved into a friendly smile, and a firm enough grip seized his outstretched hand.

"Yes, I'm Knollis. Nice of you to come down. Quite a case you've got on hand, I believe."

Wilson sought for a word, and waved a vague hand when Knollis released it. "It's—unusual. Not what you'll regard as a difficult case, but unusual. You've seen the morning papers on your way down?"

"There's little enough in them," said Knollis as he fell in step beside Wilson on the way to the barrier. "Merely said this Batley man, missing for a month, had been found in the garden of an unoccupied cottage on the outskirts of Newbourne village. You didn't tell my Super much, apart from the fact that the man was found in the well."

"That was the C.C.," grumbled Wilson, referring to the Chief Constable of the County. "I think he's a bit scared of the job. First real murder we've had while he's been at Mottingley. All the usual kid murders, and hot-blooded bashings, of course, but not a story-book affair like this."

Knollis surrendered his ticket at the barrier and followed Wilson to the waiting car. "Found in a well, eh?" he murmured.

"Two feet six of water in it," Wilson said laconically. "The well itself twenty-five feet deep and three feet in diameter. He'd a canister of cyanide in his pocket—or what was left of it, a cardboard affair with a tin bottom and tin lever lid, and two inches high and three-quarters of an inch across. He'd been socked behind the head, dropped down the well, and left. The water penetrated the canister, gas was generated, and that was the end of him! Two flagstones had been taken from a path and placed over the mouth, and a beehive had been stuck over the stones."

"Not a very wide well, surely?" asked Knollis, trying to visualize it.

Wilson shook his head as they were driven away from the station. "I asked about that. It was sunk years ago to tap a spring for garden-watering. There used to be a hand-worked rotary pump over it, with a narrow-bore pipe down the shaft—y'know the kind of thing!"

"And he vanished a whole month ago," Knollis said in a wondering voice.

"Seventh of June," said Wilson. "He was courting Daphne Moreland, daughter of the town's star lawyer. Bit of a philanderer was Batley, but he was sticking to Miss Moreland. She's money of her own, and will have a lot more when the old man pegs out. The cottage was his late aunt's—she was Roxana Doughty, the writer of romantic love novels. Believe she made a packet from the things. She left him the cottage in her will."

"He was living there?" asked Knollis.

Wilson pulled doubtfully on his ear. "Dunno for sure. I think he intended doing so—in fact he might have just moved in. It's uncertain. There was a hat and an unpacked suit-case in the cottage, and an unpacked parcel of food in the kitchen cabinet. The loaf of bread was hard and mouldy. Oh, and a queer thing! Both doors were locked on the inside, and the kitchen window was closed, but unlatched."

"He hadn't settled in then," said Knollis.

"Looks that way," said Wilson, "although it also looks very much as if he intended staying, doesn't it? There were two bedrooms, a single one and a double one. The sheets of the single bed were turned down, and there was a hot-water bottle in it."

"I see," murmured Knollis as the car drew up outside the police station, which was the divisional headquarters.

Neither he nor Wilson made any move to leave the car.

"Who reported him as missing?" asked Knollis.

"Miss Moreland," replied Wilson. "According to her story, he was supposed to be taking her to a flannel dance on the night of the eighth. He didn't call for her, so she rang him. No reply, so she went round in her car—she runs a sporty little aluminium-bodied Oberon. She seems to have known of his liking for the girls, and wondered if he'd cooked up another date and was letting her drop for the occasion. She got no reply to her ringing and knocking when she got to his flat—we've a block of service flats in Grafton Gate, and he occupied one on the second floor—so she went off in a huff to the dance and alone. He didn't show in.

"Next morning she rang again, to give him the works, and then rang his office when she couldn't get him—he worked as chief assistant to Shipley, an auctioneer, estate agent, and valuer. The office boy reported that Batley hadn't shown in for two days, so she went to see her father at his office. Moreland rang me, and sent his daughter round. I had a chat with her, and then went to the flat to make inquiries . . ."

He paused, and then added: "I could kick myself now!"

"Why?" asked Knollis. It was evident he was expected to ask something, and then attempt to mollify his new colleague.

"I never suspected it would end in murder," Wilson said, glumly. "I got the caretaker to let me in with the master-key, and the place was upside down. Looked as if he'd made up his mind in a hurry, turned all his belongings on the floor, sorted out what he wanted, and then scrammed. I rang Miss Moreland from there, and she was able to tell me what he had in the way of suit-cases, travelling trunks, and so on, and so found one suit-case missing. There was nothing I could do; he'd apparently cleared out on his own choosing, and that was all there was to it."

"Why should he?" asked Knollis, staring straight through the wind-screen.

"Quite frankly," replied Wilson, "I thought he'd done a bunk with some married woman and her husband was keeping quiet to save his own face. Batley had quite a reputation that way. Shipley'd threatened to sack him more than once—and that makes you wonder how a nice girl like Daphne Moreland could get stuck on him. Still!"

"They do it," Knollis said softly. "The way of a man with a maid. Some girls like treating badly."

"Shipley was darn decent to him," added Wilson. "He took him on when he first started work, trained him, and when Batley went into the Navy during the war, Shipley paid his salary as usual. Batley was a lieutenant in destroyers. Shipley took him on again when he was released, and, although fed-up with his making love to clients, had to admit the fellow knew his job and wasn't afraid of work."

Knollis nodded absently. "What's Miss Moreland like?"

Wilson toyed with the door handle. "Nice girl. One of those tall and willowy wenches with long arms and legs and a high waist. Fair almost to blondeness, china-blue eyes, and a delicate complexion. A high-cheeked intellectual type who reads the Book of the Month, *John o' London's*, and *The Times Literary Supplement*. She's in the Amateur Dramatic Society, and the Musical Society. High-cheeked, high-waisted, high-breasted and high-minded; that's Miss Daphne Moreland!"

"Doesn't seem to match with all you've told me about Batley," murmured Knollis. "Must have been the attraction of opposites."

Wilson smiled a dry and almost sardonic smile.

"You didn't know Batley, of course, and you won't get much of an idea of his physical attractions from what's lying in the mortuary. A month in water doesn't improve the appearance of humanity!"

"You're telling me," said Knollis. "Water's as bad as fire in a different way."

"Anyway," went on Wilson, "Batley was a sort of Byron without the intellect or the deep soulfulness. Tall bloke with handsome features, and lovely shiny black hair with natural waves—many a girl would have given her future for hair like his! And he'd deep blue eyes with dark lashes. The debonair and nonchalant type. Played tennis with a dash and a gesture, and walked about Clevely as if he owned it instead of trying to sell it for Shipley. Gerald Batley was a personable type. Had to put my thumb on my own daughter last year when she got a crush on him."

"And you got no clue to his whereabouts until his body was discovered?"

"Not a sausage," Wilson said in a tone of deep disgust. "I didn't know about the cottage then. That was where Shipley slipped. He'd handled Mrs. Doughty's affairs for years, and must have known it had gone to Batley, so surely he could have suspected that Batley had returned the compliment and gone to the cottage! Incidentally, there were six labourers' cottages in Newbourne; Shipley was to sell them, and the proceeds were to go to Batley with the rest."

"Perhaps Shipley didn't want to think about it?" Knollis suggested.

"That's it," nodded Wilson. "Probably suspected he was there with a woman, and didn't want to get mixed in any trouble that might follow. Can't blame him, really."

"Who found the body?" asked Knollis.

"Talkative old man from Newbourne, a bee-keeper. One of his hives swarmed and instead of staying at home took off across country to the Doughty cottage. He got a lad on a bike to follow them, and eventually found them setting up home in an empty hive—the one I've told you about. According to his story, bees aren't supposed to live in damp spots, and there was moss round the bricks under the stones. He investigated, and found Batley. He had a young couple with him, having decided to give the swarm to them, and having sent the lad to 'phone them and bring whatever tackle was needed."

"Know 'em?" Knollis murmured.

"They're a nice young couple by the name of Maynard. Mrs. Maynard was Batley's cousin. Mrs. Doughty, Batley's mother, and Mrs. Maynard's mother were sisters."

"I see. What's the medical report?"

"Post-mortem's this afternoon, but interim report says he's been dead three weeks to a month, and death was caused by the cyanide. The knock on the head could have done no more than lay him out."

Knollis's right hand played the piano on his knee. "Mm! He disappeared on the eighth of June. . . ."

"I didn't say that," Wilson corrected him hurriedly. "I said Miss Moreland missed him on that date. She wasn't due to see him on the seventh. On the other hand, Shipley's report that he didn't turn up for work on the seventh indicates that he went missing on that day."

"He lived in a service flat," said Knollis. "What about his meals? Have they been checked?"

"He took breakfast on the seventh, but the girl got no reply when she tried to get in on the morning of the eighth, so it would seem he went between breakfast-time on the seventh and ditto on the eighth. Oh, and some grub was missed from the kitchen during the morning of the eighth. The house-keeper says she's never had occasion to lock food up, and so we'll assume he helped himself to the stuff found out at the cottage."

Wilson wound the window to the top and then wound it down again.

"There's another interesting point, Knollis. His car is kept in the garages at the rear of the block, and it wasn't taken out."

"This cottage is in the country?"

"That's the case," said Wilson. "Newbourne's three miles from us, and the cottage is up—or down—a nice quiet lane, Windward Lane, half a mile through Newbourne. You go into the village and turn right up the Mottingley Road; the lane's off to the left."

"Bus service?" Knollis asked briefly, still staring at the windscreen as if it was a cinema screen.

"There is one," said Wilson, "but the first bus from Mottingley to Newbourne, and its counterpart working the opposite way, doesn't start until ten-thirty. You see, in that case he'd have to get from here to Newbourne, and either walk to the lane-end, or catch the first bus, and, in that case, as I see it, he couldn't have got to the cottage without somebody noticing him. And again, I can't see Batley walking, especially with that suit-case. He wasn't renowned for taking exercise unless there was a crowd of females present to watch and admire him—hence his passion for tennis. No, I've got chaps checking that walking angle, but don't expect positive results. My guess is that he went in some-body else's car."

"The one owned by the bloke who bumped him off!"

"That's it," said Wilson.

"I'd like to see the cottage, and the old man who found him," said Knollis.

"Then let's get going before the County blokes catch you," said Wilson. He bent forward and touched the driver on the shoulder. "Newbourne, Dexter, and please slow down passing the Maynard home."

Knollis's thoughts were his own as they drove along, and ac-companied by, of all things, a lullaby hummed by Wilson in a minor key.

"On your right," said Wilson, after a few minutes. "That's the Maynard apiary; you'll hear more of it when we meet the old man."

He indicated an orchard of twisted and gnarled apple and pear trees, among which were set several rows of white and whitish hives.

"Quite a picture!" Knollis remarked appreciatively.

"The meadow between here and the house doesn't belong to them," said Wilson, "but here's the house."

Knollis liked the look of it. It was an oblong building of plum-red bricks, with tall chimneys and a mansard roof. The front lawn was well-cut and neatly trimmed round the edges. Looking quickly down the drive that ran along the right side of the house he saw long herbaceous borders, alive with flowers, and beyond them a glimpse of a large lawn behind the house.

"Nice place, Wilson!" said Knollis. "So Mrs. Maynard is Bat-ley's cousin."

Wilson looked curiously at him as the car was slipped into top gear again. "Yes. Why?"

"The Maynards are bee-keepers."

Wilson nodded silently.

"There was a beehive standing over the mouth of the well."

"Yes, I said so."

"Batley was coming into his aunt's money."

"That's a fair recapitulation of what I've told you."

"And the Maynards are nice people. . . ."

Wilson half-turned in his seat. "What are you getting at?" he demanded.

"Merely reciting the facts as given," Knollis replied blandly. "The facts of a murder case are like the lines of a poem or song—they make sense only if you get them in the right order."

Wilson grunted, and stared at the passing scene as they drove into Newbourne village and pulled up before Old Heatherington's cottage. He left the car and went to the back door, returning with the old man, who nodded to Knollis and stood looking down at him through the side-window with a quizzical expression, meanwhile stroking his close-cropped grey head and fingering his wispy and tobacco-stained moustache.

Knollis opened the door and smiled into the old man's pale eyes. "Mr. Heatherington?"

"Aye," said the old man. "The Inspector tells me you're from the famous Scotland Yard, and that means you're an expert. I like meeting such, because I'm one myself, but on bees only, mind you, only on bees!"

"On crime only," Knollis smiled back. "Only on crime."

Old Heatherington chuckled. "Make room for an old chap, sir—or perhaps I'd better sit in front with the driver. My legs take up a lot of room. You'll have to spare me an hour some time to tell me about your adventures with murderers."

"And you must do the same about bees," said Knollis. "For the time being I want to know how you found the body yesterday."

Wilson muttered directions to the driver, got in, and slammed the door.

"The bees led me to him," said Old Heatherington, glancing at Knollis through the driving mirror over the wind-screen. He plunged his hand into the pocket of his once-white linen jacket and went to work with pipe and pouch. "I think they wanted me to find him, sir. The Inspector shut me down when I wanted to tell him what Shakespeare said about them—"

"I was busy with other things," snapped Wilson. The old man smiled. "You can never be too busy to listen to William Shakespeare, sir. He's wisdom and advice for every occasion."

"That's true enough," said Knollis, "but he hadn't met a modern murder case!"

"You call 'em modern just because they happen now instead of then," the old man retorted calmly between puffs as he lit his pipe. "A murder in his day would be called modern then—if you don't mind me correcting you. Modern just means the new thing at the time, and I wouldn't like to say that murders were done for any different reasons now than then."

"You're right, of course," Knollis granted, "but about this business yesterday—you had witnesses to the discovery, I understand."

"My young friends, the Maynards, sir. I wanted to help them by giving them the swarm. They've had some real bad luck this year, until it looks as if Providence doesn't want them to get on, or is trying them to the utmost for some reason or other."

"I can tell you all that later, Knollis," Wilson interrupted impatiently. "Mr. Heatherington told me the whole thing yesterday."

"Aye, but the gentleman perhaps wants to know now," the old man chided him. "You see, sir, it started with the currants, rasps and gooseberries. They just went wrong, with the leaves hanging off them like bits of brown paper. Virus trouble, Philip said it was. He dug up the lot and burned them, and although he's put new canes and bushes in another part of the garden he'll get nothing from them this year. Then some blight hit the pears and apples just as the fruit was setting, and whatever it was it doesn't look to me as if the trees'll be any more good. After that came the bee trouble . . ."

"What was that?" Knollis asked as the old man paused to suck his pipe.

"Foul brood, the American sort. It's the disease that sends larvae rotten in their cells, and you have to kill off and burn all your stocks. Goes through the apiary like a dose of salts."

"Bad luck," said Knollis. He was suddenly aware of the car running slow, giving the old man time to tell his story before they arrived at the cottage. He then realized that Wilson was not so impatient or bad-tempered as he appeared to be. He'd arranged this as they left the village, knowing he'd get more information out of the old man by trying to stop him talking than by encouraging him.

"They were starting two out-apiaries," went on Old Heatherington. "They built a sectional honey-house at Wellow Lock, and moved there all the stuff they'd need—everything barring bees. It was all stored in the honey-house and the lot went up in flames one night last month."

"What night?" Knollis asked quickly.

"The night she went in hospital."

It was Wilson who spoke next. "The morning of the seventh!"

The old man nodded. "Aye, the early hours of the morning it was, but you call it night, don't you?"

"Common usage," said Knollis.

"The police fetched him out," went on the old man. "They called for me on the way, but it was too late to do anything although the firemen played on it for an hour. The lot went up, and I reckon they lost the worst part of a hundred pounds that night. Mrs. Maynard—Georgie as I call her, was expecting a baby, and she was taken ill after they got home and had to be rushed into a nursing home for an emergency operation. She lost the baby and can't have any more," he ended laconically, and puffed stoically at his pipe.

At the cottage Wilson led the way to the far end of the orchard, and indicated the well. "We had a job getting him out. I daren't risk sending a man down, so we had to fish for him. He got damaged in transit. You know what water does to a corpse, as we've already agreed."

Knollis turned from the well to the hive, now re-assembled and standing under the hedge. "Mrs. Doughty kept bees, Mr. Heatherington?"

"Couldn't bear 'em, sir!"

"Any idea where the hive came from?"

The old man shrugged. "Could have come from almost anywhere. It's a W.B.C., called after the initials of the inventor, William Broughton Carr. Thousands of bee-keepers all over England use 'em. I've twelve occupied and six spares myself. The Maynards must have nigh on forty all told. There are fifty-odd members of the county association, and you can reckon a good two-thirds use this sort of hive."

"It isn't a new hive?"

"You can't go by the paint," said Old Heatherington. "They soon go grey, standing outside in all weathers, but I can tell you it isn't a new one. You generally clean the hives each spring. General method is to take a new or clean one, put the first stock of bees into it, then clean the one you've taken them from, and use it for the next, and so on. A good bee-keeper scorches the inside surfaces with a blow-lamp to kill any wax-moth egg there might be in the cracks and crevices. This one's been cleaned a good many times to my way of thinking."

"The Maynards go to that trouble?"

"I taught them their bee-keeping," the old man said simply. He added: "I don't think this is one of theirs, because they haven't been at it long and had all new stuff to start with."

"Mrs. Maynard was Batley's cousin?"

"Don't hold that against her, sir," pleaded the old man. "She should be having the money the old woman left to young Jerry. Hard as a flint was Mrs. Doughty. Saw 'em in a mess, and wouldn't help. I was wondering, sir," he said, half-turning on his seat and scratching his head. "Who'll get the money now this fellow's dead?"

Wilson glanced at Knollis. Knollis shook his head and in an expressionless voice replied: "That's a matter for the lawyers, Mr. Heatherington. We're only interested in his death."

Old Heatherington wagged his head. "I surely hope young Georgie gets it. She and her husband can do with every penny they can lay their hands on."

Knollis was searching the grass floor, and ignoring the old man's uncomfortable-looking perch on an upturned bucket. He said to Wilson: "See these deep triangular depressions? The flagstones were walked here, first one corner, and then the next, being too heavy to be carried. That means it was a one-man job, for two people could carry one easily enough."

"That's true," agreed Wilson. "We've done it."

Knollis looked up, realized Old Heatherington was with them and looking vastly interested, and his lips tightened.

"I think your man can run Mr. Heatherington home, Wilson. We don't want to tire him, and he may have other things to do."

The old man smiled and eased his long legs. "I'll walk it, thanks. There's a stile a bit further down the lane, and a walk back through the neck of the woods and across the meadows won't do me any harm. I've all day and nothing else to do."

"As you wish," said Knollis.

The old man began to walk away. At ten yards he turned and took the pipe from his mouth. "Don't forget William Shakespeare, sir."

"We won't," nodded Knollis.

"And you know where I live if you want me."

"I don't think we shall want you, thanks," said Wilson.

The old man smiled, a curious, secret smile. "You know where I am when you want me. Good day!"

CHAPTER III
MISS MORELAND IS BLASÉ

DAPHNE MORELAND had an even longer and thinner nose than Knollis, and she looked down it with unconcealed contempt when she consented to be interviewed by him and Wilson in her mother's drawing-room. Knollis quickly summed her up, cut across Wilson's comments on the weather, and went to work on her, determined to show her that the police had more brains than she suspected. He didn't like her.

"Inspector Wilson tells me you were engaged to Gerald Batley, Miss Moreland . . ."

She lolled against the mantel, a cigarette between her thin lips, and tugged at the jacket of her blue-grey cardigan suit while she screwed her china-blue eyes up against the spiralling smoke. "Yes, Jerry and I were engaged to be married, Inspector," she said, and made no attempt to enlarge on the subject.

Knollis nodded to himself. She was going to be difficult without making the fact too obvious. "A date had been fixed for the wedding?" he asked.

She hunched her shoulders in a fatalistic gesture. "The wedding should have been on the eighteenth of last month."

"The eighteenth of June," murmured Knollis.

"You missed him, according to Inspector Wilson, on the eighth?"

"Yes," she said, lowering her head.

"He was due to escort you to a dance that night, and didn't turn up? You rang his flat, received no reply, and went round to find him, which you didn't do? All that is substantially correct?"

"Definitely correct," she replied. "I rang the office the next morning—"

"Which would be the ninth," interrupted Knollis with his passion for absolute fact.

"The ninth, yes. I rang the office and then went to see my father. He rang Bob Shipley, and went to see him. Jerry hadn't been at the office for two days."

"You didn't see him on Monday, the seventh?"

"No, Inspector."

"You called on Inspector Wilson after seeing your father and Mr. Shipley," said Knollis. "Now tell me, Miss Moreland; you knew of the existence of the cottage at Newbourne?"

She lifted a thin-pencilled and languid eyebrow at the question. "But, yes, of course! We were to spend our honeymoon there, and hang on for a few months until we could find a decent house in town. You know how difficult houses are!"

"No honeymoon in Switzerland?" asked Knollis.

Daphne Moreland shrugged, and flicked the ash from her cigarette. "With currency regulations as they are? We wanted a holiday, not a pauper's outing."

"Knowing the existence of the cottage, and knowing it was Gerald Batley's under the terms of his aunt's will, you, of course, went out to see if he was there?" suggested Knollis.

Wilson looked up, and shifted his feet.

Daphne Moreland gave Knollis a long, searching look, and fixed her eyes on her tan walking shoes. "You know that?" she asked.

Knollis didn't bother to admit that he knew nothing of the kind, but was making a shrewd guess.

"That was on the ninth," he said, stolidly.

"The cottage, yes," she replied, and turned to flick more ash, this time into the empty grate, so that her face was turned away from them for a second or so. There was more respect, and a certain caution, in her eyes as she turned back again.

"The cottage was locked, Miss Moreland?"

"The doors were locked, and there were no signs of Jerry, Inspector."

Knollis regarded her thoughtfully with his head askew, as if looking at her from a new angle both mentally and physically. "Tell me about the kitchen window, Miss Moreland."

She blinked before she had time to conceal her surprise. "You know about that as well?"

Knollis nodded. "It was open."

"Yes, swinging open," she admitted. "It struck me as queer because I'd looked in the keyholes and the keys were in the locks. . . ."

"You went in through the window," said Knollis in a blunt tone that challenged her to deny the fact.

Wilson grunted again.

"Ye—es," she said, reluctantly. "I found an empty beer-crate in the outhouse, and stood on that. It was quite easy, really, although I laddered a stocking."

Knollis lolled back in his chair, raised one knee, and locked his fingers round it. "Now tell me what you found in the house, Miss Moreland."

She waved a vague hand. Her china-blue eyes stared at some point above Knollis's head. "His hat was on the sideboard—his grey velour. It wasn't often he wore one, which made me think he was moving in to stay. I went upstairs and found his suit-case lying on the single bed—"

"Which tended to resolve your doubts," Knollis said quietly.

"My doubts, Inspector?" she asked in an incredulous tone that failed to deceive him.

"You thought he might have taken another girl to the cottage, Miss Moreland," said Knollis. His manner indicated that he was making a statement of fact rather than a suggestion.

"Jerry—" she began, and then bit her lip and turned away to shake the near-finished cigarette into the hearth.

"There was a hot-water bottle in the bed, and the sheets were turned down."

"I did that," she said simply. "The bed was damp."

"I see," said Knollis. "Tell me, Miss Moreland; did you investigate the kitchen cabinet?"

"Yes," she nodded. "There was a parcel wrapped in brown paper. I didn't open it, but felt round it and was satisfied that it contained food. Then I climbed out again, and came home."

"You didn't look round the garden?"

"Why should I?" she asked in a surprised tone.

"Why should you indeed?" Knollis smilingly agreed. "I wondered if you might have noticed a beehive at the far end of the orchard?"

She threw the remains of the cigarette in the grate, and posed a long finger on her lip. "No—o, I can't remember noticing one."

"You got the beer-case from the outhouse. Did you notice whether or not the path was flagged?"

Her eyebrows lifted once more. "No, it wasn't, not completely. I remember I had to go round the last yard or so because it was all wet and squashy, with lots of those nasty little bug things running about."

"And this was at what time?"

She paused to reflect. "I seem to remember getting back to town shortly before noon. Is that important?"

"You never can tell, Miss Moreland," said Knollis. "It may be."

He turned to smile at Wilson, who was muttering something about bugs and dampness to himself.

"Miss Moreland," Knollis said hastily, "I must ask you this. You've virtually admitted the suspicion that Batley might have been philandering at the cottage. With whom did you expect to find him?"

"I—I can't answer that!" she protested.

"You had a rival, despite your engagement," Knollis persisted. He waved towards Wilson. "The Inspector is able to tell me . . ."

She looked from one to the other and said: "Oh!"

"I'm a stranger to Clevely," said Knollis, "but Inspector Wilson knows nearly everyone in town, and what they are doing. His department is remarkably well-informed. You will realize that of course."

She nodded slowly and pensively. "He used to run across his cousin now and again," she said, reluctantly. "Years ago he was very fond of her, and I wondered . . ."

Knollis glanced at Wilson. "That will be Mrs. Maynard?"

"Mrs. Maynard," said Wilson.

"Tell me the rest, please," Knollis said to Daphne Moreland. "We may as well clear the decks completely, having gone so far."

She walked from the hearth and took a seat, her elbows on her knees, her chin cupped in her long hands. "I was worried about it," she said in a low voice. "I knew he'd met her in town recently, and had lunched with her at the Devonshire in Castle Street."

"They were cousins," Knollis remarked.

"I know, Inspector, but you didn't know Jerry as well as I did."

"Twenty-second of March he lunched her," Wilson said authoritatively. "Fourteenth of April he met her the second time. She slapped his face for him a few yards south of the Devonshire Café-Restaurant."

Daphne Moreland turned with amazement on her oval face. Knollis sat with a face like a mask, expressionless.

"The face-slapping incident was witnessed by one of our constables, and he reported it in case a summons was issued," added Wilson.

Daphne Moreland continued to stare at him. "Georgie slapped his face! But—but that makes all the difference. And yet he told me Georgie was making up to him. That was after my friends told me he'd taken her to lunch, and I'd taxed him with it. He first excused himself because she was his cousin, and later said she was making advances because she was fed up with her husband!"

"And so, of course, you've since harboured the private opinion that the Maynards were responsible for his disappearance, and later, his death," said Knollis. "Or that Mr. Maynard was responsible," he added in slow-measured tones.

Daphne Moreland got up and strode to the hearth again, where she stood with her hands clasped behind her back. "I—I don't know where I am now. You can read my thoughts! I really did think that—and, yes, I still think so! His aunt's money was to go to Georgie if he died before the will was proved."

"And the will wasn't proved on the seventh of June?" asked Knollis.

She shook her head. "It still isn't proved. The law takes its time."

"And if he didn't die before then, but some time after, Miss Moreland?"

"To me if we were married, naturally, and his heirs and assigns. I asked my father about that—he's a lawyer, you know."

Knollis leaned forward, his lean features tense. "Tell me, Miss Moreland, did Jerry Batley propose marriage to you before or after Mrs. Doughty's death, or, alternatively, before or after he knew the terms of her will?"

"Why, before, of course!"

"He was then in an impecunious state," said Wilson, apologizing with a glance for butting in on Knollis.

"He only had what he earned, of course," Daphne Moreland said quickly.

"And living far above his income!"

"I offered to help him, Inspector Wilson!"

"He'd have none of it?"

"Jerry was far too independent, Inspector. He said it would be time enough for me to help him when we were married and he had to keep up to my standard of living. He was going into partnership with Bob Shipley, you know!"

"Oh, yes," Wilson said, non-committally.

Her lip curled as she said: "It was my father's idea. He said a mere clerkship wouldn't do for his son-in-law, and so we were going to buy him a partnership between us. He could soon have paid us back. Jerry had brains."

Knollis inched forward on his chair. "Was there any change in his attitude towards you after his aunt's death, Miss Moreland? After he knew the terms of the will?"

She grimaced her distaste. "It's a horrible thing you're asking me, Inspector Knollis!"

"I'm investigating a murder, Miss Moreland, and murder is more horrible than hurt feelings. I repeat, was there any change in his attitude after he knew he was to inherit his aunt's money?"

"You've an uncanny power of insight, Inspector," she said. She took a cigarette from an enamelled box on the mantel, and lit it, meanwhile staring reflectively at Knollis over her hands.

"It's sheer damned treachery," she said softly as she blew the smoke down pinched nostrils. "Yes, there was a change—not in his affections, and I'm sure of that—but he was more—more, how can I put it? More off-hand, more casual? Previously he'd been punctual and punctilious, and then he started turning up late for dates."

"He was feeling his feet?" suggested Knollis.

"The reins were changing hands," Daphne Moreland said with a cynical gesture.

"I see," said Knollis.

He saw a great deal. A young and ambitious man looking for social and professional advancement, and finding the chance of achieving both through the daughter of the town's leading lawyer, and then discovering that in hitching himself to them he'd allowed himself to be harnessed to their ambitions instead of his own.

He saw a girl and her father both wanting a personable young man in the family, and insisting that he follow their plans for his life. Then a sense of freedom as he realized that with his aunt's money he could still marry the girl, and her money, and retain his self-respect—or the substitute that represented it.

He saw the girl suddenly realizing that her grip on him was failing, and striving her utmost to hold him even when she believed he was having an affair with his cousin. In which case she had been rapidly losing her own self-respect, and that meant she was passionately in love with him despite the ice-cold façade she showed to the town in particular and the world in general.

Knollis fingered his chin. Now if there was another woman, his cousin or anyone else, and this Daphne Moreland knew about her ... The cold façade and the concealed inner passion ... Intellectual deliberation backed by emotional driving force ... Sooner than lose him to another woman she might well contemplate murder.

"You were educated here in Clevely, Miss Moreland?" he asked gently.

She almost recoiled from the suggestion. "God, no!" she ejaculated. "I went to Mottingley High, and then on to Queen's!"

Wilson turned to Knollis with a blank face behind which any emotion under the sun might have been lurking. "Miss Moreland holds an M.A. with distinctions in—"

"Literature and logic," she said, grandly.

"I was thinking of something like that," said Knollis. "Er—when did you last see Gerald Batley, Miss Moreland?"

She gave him a cold smile. "I remember that. Inspector Wilson asked me when I called on him that day. It was the evening of the sixth. He took me into Mottingley to the International Ballet. They did *Twelfth Night* and the usual excerpts from *Swan Lake*. Then we fixed up for the dance on the eighth."

"You didn't see him at all on Tuesday, the seventh?"

She shook her head. "Literally, no. He left me well before midnight on the Monday, the sixth."

"You're very certain," said Knollis.

"Inspector Wilson pressed the same questions."

"True enough," interrupted Wilson.

"He was in the habit of ringing you for a chat on the days when you weren't due to meet?"

"If I was to be at home, yes. I go golfing now and again."

"You weren't at home on the seventh?"

"I was."

"Any idea where he was supposed to be going that evening of the seventh?" asked Knollis.

"Yes," she replied. "He was going to join the Photographic Society. They had a meeting in the Museum Lecture Hall."

"He didn't go?"

She wrinkled her nose at him. It almost amounted to an insult. "You're asking questions, Inspector, but I wonder how much you already know?"

"Knowledge is comparative," Knollis countered. "He did go—or didn't he?"

She lit another cigarette from the remains of the one that was nearly burning her fingers. "I'm beginning to hate myself. I don't think he went!"

"Why not, Miss Moreland?"

"I have a friend who's a member, and she didn't see him there."

"When did she tell you this?"

"Oh, quite early the next morning!"

"The eighth."

"Yes, she rang to tell me."

Knollis sniffed. "You have nice friends, Miss Moreland."

"Inspector!" she exclaimed, bridling.

"Where do you think he went that evening?"

She stared at the end of her cigarette and did not deign to answer.

"The cottage?" suggested Knollis.

She still did not reply.

"I think I see how you reasoned this thing out," said Knollis. "I think I see why your interest in his disappearance cooled after the first shock. You thought he went to the cottage to prepare it, not for your honeymoon, but for a week-end with someone else, and if he was so low as to take another girl to the cottage in which you were going to spend the first days of your married life ... Need I go on, Miss Moreland?"

"I didn't realize he'd gone to his death, Inspector, or I should have haunted the cottage. You must understand that," she said in a low voice, and bit her lip hard.

"Why do you think he was killed, Miss Moreland?"

She turned away, and looked at him through a convex mirror in the corner of the room. "I've told you—for his aunt's money. Either that or because someone else didn't want him to marry me!"

Knollis watched her face, a mere white point in the silvered reflection of the room.

"Are you sure it was the ninth when you went to the cottage, Miss Moreland?" he asked gently. "Are you sure you didn't ring him on the morning of the *eighth*? Are you sure you didn't want to tax him with deception after your friend told you he wasn't at the photographic meeting? Are you sure it wasn't the eighth when Shipley's office boy told you Batley was not at business? Are you sure you didn't think he'd been out all night—on the tiles, in the popular phrase? Are you sure you didn't take that Oberon of yours and chase straight out to the cottage to catch him *flagrante delicto*, or, to descend to the vernacular, red-handed? Are you really sure of all those things, Miss Moreland?"

She swung round, her face pale, and her lips tightly compressed. "It was the ninth, Inspector Knollis!"

"Suppose it became necessary to account for your movements on the seventh, Miss Moreland? Could you do so?"

"I—I think so," she stammered. "I keep a diary."

"Tell me," said Knollis; "was Batley a keen photographer?"

The frown vanished from her forehead, leaving it smooth as marble. "Frankly, I'd never known him display any interest in photography! I was surprised when he said he was going to join the society. He said he was preparing for a quieter life—and grinned at me as he said it."

"Ah!" said Knollis, while Wilson looked curiously at him.

"When did he tell you of his intention to join?"

"Why, when he was leaving me the previous night. He said he wouldn't be seeing me, and explained why."

Knollis smiled blandly. "And you didn't believe him, did you?"

She stared at him for a moment, and her expression did not change as she said, very frankly: "No, I didn't!"

"And you think you could account for your movements on the seventh of June, Miss Moreland?"

She nodded vigorously. "Please excuse me."

She walked briskly from the room, leaving Wilson staring in a perplexed manner at Knollis, and Knollis staring idly through the window at a thrush perched in a buddleia.

"Lovely markings," said Knollis.

"What is?" demanded Wilson.

"The thrush. See the flecking on its breast! By the way, what were you saying about bugs and damp?"

"Oh, that!" said Wilson, throwing his mind back half an hour. "I was thinking those bugs only stay in damp places. The earth under those flagstones would have dried quickly in the sun we're getting, so if she went there on the ninth, and the ground was damp, it means that Batley wasn't murdered until the ninth, or the eighth at the earliest!"

"And by the same rule," said Knollis with a mysterious smile, "if the earth was damp, and Batley was murdered the day he went out to the cottage, which seems to be the seventh, it means that Miss Moreland went to the cottage at least one day, if not two, earlier than she wants us to think!"

"Good Lord!" said Wilson. "That's true enough."

He looked suspiciously at Knollis, and asked: "You don't trust her story then?"

"She started by putting on an act," replied Knollis in a matter-of-fact voice. "She was the superior among us, the daughter of a prominent townsman condescending to two poor coppers. Then she realized I was pricking her balloon, and started lying. She's still lying, but I'm going to trap her into giving the truth—not necessarily now, but later."

"It's a difficult business," said Wilson, with a forward jerk of his head. "Moreland's influential—and why shouldn't she come clean with us, anyway?" Knollis smiled. "Confucius say, girl who wash in public lose face. Isn't it obvious what she's doing? Isn't she only telling us what the rest of her set know? Anything they don't know, she's keeping quiet. She's now putting on an act of being perfectly straightforward with us. All her friends knew Batley was making a mug of her, and the only way she can protect her feelings is by making out she knew about it all the time, whereas the penny didn't actually drop until after he vanished."

"I see that," said Wilson, "but why your suggestion that she went to the cottage on the seventh?"

"Look," Knollis replied patiently, "doesn't his story, as told to her, stink? Here you have an engaged couple, within a few weeks of getting married. Wouldn't you expect 'em to spend practically every living minute with each other?"

"Well, yes," Wilson admitted.

"Whereas Batley, leaving her after an evening at the ballet, calmly proposes dropping her the next evening to attend a photographic society meeting. It doesn't make sense. She was probably too surprised to say anything when he told her, but what was her reaction next morning? Isn't it obvious?"

"She rang him up to give him the works?"

"Well, that's how I see it. She got no reply from the flat, so tried the office, to be told he wasn't there. Where else could she logically expect to find him?"

"At the cottage!"

"Fair enough, Wilson. And would you logically expect her to wait two days before going out there to look for him? You wouldn't! As things are at present, she's trying to be blasé, trying to say, in effect: *My dear Inspectors, I knew on the morning of the seventh, in fact on the night of the sixth, that he was trying to ditch me, but it wasn't so very important to me, and so I just didn't bother to hunt him up for two more days.* All very sophisticated and modern—in the worst sense of that word."

"Quite so," agreed Wilson. "It makes sense, but did she push him down the well?"

"I don't know," Knollis said frankly. "We can't really suggest anybody until we know where the cyanide comes from. All I'm trying to do at the moment is establish the last time he was seen—by anybody, and this girl is obstructing me in trying to save her face. It's a very simple issue."

Daphne Moreland returned and thrust a small diary into Knollis's hands. "There you are, Inspector. Now you'll know what I did on the seventh!"

Her manner was smugly triumphant.

Knollis flashed a quick glance at the opened diary and handed it back to her. "There's no need for this, Miss Moreland," he said with a smile. "I was merely voicing a rhetorical question when I asked if you could account for your movements on that day. Still, thanks for your patience under fire. Now let's be going, Wilson. I'm sure we've hindered Miss Moreland enough for one day."

Outside, walking to the car, Wilson asked irritably:

"Why the heck didn't you take the diary? We could have checked on her!"

Knollis went round the car and got in. As Wilson slid under the wheel he said to him: "Have your men check her movements for the seventh. Boots' Library at ten. Coffee with some Mrs. Davenport half-past ten to eleven. Call on some dentist named Dearing to make an appointment; that was between half-eleven and noon. Tennis at three-thirty—you'll know where she plays. Afternoon tea with Sally P. and Linda M. at the Devonshire Café. Rehearsal with the C.A.D.S. at six-forty-five."

"Lord! You memorized them!" exclaimed Wilson.

"That's beside the point," said Knollis. He was sitting bolt upright in his seat, his eyes near closed, and his chin pushed slightly forward in a stubborn attitude. "You'll find she didn't keep some of those appointments, Wilson, if in fact she ever made them. The diary was made of thin india paper, and you could see through the pages. There was one entry, in pencil, for the previous day; there were none for the next day on the opposite page, and no entries for the next two days. She filled in the seventh while we waited, with one of these new ball-pointed pens that use quick-drying ink."

"Mm!" murmured Wilson.

"I mean," said Knollis. "You either keep a diary conscientiously, or not at all after the first week of the year. You do see what I mean?"

"I see a great deal," Wilson said grimly. "Where do we go from here?"

"Batley's flat."

Wilson neglected his driving for a second and then swung the car back from the crown of the road. "Not to see Mrs. Maynard?"

"No, to Batley's flat," said Knollis. Without turning his head or breaking his rigid pose he added: "You see, Wilson, we know where the bird is if we want her. As it is, I think it might be worth while looking round the flat for evidence declaring whether she was there or not early that morning of the seventh. Birds are inclined to drop feathers, and we might find one or two."

"Feathers!" said Wilson.

CHAPTER IV
MR. BATLEY LIKED THE LADIES

THE CARETAKER of the Grafton Flats was a weaselish little man with a stringy neck and protruding eyes. He wore a soiled soft collar and green-spotted tie to his shiny blue suit, and his hair stood straight up on end as if the arrival of Knollis and Wilson had scared him.

They asked him for a key to the flat, whereupon he stared at them, and his Adam's apple went up and down like a crazy lift.

"Good job it's you, Inspector," he said to Wilson, "or I shouldn't have let you have it. Others have been after it, but I wouldn't let them have it. No, sir, not me. Two ladies they was, and that makes you wonder, doesn't it?"

Knollis agreed that it did. "They came together?" he asked.

"Separate, sir, and on different days."

"You knew them?" Wilson asked anxiously.

"Only the one he was going out with, sir," said the caretaker. He snapped his fingers. "What's her name now—the lawyer's daughter?"

Neither Knollis nor Wilson made any attempt to help him, suggestions and leading questions being calculated to stimulate the imagination rather than the memory of a witness.

The caretaker suddenly smiled. "Miss Moreland—that's her. She's been up here several times trying to get in."

"And the other?" asked Wilson. "Can you describe her?"

The caretaker cultivated the back of his neck with long finger-nails, and if his contorted expression was any guide he was having a struggle either with his memory or his power of description. "She was sort of not so tall as Miss Moreland, and dark—her hair, I mean. And then she was slimmish, and had legs."

"Haven't they all?" asked Knollis.

"These were legs, sir! Racehorse sort. She was a bit on the haughty side, different sort of 'aught to Miss Moreland, if you understand."

"What was she wearing?" Wilson asked with some impatience.

"Well, every time I saw her she'd a fur cape thing on—this weather an' all, and high-heeled shoes, and that's all."

"She obviously needed the cape," Knollis said without changing his expression.

The caretaker gasped. "I didn't mean that, sir. I meant that was all I could remember, although now I come to think back she had a blue frock on."

"Even seen her before?" asked Wilson.

"Aye, somewhere, sir, but I couldn't say where it was, and I wouldn't say it was here."

"Then don't," said Knollis. "Now, before we get on with our work, when did you last see Mr. Batley? Can you remember that?"

"Miss Moreland asked me that, sir. It was the night before he went missing. I saw him driving the car out early on—about half-past six it'd be."

"He brought it back that night?" asked Wilson.

"It was there next morning, sir."

"And was not taken out again," said Knollis with a light nod.

The caretaker blinked. "Not taken out again? But it was, sir. It was out all day Tuesday, the day he went missing!"

Wilson took half a step forward, thrust his chin out, and stared straight into the little man's protuberant eyes. "You told my sergeant the car hadn't been out at all!" he said, in accusing voice.

The caretaker backed away from him. "Not me, sir! The sergeant saw my mate, not me. I told him he'd made a mistake when he told me about it, and said he'd better let you know. Mr. Batley's car was out half an hour after I came on that morning, and it was there when I looked in the garages at eight o'clock! It was out all day, and it was out when I went round the stokehold and the garages before knocking off at ten that night, and then it was back in the garage next morning, because I opened up to sweep out."

Knollis stepped between Wilson and the little man. "You say you have a mate. Are you both on duty at the same time?"

"Nights one week, days the next, sir. We do porter as well as caretaker. Ten to eight on nights, and eight to ten—official—on days, although we often take an hour off now and then."

Knollis cocked an eye at Wilson. "That's interesting. Tell me, Mr. er—?"

"Marston's the name, sir. Bert Marston."

Knollis nodded. "I understood you to say, Mr. Marston, that both these women tried to get in the flat. You mean they tried the door?"

Marston shook his head. "I mean as they tried to get me to let them in. Miss Moreland tried it with a ten-shilling note, and the other tried to la-di-da me. I wasn't having any."

"Suppose you let us in now," suggested Wilson. "We shall neither bribe nor coax you."

Marston unlocked the door. "I can let you have a key later, but not now. It's a latch-lock. When you come out, just pull the door and it'll lock itself. It's what they call a latch-lock."

"Thanks for telling us," Knollis said gravely. He smiled as the little man trotted off with an air of importance to the self-operated lift.

Once inside the flat, with the door closed, Knollis was all business. The living-room was as Wilson had described it, a mess of littered books and papers, clothing and cushions. Two chairs were overturned in the middle of the room. Knollis looked round, and turned to Wilson with a peculiar expression on his lean features. "I thought you said he'd turned the place inside out!"

Wilson waved an all-embracing hand. "Well, look at it! Doesn't it speak for itself?"

"There's been a fight here," said Knollis, and sniffed. "A heck of a fight. I'll lay a pound that Batley was knocked out, and his assailant then searched the room. I mean, Wilson, if you're looking for something in your own home you've a good idea where it might be, and you don't throw cushions all over the room, and overturn chairs. It might be as well to interview the people who live under and above him."

As he was talking, Knollis was prowling about the room, his gaze travelling over every single item. He came to rest before the settee, and with his back towards Wilson asked: "Ever read Maeterlink, Wilson?"

Wilson pondered. "Ye—es, I read *Blue Bird* to my daughter when she was a kid."

"I was thinking about his *Life of the Bee*," said Knollis.

"I read it years ago, but can't remember much of it. Why?"

Knollis turned. His hands were clasped behind his back, and his eyes were almost hidden behind slitted lids.

"Know anyone in town who keeps bees?"

Wilson scratched his head. "Not actually living in town, but there are people working in town and living in the outer suburbs who do. Why?"

"One you can get hold of straight away?"

"Ye—es, there's Normanton. He's the chemist at the brewery two streets away."

"He could spare half an hour for us?"

Wilson paused before answering. "Look, Knollis," he said, "what are you getting at? What do you want to know?"

Knollis smiled. "I want to know how far a bee can, or will, fly from its hive."

Wilson shook his head sadly. "Your methods are queer ones to me. Still, if you want Normanton I'll get him on the blower. You couldn't ask him without bringing him across, could you?"

"I'd like him here," said Knollis.

Wilson shrugged and went to the telephone, picking his way through Batley's strewn belongings. Three minutes later he announced that Normanton was willing to come over.

"I wonder what the two women were after?" he asked, irrelevantly.

Knollis rubbed the palms of his hands together. "It might have been the same object Batley's assailant was looking for. In which case it may or may not be here. We'll attend to that when Normanton's been."

Hedley Normanton was a good-looking and friendly man in the early thirties, and interested in the reason for which he'd been invited from his work.

"It's Inspector Knollis who wants you," said Wilson as he introduced them. "He's got a bee in his bonnet."

Knollis grinned, and offered his cigarettes. "How far will a honey-bee fly from her hive, Mr. Normanton?"

"Depends," said Normanton. "If there's plenty of nectar at hand she won't fly far—her span of life depends on how soon she wears her wings to shreds. If the hive's badly off for food—well, it's said she'll fly two miles."

"Inspector Wilson tells me there are hives in the suburbs of Clevely," said Knollis. "Tell me, Mr. Normanton, do those bees have to go far afield for their nectar?"

Normanton shook his head. "It's not bad bee country round here, Inspector. Clevely's a compact town, and the outer suburbs are on the edge of open country. We run into meadowland to the west, and to the east there's a goodish stretch of ling heather."

Knollis nodded his satisfaction at the explanation. "This is a good season?"

"If we don't hit a damp cold patch of weather there'll be a good honey take," Normanton said, happily.

"There's no possibility of starvation?"

"None at the moment."

"And since the beginning of the season?"

"It's been good all the way through."

"I see," said Knollis, "and even if the Clevely bees found a shortage of nectar in their immediate neighbourhood they wouldn't be inclined to fly back into town in search of food?"

"Heavens, no!" said Normanton. "They'd go further out into open country. Can I ask what you're getting at, Inspector?"

"That's my question as well," grumbled Wilson. "The man is playing at being the Sphinx."

Knollis smiled. "I'm secretive because I don't want to make a fool of myself. Now perhaps Mr. Normanton will tell me something else! Where is the nearest hive to this flat, and how near is it?"

Normanton looked at Knollis, pulled on the lobe of his ear, and looked across at Wilson. "Won't Debenham's be the nearest? That's at the top of the London Road, a good mile away."

"One more question," said Knollis. "Could you, by examining a bee, say whether it had or had not come from a particular hive?"

Normanton laughed. "There's no finger-print system you can apply to bees, Inspector!"

He puffed at his cigarette, and then blinked. "I'll tell you what I could do. I could tell you whether a particular bee could have come from a certain hive, or whether it definitely couldn't! That's a different matter, of course."

"Sounds like the blood-group test in a paternity case," Wilson remarked sarcastically. "That can only tell that a man could have been the father of the child, or definitely wasn't."

"Explain, please," Knollis said shortly to Normanton.

"There are various varieties of bees, Inspector. The Italian is a yellow-banded bee. The Caucasian is of two kinds, the grey-banded one from the mountains, and the brownish one from the lowlands. Then there's the French bee, and the Carniolan, and the Dutch bee, and—"

"Obviously an enthusiast," commented Knollis. "Equally obvious is the fact that you're an expert."

"Technically, I am," replied Normanton, "although I don't think anybody can claim to be one under fifty years' experience."

"Like Old Heatherington, as he seems to be generally called?" suggested Knollis.

"What he doesn't know isn't worth knowing," Normanton said enthusiastically. "He can read their minds—but, of course, they constitute his main interest in life!"

Knollis turned away, bent over the settee, and turned back with a dead bee in his hand. "What's that, Mr. Normanton?"

Normanton took it from him and poked it with a finger. "An old bee, and a cross between an I tie and a Caucasian. See the yellow thorax and the brown-banded abdomen? Further to the point, it stung something or other before it died."

Knollis opened his eyes. "Oh?"

"It's elementary," smiled Normanton. "A bee sting is barbed, and when a bee digs it in it generally pulls away from the stung object. The sting stays put on account of the barbs, and the bee leaves behind its entrails, and consequently dies."

"Leaving the sting in whatever it has stabbed?"

"That's it, Inspector!"

A second later Knollis was on his knees, peering closely at the moquette-covered settee. "You know what to look for, Mr. Normanton. See if you can find the sting for me, please."

Normanton eventually admitted that there wasn't one. "The bee was probably carried dead into the room clinging on somebody's clothing."

Wilson fixed Knollis with a challenging stare. "So what?"

Knollis went through to the kitchenette, returning with an empty match-box into which he popped the dead bee. "That's probably going to hang someone," he said.

He thanked Normanton for his assistance, and hustled him off the premises, venturing the opinion he might be needed again, and would he please keep his own counsel. He returned to Wilson wearing a light smile on his sharp features.

Wilson sank into the comfort of the settee and looked appealingly at him. "Would you really mind telling me all this is about?"

Knollis propped himself against the table, and with his eyes half-closed ticked off a variety of points on his fingers.

"Batley vanished on the morning of the seventh of June, Wilson. We're agreed on that?"

"The date haunts me," sighed Wilson.

"Mrs. Maynard was taken to hospital early in the morning of the same day."

"Granted."

"Still earlier the honey-house at Somewhere Lock was burned down."

"Wellow Lock, yes."

"Here we have all the evidence of a first-class scrap, and a thorough search."

"True," said Wilson.

"And a dead bee which apparently didn't live here in town."

"Fair enough."

"Now what kind of person would be most likely to have a dead bee clinging to his clothes?"

"I'll take a bee-keeper," Wilson said sarcastically.

"And a bee could get knocked off a coat or jacket in a fight!"

"Ye—es," said Wilson slowly, as if the sun of understanding was dawning.

"Now, on the fourteenth of April the dead man was slapped in the face by Mrs. Maynard—and why does a woman slap a man's face, Wilson?"

"Because he insults her, of course."

"And there, in those facts, you have the whole thing, Wilson," Knollis said intensely. "Put them in the correct order of sequence. Mind you, there may be nothing in this bearing directly on the cause of his death. It's simply that these items link themselves in my mind, and raise certain suspicions."

Wilson stared at Knollis as if he was an illusionist.

"'Struth, yes! Mrs. Maynard is chased by Batley. She slaps his face for making an improper suggestion. Batley burns down the honey-house for spite. The shock makes her ill and she goes into hospital. Philip Maynard comes down here, beats up Batley, and then—but he couldn't have bumped him off," Wilson protested, "because Batley had his breakfast here before vanishing!"

"Quite," Knollis said softly.

"And two full months elapsed between the presumed improper suggestion, and the burning down of the honey-house!"

"Other things happened in between, if you'll only think back," Knollis reminded him gently.

Wilson lit a cigarette and allowed it to burn between his fingers as he stared at the carpet. "Then there's the beehive at Doughty's cottage!"

"Which could be one of two things—in significance, I mean," said Knollis.

Wilson said: "Hm?"

"Either an attempt to disguise the presence of the well, or a hint from a third person that Batley's murder was concerned with bees."

"This is a real number one case," said Wilson.

Knollis left the table against which he was resting.

"Well, let's go through Batley's belongings, shall we? Our man probably didn't find what he was looking for, since all the drawers and cupboards are opened. If he'd found it, then some at least would be closed, wouldn't they? Care to do the bedroom and bathroom, Wilson?"

Wilson got up as if in a trance, and disappeared beyond the panelled cream door leading to Batley's bedroom.

Knollis went to work on the bureau, taking out each of the drawers in turn and feeling behind them. An oblong package met his finger-tips as he ferreted under and behind the bottom one, and, after retrieving it, he hailed Wilson, who joined him.

They opened the package on the table.

"Photos, Knollis!"

"All girls," said Knollis. "His many conquests, I suppose. Good job he didn't marry 'em all, or he'd have rivalled a sultan's harem! He had to hang on to the photos, though, even when getting married. *Vanity of vanities, all is vanity!* The Preacher was a wise man, Wilson—and he hit the spot every time."

"He and Old Heatherington's friend from Stratford," grinned Wilson.

"Girls, girls and more girls," said Knollis. "See the inscriptions, Wilson! Passion in ink! *Always—Ever—Yours, Sally*. She probably married an iceberg in the end and is now suffering from a neurosis. *Night and Day, Bobbie!* She looks that type, too. Must have been on twenty-four hour shifts. The next one's more sober. *Jerry with love, Georgie*. Haven't we a Georgie somewhere in the case, Wilson?"

"Whoa!" Wilson exclaimed. "That's Mrs. Maynard. Chubby little piece, isn't she?"

"Something like a koala bear," said Knollis. "Very snuggly, very cuddly. We'll put that one aside. Now look at this one from *Ever-Devoted Doreen* in purple ink and six kisses. Different type altogether. Must have been a queer bloke, this Batley. In my experience they mostly go for the one type. Still, my experience isn't as extensive as his—"

He broke off to ask Wilson what was wrong as he suddenly dived at his hands.

"That one!" exclaimed Wilson. "The one you've just passed. Yes, that's right! Now I wonder . . ."

"What do you wonder?" Knollis asked patiently.

"There's a time for all things, according to your Preacher," said Wilson. "This is my time to be mysterious!" There was an extra flush on his fresh-complexioned cheeks. "Back in a minute!"

Knollis shrugged, and carried on with his examination of the trophies of Batley's life-long chase. Wilson returned with Marston, the caretaker.

"Shuffle 'em together, Knollis!" said Wilson. Knollis then realized Wilson's game, but tactfully registered wonderment, allowing his colleague his moment of triumph.

Wilson thrust the pack of photographs into Marston's hands. "Look through those, Mr. Marston!"

"What for, sir?"

"Look through 'em!"

Marston obeyed, passing a remark on each one, and some of his comments were not what might have been expected of a man of his age. Once he grunted, twice he gave a long whistle, and then he suddenly held out one of the photographs. "That's her as tried to la-di-da me into letting her in here!"

"Sure?" asked Knollis, moving round to look over his shoulder.

"On my davy, sir. I'd swear it in court!"

"You may have to do just that," Wilson warned him.

"I'd do it, sir. I know it's her!"

Wilson gave him half a crown for a drink, and turned him out unceremoniously. He was a happy man as he turned from the door.

"Good work, Wilson!" Knollis said softly.

Wilson flushed with pleasure. "Know who she is?"

"I'm a stranger in a strange land."

"And this is Mrs. Maynard's sister-in-law, Mrs. Lanson. And her photograph here in Batley's collection. What a photograph, too! There's only a yard of muslin between her and pneumonia! What a turn-up for the book!"

Knollis gently relieved him of the photograph and turned it over. "Grecian Studios, Castle Street, Clevely," he read. "So Mrs. Lanson didn't want us to find her photograph here, Wilson. How long has she been married?"

"Dunno, quite," replied Wilson. "Shipley can tell us. He was at the wedding. In fact, nearly all Clevely was at the wedding, so I don't know why I mentioned Shipley. It was a slap-up do with a reception in the Masonic Hall, with gold plate and red carpets."

"A year?" asked Knollis.

"Longer than that!"

"Find out," said Knollis. "The local paper's the best bet. They won't talk, and Shipley might."

Shortly afterwards Wilson announced. "Three years and eight months."

Knollis took his arm and led him to the door. "The Grecian Studios, my friend. We can come back here after tea. See, according to Mr. Marston, we pull the door and it locks itself. It's a latch-lock, Wilson, so file the information; it might prove useful some day!"

Wilson laughed, and slammed the door hard. Knollis primed him as they walked the short distance to the studios, and effaced himself during the interview with the manageress, since Wilson knew her well.

"This photo," said Wilson. "You know the lady?"

"Mrs. Rodney Lanson, of course. It's one of our photographers—one of our studies."

"Could you tell us when it was taken?"

"In three minutes, Inspector. I'm proud of my filing system."

They looked up curiously as she returned with the photograph and three white envelopes.

"July the tenth last year, Inspector," she informed them. "Er—is there something fishy about it?"

"There is, and we must rely on your discretion."

The manageress nodded a well-coiffeured head. "I wondered. You see, odd incidents stick in one's mind, and one came back to me as soon as you showed me the photograph. We usually post proofs to clients, but Mrs. Lanson was insistent that she should call and inspect them here, and make her choice."

"That fits," said Wilson. "How many copies did she order?"

"One only of each, according to the details entered in the negative files. One of each of three exposures, that is. We would charge her heavily for that, of course. Small orders don't pay."

Out on the hot pavement of Castle Street, Wilson wondered: "Did she let Batley choose his own, then sign the one and burn the others, Knollis?"

"I'm inclined to agree with that theory," said Knollis. "She obviously didn't want her husband to know anything about them. Oh, well, let's take tea, and afterwards it might be as well to run out to the Maynard home instead of going back to the flat. It's a most interesting case, Wilson. Fascinating, in fact!"

"You make it sound horrible," grumbled Wilson, "almost as if we're doing you a good turn! Murders arranged to meet the convenience of investigators. Hangings arranged at the shortest notice. Quotations by return of post. Apply Police Headquarters, Victoria Street, Clevely. Bah!"

Knollis patted him comfortingly on the shoulder. "In a job like ours we have to concentrate on the purely intellectual aspects of a case, Wilson. If we paused too often to consider the emotional side we'd go mad. Don't mistake my enthusiasm. It's entirely intellectual. Somewhere in this district is a person with brains who knows how to use them. It's going to be a battle of wits—and it isn't going to be an easy case!"

CHAPTER V
MRS. MAYNARD REVEALS A SECRET

IT WAS SELDOM Gordon Knollis evolved a theory early in the course of an investigation. His method was to seek a pattern in the events surrounding the murder, a pattern which suggested, if no more, the causal factors, and a pattern in which the murder was the focal point.

The murder itself, despite its sensational nature, was not the vital factor in a case as Knollis saw it; rather was it the bubble in a swamp telling of long-repressed forces beneath the surface, the eruption telling of poisons circulating through the apparently healthy system, the molehill indicating the runs and tunnels hidden from the eye.

The decomposed body of Gerald Batley was, to Knollis, no more than a symbol of pent-up emotions that had overcome their control, and, as he pointed out to Wilson when they drove out to Mansard House, a family affair, and a complicated one into the bargain. Batley was a cousin to Georgie Maynard, and had evidently courted her at one time, ignoring the reputed dangers of consanguinity; by what Wilson was able to tell him of the affair, Batley at that time intended marrying her, which intention seemed to be absent from his more recent siege of her heart.

Mrs. Lanson had also been a Batley conquest, and she was Philip Maynard's sister, and, consequently, within the family circle. Daphne Moreland was outside, and yet attached to it, if only as a tangent, by virtue of her relationship to Batley.

"It isn't always so," he said, in his short and academic lecture, "but in this case the corpse is the centre of the web. At various points on the circumference we find these women. All three of them seem to have known of Batley's mania for women, and each of them must have known of his interest in the other two—if they lived with their eyes and ears open!"

"And of the three . . . ?" asked Wilson.

Knollis gave a sly smile. "It would appear that Miss Moreland had the strongest motive. She could have done it, you know. I told you at the cottage it was a one-person job, and I'll stick to that. Daphne Moreland's physical appearance is deceptive. She looks thin, and somewhat delicate, but I'll wager she's strong and wiry. And motive? Daughter of a prominent townsman, member of a small-town social set—"

"And Batley humiliating her!" said Wilson.

Knollis nodded vigorously. "You've hit the mark, Wilson. It wasn't jealousy as much as humiliation that moved her to action—since we're temporarily regarding her as the culprit. If Batley had favoured—save the word!—another girl, and kept it quiet, then even if Daphne Moreland had known of it she might have overlooked it, realizing the only way to save her own face was to keep her eyes closed, but Batley doesn't seem to have cared who saw him with a second girl, and if Daphne Moreland did kill him, then it was that error of not being circumspect that brought about his death."

"And the cyanide?" wondered Wilson.

"We'll find it, man," Knollis assured him. "You can't walk into a shop and buy that stuff as you buy aspirin or syrup of rhubarb."

"I keep thinking about Bernice Lanson," said Wilson, as he steered round a sharpish bend.

Knollis shrugged. "We don't know much about her yet, do we? We've established the fact that she had a minor affair with Batley, but no more. One point interests me; you said Batley was short of money."

"That's so," agreed Wilson.

"Have the Lansons any money?"

"They're not in the Moreland class, but they won't be broke by any means. You're wondering if he tried to chisel her, using the photograph as the blade?"

"Could be," muttered Knollis. "It's only an idea. This is all conjecture. She was anxious to get into the flat, of course, and we can allow ourselves to believe she was after the photograph until some better explanation turns up. We'd better forget her for the time being, Wilson, don't you think?"

"And that will bring us back to these Maynard people."

"We've heard that Mrs. Doughty's money will now go to Mrs. Maynard."

"They've had their spell of bad luck, and seem to be broke to the wide," said Wilson. "We can't forget that."

Knollis jerked his head round towards Wilson. "What is luck, my friend?"

Wilson spared a hand from the wheel to scratch his ear. "We—ell, the way circumstances play for or against you, surely!"

"Independent of any human action, you mean?"

"Yes, I think you can add that as a postscript," said Wilson.

Knollis shook his head. "It won't do, Wilson. It won't do. You're visualizing a chaotic universe, and yet everything from the atom to the universe itself is governed by law. Circumstances are the result of human actions, and not of a play of blind forces. Didn't even the great Voltaire say that chance was the name we've given to the observed effect of an unobserved cause?"

"Did he?" Wilson murmured vaguely.

"I mean," went on Knollis with a flourish of his hand, "all these things didn't happen to the Maynards without reason. Either Maynard was a rotten gardener and bee-keeper, or . . ."

His voice died away to a whisper, and then faded into silence as he stared with narrowed eyes at the road as it vanished beneath the nose of the car.

"Or what?" Wilson demanded. He put out his hand, and turned right into the drive of Mansard House.

Knollis broke from his reverie to smile. "That's it, Wilson! Or what? That's what we have to prove to ourselves."

"You've some notion floating about inside that head of yours," Wilson said accusingly.

"It's almost a conviction," said Knollis.

Wilson grunted. "You're a queer man, if you don't mind me saying so."

"Only because I don't care to reveal the ideas in my mind," said Knollis as they got from the car. "If I told you what I think about this case you'd say I was mad, and so I prefer to present you with theory and solution at one and the same time. But here's a tip. Remember that Mrs. Maynard slapped Batley's face in public, and then remember what we've said about the Moreland girl and the motive of humiliation! Batley also had his pride—in his power to handle women. And—all action is reciprocal! Do those facts tell you anything?"

They apparently didn't, for Wilson walked to the open door of the house and rang the bell, making no reply. Knollis followed a few steps behind, his chin in the air, and his fingers only pushed into the pockets of his light grey lounge jacket, leaving his thumbs free to waggle in time with Wilson's determined strides.

Georgie Maynard was dressed in blue slacks and a flowered house-coat when she opened the inner door of the porch to them. She regarded them gravely with wide, deep-blue eyes, and her full lips were lightly pursed.

"You remember me, Mrs. Maynard?" said Wilson.

She inclined her head. "Inspector Wilson, from Clevely."

"My colleague is Inspector Knollis of the Yard. We wondered if you and your husband could spare us ten minutes or so."

She touched herself on the breast. "Me, and my husband, Inspector?"

Wilson nodded.

"He's in the greenhouse," she said. "Perhaps you'll come inside, and I'll fetch him. What is it you wanted to see us about?"

Wilson produced a comforting smile. "We think you may be able to help us with a few facts about your late cousin, Gerald Batley."

"Oh, Jerry! Yes, of course," she said, uncertainly.

"So far as we can learn, you're the sole surviving relative, you see," said Wilson. "We thought you'd prefer your husband to be present at the interview," he added.

"Yes. Yes, I see," she said.

She took them into the garden room, a cream-distempered and white-painted room with french windows opening on a large square lawn.

"I'll fetch Phil," she said.

"A nice little woman," Wilson murmured in an appreciative tone as he watched her hurrying down a set of stone steps beyond the lawn to a lower terrace.

"Very attractive," agreed Knollis, "and the only person I've heard of in the case so far who couldn't possibly have murdered Batley. She was busy trying to produce life while someone else was making sure of extinguishing it. She's got good eyes!"

"Nice big blue ones," said Wilson.

"I was thinking more of their directness, of their usefulness to a poor detective as mirrors of the soul," Knollis said dryly. "I'm not susceptible to prettiness, although I'll grant she's a lovely young woman."

"Round and cuddly," murmured Wilson in a partial daze. "Her husband's a lucky man."

"Tell me," said Knollis, "what amount of rain you've had in this district in, say, the last two months."

Wilson stared at him, and then shrugged in a hopeless manner. "Oh, very little. It's been fairly dry over the whole country, hasn't it?"

"Some districts have had rain," said the literal-minded Knollis.

"You can be most exasperating, Knollis," snorted Wilson. "From women to weather in a matter of seconds!"

Knollis smiled. "Oh no, you're wrong. I was thinking about the weather all the time. It was you who was thinking about Mrs. Maynard! And here she comes with her husband . . ."

The Maynards came in holding hands. Philip Maynard was a slim, languid-looking fellow, with lank brown hair and almost colourless eyes. Knollis quickly summed him up as a quiet, thoughtful man who got on with the jobs to be done without any fuss. He fixed his age at thirty-odd.

Georgie Maynard suggested they might as well be seated.

Knollis turned to Philip Maynard. "We've really come to see your wife," he began in his best conversational manner, "but thought it only fair to have you present at the interview. She is Batley's only surviving relative, I suppose?"

Georgie Maynard answered his question, holding tight her husband's hand. "That's correct, Inspector. Aunt Roxy had no children. I was the only child in our family, and Jerry in his."

"Your mother had no brothers, Mrs. Maynard?"

"No, Inspector. There were just the three sisters."

Knollis inspected his knuckles before looking up with a friendly smile. "Tell me, Mrs. Maynard, will the Doughty money come to you now your cousin is dead?"

There was an awkward silence in the room, during which Georgie Maynard looked at her husband with troubled eyes, and moved an inch closer to him. He answered for her. "We hope so, Inspector, although we've heard nothing from the solicitors. I'm frank about it; we hope so."

"You've had a fair amount of bad luck this year, haven't you?" asked Knollis, while Wilson cocked a curious eye at him.

Philip Maynard swept his hair back from his forehead with his free hand, still holding his wife's hand with the other. A twisted smile came to his lips. "There's nothing left to go wrong, Inspector. We've lost our fruit, our bees, and our baby, and we're flat broke."

"Tell me about the fire at Wellow Lock," said Knollis. "I understand you lost quite a lot of money there."

"You've seen Mr. Heatherington, of course," said Georgie Maynard. "He's been a grand friend to us, hasn't he, Phil?"

"The fire, please," said Knollis.

Philip Maynard freed his hand, and imprisoned both between his knees. "It was about one in the morning—"

"The morning of the seventh of June."

"Yes," Maynard nodded. "Sergeant Thorpe rang me. He and a constable had spotted it and reported to the fire station. We went out in the car, picking Old Heatherington up on the way. The fire was about out when we got there, and a hundred pounds' worth of equipment had gone up in smoke."

"Any idea how it started?" asked Knollis.

Maynard looked up quickly, met Knollis's keen stare, and looked down at the carpet again. He shook his head. "No idea at all, Inspector. I hadn't been out for three days. There's been no need to use the smoker since we'd no bees there, and as for cigarettes—well, I smoke very little, and not at all when in the apiaries."

"The contents of the honey-house were highly combustible, Mr. Maynard?"

Maynard grimaced. "The brood body boxes and super boxes were seasoned red cedar, and the frames all held either wax comb or wax foundation."

"Wax foundation?" murmured Knollis.

"That's sheet wax with the pattern of the cells embossed on both sides. The bees draw them out into combs."

"How could the fire have started?" Knollis persisted. "Surely you've some theory?"

Maynard looked up, his pale eyes expressionless. "I haven't a clue, Inspector."

"The insurance company? Didn't they investigate?"

"Most thoroughly—and questioned us for days," said Maynard. "They were as baffled as we were."

"Did you hold any suspicion of deliberate arson, Mr. Maynard?"

Philip Maynard hesitated, and for just a fraction of a second too long, so that Knollis realized the truth he had suspected.

"You did suspect arson!" he said.

Maynard shifted uncomfortably. "Well . . ."

"Was there any reason to believe in a spontaneously generated fire, Mr. Maynard?"

"No—o, I suppose not," Maynard said in a resigned voice. "No, there wasn't."

"Your wife was taken ill that morning," said Knollis. "To what was her illness attributed?"

Georgie Maynard sought her husband's hand again, and her eyes rested on him nervously.

"Worry and shock," Maynard said grimly. "As I've told you, we've had the devil's own luck this year!"

"Have you a name for the particular devil?" asked Knollis.

The Maynards looked through him, apparently not understanding his question.

"Before the fire," said Knollis; "what was the previous stroke of—er—bad luck you experienced?"

"The soft fruit. Virus trouble. It went like that in a matter of a day or so," he replied, snapping his thumb and finger.

"And then—or perhaps I should ask what went before?"

"Well, actually, the fruit was the first patch of trouble, together with the failing of the hard fruit. Then came the bees. We got foul brood in the home apiary."

"That's a notifiable disease?" asked Knollis.

"Not to the police. We report it to the expert of the local Bee-Keepers' Association, and he reports to the War Agricultural Committee. Some counties have an official Foul Brood Inspector; others leave it to the association. The end's the same; we have to destroy our bees and burn them together with some of the equipment."

Knollis screwed up one eye and looked into and through Maynard for a minute or so, after which he asked: "Mr. Maynard, are your bees ever inspected by anyone other than your wife and yourself?"

"Why, yes," Philip Maynard replied readily. "Old Heatherington started us, and still keeps an eye on our activities."

"He'd looked into your hives shortly before you found signs of the disease?"

"Only the week previous. That's what puzzled us. My wife and I might have missed it, but he certainly wouldn't. He's an expert."

"I see," said Knollis. "I wonder if you'd care to show us the area on which you grew the soft fruit? I'm rather interested in your remarkable run of ill-luck."

Maynard got to his feet as if only too ready to do anything which would put an end to the seemingly interminable questions. He helped his wife up, and led them across the lawn, down two terraces, and to the far end of the miniature estate, which Knollis roughly estimated as covering two and a half acres.

Philip Maynard threw a pointing finger to a patch of bare ground, perhaps thirty yards square. "That was all rasps—a small fortune gone west, and in a good fruit year!"

Knollis ignored him, and walked ahead to inspect the grass paths that bordered the bed. He bent down and plucked a handful of blades and eyed them as they lay in his open palm.

"Do these fruit virus diseases affect grass, Mr. Maynard?" he asked solemnly. He held Maynard's eyes and was satisfied that he was uneasy if not actually afraid of the question. "Do they, Mr. Maynard?" he pressed him.

"I—I don't think so," said Maynard. "Do they, Georgie?"

She, too, was staring fixedly at Knollis.

"Tell me, Mr. Maynard," said Knollis; "has this ground been dug over since you pulled up the raspberry canes?"

Maynard said: "No."

"Your currants went the same way?" Knollis asked in a clipped, cold voice.

"At the other side of the hedge, Inspector," Georgie Maynard whispered. "The strawberries, too. We'd six hundred strawberry plants."

"The grass paths round your currant and strawberry beds? Have they gone yellow and dry like these?"

Both Maynards nodded, and drew closer together again, like two children being chided by a stern father.

Knollis waved a comprehensive hand round the scene. "All this, and the trouble with your bees, and the fire at Wellow Lock were caused by some nameless god who wanted to afflict you," he said caustically. "Circumstances were against you!"

He put his hands on his hips and thrust his head forward. "I don't believe it, Mr. Maynard! You don't believe it! You believe, as I believe, that you've been the victims of petty spite wreaked by an adolescent—whatever his physical age!"

Maynard licked his lips and said nothing.

Knollis suddenly relaxed. "Shall we go back to the house?"

He gave Wilson a wink and pushed him forward to cover him as the Maynards began the walk back to the house. He quickly emptied his matches in his pocket, and as quickly filled the box with soil from the bed before returning it to his pocket. He also pulled a handful of blades of grass and put them in his wallet.

Back in the garden-room he was more sociable.

"You've had a rotten spell," he said, easily. "How long had you been home from Wellow Lock when your wife was taken ill?"

"Oh, half an hour or so," Maynard replied. "I dropped her off here, and then took Old Heatherington home. When I got back I found her lying unconscious across the dining-room floor."

Knollis closed his eyes and tried to visualize the map of the district shown to him by Wilson during the lunch-hour. "But surely you come through Newbourne, and past Mr. Heatherington's house, when returning from Wellow Lock?" he inquired, mildly.

"There's a slip road," said Maynard. "I wanted to get Georgie home first. She wasn't looking too good."

"Quite understandable," said Knollis. "Experience much trouble in getting her to hospital?"

"The nursing home," Maynard corrected him. "No, the ambulance came straight out, Inspector."

"An admirable service! How long did you stay at Wellow Lock?"

"Oh, perhaps an hour," replied Maynard, turning to his wife for confirmation.

"We left at a quarter past two," she said.

"Seven miles out, isn't it?" asked Knollis, guessing.

"Five," Wilson said shortly.

"I see," said Knollis. He turned back to Maynard. "That must have been a heck of a day for you. The fire, and then your wife's collapse. I suppose you hovered round the nursing home most of the day?"

"Yes, but they wouldn't let me stay," replied Maynard. "I went back again after breakfast, and again in the afternoon."

"They let you see her?"

"I saw her as she was wheeled from the theatre to the ward, and then not again until evening. They said she wasn't out of the anaesthetic . . ."

"So you had to come home again?"

"I couldn't face the empty house, so went to a cinema," Maynard said shortly.

"A good idea," said Knollis. "I hope it was a film capable of taking your mind off your troubles for an hour or so?"

"Yes, a thriller. The film of Raymond Chandler's *Lady in the Lake*. I like a good mystery."

"So do I," Knollis remarked ambiguously. "A good one can supply intellectual pleasure as well as escape." He brought the photograph of Bernice Lanson from his inside breast pocket and thrust it under Georgie Maynard's nose. "You know this lady?"

She turned to her husband with wife eyes. "I haven't seen this before! Where has it come from, Inspector?"

Knollis leaned forward, a deceptively innocent expression on his lean features. "Tell me, Mrs. Maynard, how long did the affair between your husband's sister and Gerald Batley last?"

Philip Maynard stared at him, and then got slowly to his feet, a flush on his pale cheeks. "How—how dare you accuse my sister of any such thing! It's a damned vile suggestion!"

Knollis gave a careless shrug. "Read the inscription, Mr. Maynard. Ask Inspector Wilson where we found the photo."

"In a packet of girls' photos, all signed, in Gerald Batley's flat," said Wilson, as Maynard turned on him.

"Mrs. Lanson has been trying to persuade the caretaker at the Grafton Flats to let her into Batley's rooms," added Knollis.

Maynard sat down again, and turned to his wife. "This is the little mystery—as I thought it!—you wouldn't let me into!"

Tears were welling in Georgie Maynard's blue eyes as she replied: "How could I, Phil? I knew it would hurt you . . ."

Knollis and Wilson sat back, temporarily forgotten by the Maynards, letting the drama take its own course.

"The odd remark passed by Bern that day in the kitchen," muttered Maynard. "I wondered, and then walked away from the window, chiding myself for misconstruing a simple sentence! I was right, then! Bernice of all people. I'll—I'll ring Rod and tell him straight away. No sister of mine is going to make a fool of a decent man!"

Georgie Maynard jumped up and caught his arm. "You can't do it, Phil! It wouldn't do any good now, and would only wreck their lives. Bern's playing straight with him now—I swear it! You mustn't tell him! You simply mustn't!"

Philip Maynard flopped back again in his seat, mumbling to himself. "I suppose you're right," he said, "but it's damned rotten of her. What happened, anyway?"

Without as much as a glance at Knollis and Wilson she explained: "Oh, it was a temporary infatuation. She got it bad while it lasted, and was going to run away with him. She changed her mind at the last minute. It was when she was going for that holiday alone—"

"And then told Rod she couldn't bear the thought of a holiday without him!" Philip Maynard said bitterly. "I'll tell her what I think when I see her alone!"

"You can't even do that, Phil," said Georgie Maynard. "She made me swear never to tell you, and you can't let me down!"

Maynard looked across at Knollis. "You knew all this, and I didn't—her brother!"

Knollis admitted no such thing. Instead, he asked a question. "Didn't you have occasion to slap Batley's face in April, Mrs. Maynard?"

She covered her face with her hands. "He was hateful! Phil knows about it. He wanted me to meet him in town—regularly. I asked him about the girl he was engaged to, and he said she didn't matter; he was marrying her for her money, and she was marrying him because he had prospects, and it was only to be a marriage of convenience."

"Miss Moreland didn't think so," Knollis said grimly.

"Finish the story, Georgie," Maynard said wearily. "They might as well know the whole thing—if they don't already!"

"I—I can't, darling!" she stammered.

"I will then," snapped Maynard. "Inspector Wilson knows I was shipped home from Burma with T.B., and spent two years in Rossall Sanatorium, so I'm admittedly not the man I was when I joined up, but Georgie was told by Batley that I was only half a man, and a robust and vigorous young woman like herself needed a man and a half—like he always thought he was. That was where she bounced him!"

"She'd got something, too!" Wilson said, warmly. "You know, Knollis, he was a rotten swine!"

"He was murdered," said Knollis.

"My wife—and my sister," said Maynard. "He deserved to be murdered."

"When did this business start, Mrs. Maynard?" asked Knollis.

"I first re-met him in March," she explained in a small voice. "It was the day before Phil's birthday, and I went into Clevely to find a present for him. I went to lunch with Jerry, and he threw out a hint then that he'd like to see more of me, but I ignored it. It was April when he got me mad, and that was the second accidental meeting."

Knollis gently drew the photograph from her hands and moved towards the inner door of the garden-room. "Sorry to have upset you both so much, but these are upsetting affairs at the best. Ready, Wilson?"

On the way through the hall he paused to glance at a pile of magazines standing on a side-table beside the telephone. "*The Reader*, eh? One of my favourite periodicals. There's some interesting reading in them. Oh, well, we'll bid you good evening."

On the way back to Clevely, Wilson asked: "What have we got when it's sorted out?"

"A wallet full of grass, a match-box full of soil, and a handful of facts. They all need analysing."

"I'll get a rider to run the grass and soil into the Home Office lab. at Mottingley tonight," said Wilson. "What do you expect 'em to find?"

Knollis sighed. "Well, Wilson, I have a little garden of my own in the northern suburbs of London, The paths are stone, and tend to get clogged with weeds. Picking 'em out with a nail is a fiddling job, so I use sodium chlorate. It's non-selective, and kills everything it touches, so I have to make sure I don't so flood the paths that the stuff works into the borders. It's also hygroscopic, you know, drawing moisture from the atmosphere. You usually use it in solution, but if thrown on in its crystalline state it would soon deteriorate, leaving no visible trace. That's why I asked you about the rainfall earlier in the evening."

"So you knew what to look for before we got there?" Wilson asked in amazement.

"I'd a rough idea," Knollis admitted. "Using the stuff twice a year, I know what I'm talking about. Rainfall apart, heavy night dews would cause the stuff to deteriorate. Get your blokes to check with the chemists and horticultural suppliers. We shan't get a report for twelve hours, but I know I'm right. Somebody bought a lot of the stuff, and the purchase should be easy to trace."

"Batley's death could have been arranged even before Mrs. Maynard went in hospital," Wilson said smoothly. "That would give us a conspiracy!"

Knollis smiled. "Oh, yes, there was a conspiracy. Well, not actually a conspiracy, but a plot to murder. A conspiracy entails two or more persons, you know. I've said all along it was a one-man job. I'm beginning to see light at last."

"Maynard, of course?" murmured Wilson uncertainly.

Surprisingly, Knollis said: "No! It was Batley who was planning murder, my friend. That's why he persuaded Daphne Moreland to spend the honeymoon at the cottage in Windward Lane."

Chapter VI
GORDON KNOLLIS HAS A THEORY

Inspector Wilson had a fair amount of information, gathered by his staff, to put before Knollis when they met at Divisional Headquarters the next morning.

"First," he said to the somewhat sleepy Knollis, "we learn that Miss Moreland kept only one of those Tuesday morning appointments—that with the dentist at eleven-thirty. It wasn't an appointment actually, since she only called to make an appointment."

"That's something," said Knollis. "What else?"

"We've got her on the hip with the rest of the doings in her diary. She did not change her book at Boots on that day. She didn't take coffee with Mrs. Davenport. Sergeant Collier went to work at the Moreland home, and the maid is prepared to swear Daphne phoned Batley at twenty past eight that morning and got no answer. Oh, and she'd had no incoming call!

"In short, she'd slept on his brief notice to the effect that he wasn't turning up the next night, and didn't like it!

"Collier says the maid is certain it was Tuesday, the seventh," added Wilson.

Knollis smiled of gratification.

"Then the cyanide," said Wilson. "We started checking poison books an hour after the body was found, of course. It wasn't a difficult job, because although the canister had come to pieces we were able to rescue the bits, including the label. . . ."

"It wouldn't be sold in a cardboard container, of course," muttered Knollis. "The fact that the label was transferred is significant."

"Gregsons of Mottlingley are the only people in the area who can supply the stuff," said Wilson, "and that seems strange to me."

"It's queer stuff to get hold of," said Knollis in reply. "The supply is mainly confined to firms using it as a base for horticultural fumigants—which is why I know about it, having used it in my small greenhouse. Horticultural fumigants manufacturers, and the War Agricultural Committees for rat and rabbit extermination. Calcium cyanide needs moisture to trigger it off, and it then develops—if that's the right word—cyanogas. It's dangerous stuff to handle, and the rat catchers, or Rodent Officers as they're called in these self-conscious days, use a spoon attached to a long rod when putting it in burrows and rat-holes. The alternatives are potassium cyanide and sodium cyanide, but they both need dilute sulphuric acid to set them going, and that would have complicated our man's plan. It was calcium cyanide or nothing, and whoever bought it must have been well known to the chemist."

"Under the Poison Regulations," said Wilson, nodding his understanding of the point.

"Yes," said Knollis, "but what I mean is that whoever bought it must have been so well known to the chemist that he was able to persuade him to sell calcium cyanide instead of either of the other two."

"Know who bought it from Gregsons?" asked Wilson, a smile of triumph slowly blooming on his pink cheeks.

"Go on," sighed Knollis. "I'm waiting."

"Two lots were bought and signed for in the name of Philip Maynard."

"That's wrong!" snapped Knollis. "It can't be, or my theory goes phut!"

"Hold a minute!" Wilson warned him. "You're in too much of a hurry, Knollis. The signatures are in different handwritings. Somebody put a fast one across Gregson's man. The first entry in the poison book was dated Friday, the third of June. The second, Monday, the sixth of June."

"Oh!" exclaimed Knollis.

"Collier used his brains," went on Wilson. "He knew Maynard sold his last season's honey in bulk to a chemist here in Clevely—Harrison James, so he went along and scrounged the receipted bill. The signature on that corresponds with the third-of-June signature in the poison book."

"And the other?" asked Knollis, waiting calmly as Wilson worked his way to the denouement.

"Collier realized that Batley was supposed to be at business that day, so he asked Shipley whether Batley had official business in Mottingley."

"He had?"

Wilson nodded happily. "He was there the whole day—well, the whole afternoon, which is near enough for us. Collier then got a sample of Batley's signature from Shipley, and went back to Mottingley. While it will need the usual expert to declare that the poison book entry is a clumsy forgery perpetrated by Batley, there's no doubt he did the job."

Knollis smiled. "Wait a moment, Wilson. All this is interesting enough, but we still don't know whether it was the stuff he bought, or the stuff Maynard bought, that snuffed him! We can, of course, tackle Maynard for his reason for buying the stuff, asking to see the canister, and so on—"

"Oh, I know why he bought the stuff," Wilson interrupted with a note of pride. "I got in touch with Normanton on the blower late last night. They—Maynard and old man Heatherington—used it for killing off the bees after the disease crept into the apiary."

Knollis folded his long fingers under his chin, stuck his elbows on the desk, and stared across at Wilson. "It's good work, Wilson, but at the moment I can't make it fit in with my theory—serves me right for developing one so early in the case; it's always fatal! You see, my notion is this; Batley wanted Georgie Maynard pretty badly, and twice made overtures to her, being rejected with violence, as we know, on the second occasion. We've discussed the humiliation aspects, and we can then assume that his so-called love turned to hate, and increased his intention to get her—intensified would be the better word. He meant getting her now for sheer cussedness. He knew Mrs. Georgie was passionately devoted to her husband, so he set to work to part them—"

"He couldn't have done it!" Wilson objected.

"He was doing his best," persisted Knollis. "He was trying to get his own back by ruining them. Oh, yes, I'll grant the method was petty, and adolescent, but then, Batley was emotionally adolescent!"

"I wouldn't say that," grunted Wilson. "Considering his behaviour with certain women in this town, I'd say he was a real man-of-the-world type."

"My dear fellow," Knollis said patiently, "isn't that just the point? The lady-killer is always an adolescent. Take him back to his early youth. He's good-looking, and has what we call a way with him. He discovers he goes down well with the girls, and has the power to attract them. Once he becomes conscious of that power he develops it. Later he finds that by exercising it he can persuade his conquests to give him the privileges of marriage—"

"Mm!" muttered Wilson.

"Now if he develops normally he eventually marries and accepts the responsibilities of marriage along with the privileges. Batley didn't develop normally. I never knew the man alive, and he doesn't look attractive now, but I'll wager that any psychologist who'd analysed him would have agreed with me. Batley was the type of boy who always wanted to be the captain when he and his pals were playing football on the waste ground at the end of the street; if he had a row with them and they refused to let him be captain, then he'd as likely as not stick a pin in the ball so that nobody else could play. Now transfer the illustration. He wanted to play with Georgie Maynard—and how! She wouldn't fall, so what does he do? Tries to spoil life for her and her husband."

"True enough when looked at that way," Wilson said. "Yes, you may have something there. But, look here, Knollis! Assuming Maynard killed Batley—did he do it because Batley was responsible for his troubles, or because he tried to grab his wife? We have to consider motives!"

Knollis moved his chin from his hands and extended them in an open gesture. "Don't they mean the same thing? But we can't decide anything until we've proved that Batley was at least suspected, if no more, by Maynard of being responsible for the happenings at Mansard House. If he was aware, then the illness of his wife, brought on by worry and shock, was the last straw on the camel's back, and it would be then, on that very morning of Batley's death, that Maynard made up his mind to kill him."

He paused for a moment.

"The snag is in proving his movements. I've a notion Maynard went to Batley's flat to beat him up *after* the fire at Wellow Lock, but *before* his wife collapsed. We know he dropped her off at home, and then went somewhere, ostensibly to take Mr. Heatherington home—and so we ask ourselves whether the old man went with him. The point bothering me at the moment is how did Maynard know Batley was going to the cottage, or, alternatively, how did he get him out there to kill him? Batley seems to have gone there in a deuce of a hurry—"

A knock sounded on the door, and a tall man put his head into the room, asking for permission to enter. Wilson introduced him as Sergeant Collier.

"Peel and Davidson just phoned in their reports, sir," he said. "Batley bought five pounds of sodium chlorate from Charles and Anderson either late May or early June. Mr. Charles knew him well. Batley consulted him on a suitable weed-killer to clear the moss and grass in the cracks of the paths at Mrs. Doughty's cottage. He also bought five pounds from Dennis in Linden Street about the same time, although we can't get exact dates, and five ounces of copper sulphate from Dixon's for the same alleged purpose."

"Copper sulphate?" said Knollis. "That accounts for the fruit trees—the apples and pears. This is good work. We only need the lab. report now."

"I'll try 'em on the blower," said Wilson. "May as well get this point squared up if we can."

He turned to the telephone, and even before he finished the call Knollis knew that his hunch of the previous evening was a correct one.

"Sodium chlorate!" sighed Wilson.

"That's that, then," said Knollis. "We'll have to delve into this bee disease next. For now, I want to go over the flat again, and also see Daphne Moreland and Mrs. Lanson once more."

He flung a leg over the chair arm. "Sergeant Collier, if Inspector Wilson's agreeable, I'd like you to spend the morning fishing round the nursing home where Mrs. Maynard was taken. Try to whittle down Maynard's alibi. See if you can trace his presence at the—what was the name of the cinema, Wilson?"

"The Rex. He says he went to see *Lady in the Lake*, Collier."

Collier left them. Knollis stared steadily at the blotting-pad, tracing a spiral with his finger. "I must attend to those copies of *The Reader* in Maynard's entrance hall. Yes, I must dig into them!"

"What's it mean in English, Knollis?" asked Wilson.

"I'll tell you when I've got the thing straight in my mind," said Knollis. "It's the instrument with which I'm going to burst part of Maynard's alibi—I hope! Just one copy of that periodical, Wilson."

Wilson sighed. "Okay, Sphinx, let's get going!"

Marston met them in the vestibule of the Grafton Flats. "She's been here again, gents," he greeted them. "Came yesterday afternoon about five, and said she simply must get inside the flat. I said she simply mustn't because the police were in charge. She walked to the door there, stood nibbling her fingers for a minute or two, and then stamped her foot and went away."

"She won't bother you again," Knollis smiled, "not after a friend phoned her last evening. Now we want a key. We can't be chasing you every time we want to go in the flat—"

"What's the matter?" Wilson asked as Knollis broke off and stood licking his upper lip.

Knollis hastily encouraged Marston to part with one of his precious keys, and got rid of him as quickly as possible. He then said: "Wilson, where's Batley's own key?"

"Bat—"

"Didn't you find it in his pockets?"

Wilson swore. "No, I didn't, and I never even thought about it, queerly enough. It's queer, Knollis!"

They went up to the flat in silence. Knollis eased himself on the table and sat swinging his legs, his arms folded across his chest.

"It means, Wilson, that neither Daphne Moreland nor Bernice Lanson can have had a hand in his death. Mrs. Lanson can't have wanted anything but her photograph, and even supposing she went to the extreme of committing murder she'd have had the sense to get the key before pushing him down the well!"

"While Daphne Moreland would have had no need of the key," said Wilson. "If she did him in she wanted nothing but his death."

"She's wanted something since his death," Knollis corrected him, "otherwise she wouldn't have haunted Marston. Still, she hasn't got the key—or has she?"

"Another notion meandering round the cerebrum?"

"Possibly," said Knollis. "While it crystallizes, let's go next door and make inquiries about the fight I've imagined from this mess of litter."

The lady next door was pleased to see them. Their visit was going to be something to tell her friends. She offered them coffee and biscuits, which they accepted. She knew Mr. Batley, oh, yes! Such a charming young gentleman! It was evident that she wouldn't have objected if Mr. Batley had tried to seduce her while her husband was out. He always raised his hat when he met her, and stood aside for her to enter the lift first—such delightful manners, and so considerate!

"You'll remember the hullabaloo in his flat?" asked Knollis, casually.

My word, yes, she remembered that! Turned three in the morning, and her husband wondered about getting up to see what it was all about, but she'd persuaded him to mind his own business—one has to, really, hasn't one? There'd been an awful lot of bumping about, and then a door slammed, and shortly afterwards a car drove away.

"That establishes that," said Knollis, when they were back in the flat. "You and I can't spare the time to get further corroboration, so I suggest you turn a man loose on the left-hand neighbour, and those over and below."

Wilson agreed. "I'll phone Coxon now. He's the best bloke for a job like this. He knows how to apply the soft soap and flannel and get them to talk. Collier's all zeal and hurry—like you!"

They went on to the Moreland home, where Knollis wasted no time in challenging Daphne. She was ready to go out, and received them in a long blue coat that emphasized the delicate blueness of her eyes, which looked a wee bit strained now.

"1 thought I'd seen the last of you," she said in a nonchalant manner intended to give the impression of non-concern with their errand.

"Not by any manner of means," Knollis said severely. His face was a mask of official disapproval of her.

"I'm sorry," she said, and evidently meant it.

"Where were you on the morning of the seventh of July, Miss Moreland. I must ask you that, and must insist on an answer."

Daphne Moreland giggled, surprisingly. "That sounds like a talkie detective. I told you, Inspector—at least I showed you my diary."

"Faked while we waited for you," snapped Knollis. "According to the entries you were due to change your library book at Boots, take coffee with Mrs. Davenport, and call on the dentist that morning!"

"I did all those things," she replied, earnestly.

"You did not, Miss Moreland! You called on the dentist at eleven-thirty, but the other so-called appointments you did not keep!"

She paced across the room, asking over her shoulder: "How on earth can I convince you?"

"You can't!" Knollis flashed back. "You went to the cottage at Newbourne on the morning of the seventh of June, having rung both Gerald Batley's flat and his place of business without tracing his whereabouts. You suspected him of being at the cottage with another girl, and went to catch him with her. Isn't that correct, Miss Moreland?"

She bit her lip and nodded.

"Who was the suspected woman, Miss Moreland?"

She studied her varnished nails closely and did not raise her head. "Georgie Maynard, his cousin."

"He was chasing her?"

"We've been into all this before," she replied, solemnly.

"Chasing her without any regard for her husband?"

Daphne Moreland grimaced. "Jerry had nothing but the most utter contempt for him. I had an idea which way the wind was blowing, and tried to lead him on one evening to talk about Georgie. His tale was that he was sorry for her. He said it was rotten for her having a husband like Phil. If the wind blew the wrong way once he'd rock, and if it blew twice he'd fall down and not try to get up again. . . ."

With her back towards them as she stared through the window, and her fingers fidgeting with the buttons of her blue coat, she said: "I can hear him now, in a most scornful voice, saying: *'I mean that if they get any trouble up at Mansard House he'll curl up. He's the gutless type that commits suicide when the load gets too heavy.'*"

She swung round and looked solemnly at Knollis and Wilson. "Does that suggest anything to either of you? It does to me!"

Knollis drew in a sharp breath. "So that was it!"

Wilson blinked. "What was?"

"Do you agree with Batley's summing-up of Maynard's character, Miss Moreland?"

"I most certainly don't," she answered. "That's why I'm afraid for Georgie's sake. She's a lovely girl!"

Wilson sat tight, looking from Knollis's tense face to the girl's tired one. The barriers were down at last. She looked haggard and worried, her black-rimmed eyes and sagging cheeks betraying the lack of sleep.

"You're afraid for Mrs. Maynard," Knollis said quickly. "You think Maynard killed your fiancé?"

"I can't help thinking it," she said, desperately. "This isn't helping Georgie a bit, but I'm sick of the thing running through my mind. Night and day. Night and day! I can't rid myself of it! Jerry was playing with fire and didn't know it!"

"That was possible," Knollis said. "You knew about this attempted affair with Mrs. Maynard—this is almost a rotten question to ask you, Miss Moreland, but were you of the opinion you were losing him?"

She braced herself and lifted her chin. "The marriage would have gone through as arranged," she said in a cold, deliberate voice. "We would have been married on the eighteenth of June if he'd lived—but if Georgie had shown him any favour I couldn't have held him even as my husband. And Jerry? He'd have gone through with it even while deceiving me. It was all to his benefit! A partnership with Bob Shipley! Son-in-law to Frank Moreland!"

"And wife to you," added Knollis.

"That could sound awful coming from me, Inspector."

"I said it for you, Miss Moreland. Batley was marrying above himself. So you would have gone through with it, knowing what man you were marrying!"

She stared bleakly, a thin smile on her tight lips.

"There are certain disadvantages in belonging to what is known as the middle class, Inspector. The lower classes may envy us, and even hate us, but they have freedom of a kind we know nothing about. We have to live our lives to a code—a conventional code that means nothing and yet has to be complied with! The law of the herd—our particular herd! You know the chief tenet of it? Thou shalt not let down thy father, nor thy mother, nor thy man-servant, nor thy maid-servant, nor anything that is within thy gates! The price you pay doesn't matter. Jerry Batley and I had announced our engagement. We had announced the date of the wedding. We should have been married—and I couldn't back out without making myself an object of ridicule in the set, the herd of doctors, lawyers, bank-managers, parsons—and God knows who else."

She suddenly relaxed, and smiled. "You do see what I mean, Inspector?"

"There was a way out, Miss Moreland," Knollis said, quietly.

"I did not murder Gerald Batley, Inspector!"

"You must have known a great deal about him," said Knollis, ignoring her protestation. "Did he know anything about bee-keeping?"

She gave him a long, searching look, one he failed to interpret, before answering his question. "His father was a bee-master," she said, softly.

"And he?"

"Was allergic to stings and consequently couldn't keep bees. A single sting would lay him out cold for hours. He told me once that on two occasions when he was stung as a lad the doctor had to inject adrenalin straight into his heart."

"I see," said Knollis. He took out his note-book and gravely consulted a blank page. "So you went to the cottage on the seventh, Miss Moreland?"

"Yes," she said, sighing deeply.

"And again on the eighth?"

"Yes, that was the visit I described to you."

"The one on the eighth?"

"Yes."

"And when you went on the seventh . . . ?"

"His car was standing outside the gate, and there was no sign of him either in the house or the garden. Both front and back doors were standing open. His suit-case, hat and the parcel which was in the cabinet next day were on the refectory table in the lounge. I thought he might be walking in the woods, so I backed out of the lane and came home. I went again next morning," she said dully, as if reciting a well-learned lesson. "That was when I climbed in through the window. It was then I knew he was dead. I felt it here," she added, touching her breast over her heart.

"And so?" murmured Knollis.

She raised her arms and let them fall limply to her sides. "There was nothing more to be done, Inspector."

Knollis signalled to Wilson and they left her. Hardly a word was spoken until they were back in Wilson's office, facing each other across the table.

"Well," said Wilson. "Did she, or didn't she?"

"I'm not concerned with that at the moment," said Knollis, "but with Batley's ideas. Daphne Moreland's given me the one item of verification I needed. You know what I have in mind, of course?"

Wilson sighed, and pushed the cigarette-box. "Have one, for Pete's sake. I'll have a chance to catch up with your quick mind while you light up!"

Knollis flicked his lighter, and they sat looking at each other, Knollis's long, inquisitive nose pointing to the blotting-pad as he picked up a pencil and began to doodle; Wilson's jaw sagging open as he tried to make smoke rings with hollowed cheeks.

"Somebody," said Knollis, "has saved Batley from the gallows. At first I had the idea that he might have obtained the calcium cyanide for further dirty work on Maynard's bees. And again, while I still say Batley was an adolescent, I thought his manoeuvres up at Mansard House so petty and childish as to be unbelievable, and I wondered if I was barking up the wrong tree."

"And, instead, Knollis?"

"He was contemplating murder, a double murder—or if you're pedantic by any chance, two murders. He was going to murder Daphne Moreland and Philip Maynard."

Wilson stuck the cigarette in the corner of his mouth and rubbed his cheek doubtfully. "An incredible theory, Knollis. You've read more than is justifiable into the facts."

Knollis drew a grill of four horizontal and four vertical lines, and joined the ends of the lower two with a loop. "You've remarked on my memory, Wilson, but you'll agree there's nothing phenomenal in remembering the words Daphne Moreland attributed to Batley. *'I mean that they get any trouble up at Mansard House he'll curl up. He's the gutless type that commits suicide when the load gets too heavy.'*"

"She said that, yes."

"I only dealt with Batley's emotional rating when we were discussing him earlier," said Knollis. "Adolescent he may have been emotionally, but the man had brains. When you first told me of Mrs. Maynard slapping his face in Castle Street I thought I saw the reason for the troubles at Maynard's place—sheer petty spite of a childish nature. Now I see the truth. Batley was deliberately pin-pricking Maynard, piling one straw after another on his back, and waiting until the last one broke it—as he hoped. Batley had wrongly estimated Maynard's character, *and was trying to drive him into suicide!*"

"To get his wife!" exclaimed Wilson, as if a revelation had visited him.

"To get his wife," said Knollis, looping more of the intersecting lines together.

Wilson flicked his ash on the floor, stuck the cigarette back in his mouth, and slapped a hand flat on the surface with some violence. "But Batley was going to marry Daphne Moreland! Even she's agreed on that, while admitting his infatuation for his cousin!"

"Of course," said Knollis, with a thin smile.

Wilson flopped back in disgust. "It don't make sense!"

"It makes sense if he was planning to kill her when she was his wife!"

Wilson came forward again. "That!"

"What?" Knollis tantalized him.

"That damned awful suggestion of yours! Daphne's money in his purse, he kills her, encourages Maynard to put his head in the gas oven, and then marries Georgie!" He shuddered. "It's horrible, even to a hardened old copper like me!"

"Don't you think I've outlined the truth of the matter?" asked Knollis.

"Only too blooming accurately. It's a ghastly invention, Knollis! Sure there's no catch in it?"

"Look, Wilson, Daphne Moreland's a town girl, and she's told us, not in so many words, but by implication, that she regards herself as a somebody. Batley was a man-about-town who liked life, in its social sense, as much as she did. Can you think of any sane reason why such a couple should want to spend a protracted honeymoon in a lonely country lane? Can you imagine Daphne Moreland going rustic?"

"No," said Wilson frankly, "I can't. But I could have pictured a honeymoon, even if spent in Clevely, consisting of a series of dances, dinners, theatres and the rest of it. You're right, Knollis! You're right!"

"Batley must have worked on her like a beaver, damning up her ideas of a continental holiday, and slinging in suggestions of romantic rusticity, with moonlight glades, and—"

"Green fairy-rings and the merry, merry pipes of Pan!"

Knollis laughed. "That's the general idea."

"And calcium cyanide in the trousseau!"

"It really is grim, Wilson!"

Wilson gave him a quizzical glance. "How do you think it would work out?"

Knollis stubbed his cigarette. "Philip Maynard goes first, leaving Georgie a widow—obviously! She's an emotional type, warm-hearted, loving, and needing love in return. Suddenly bereft, she's lost to the wide. Then Daphne Moreland dies, and this bereaved couple find much in common. The rest needs no outlining."

Wilson's voice dropped to a whisper. "It's going to take some proving, Knollis, but there's light at the end of the tunnel all right. I told you I had a chat with Normanton on the blower last night? Well, suppose Batley took the hive to the cottage? Suppose it was to be filled with bees—"

"Suffering from the same disease that afflicted Maynard?" said Knollis.

Wilson snorted. "You're ahead of me all the way. Any way, there's the excuse for having cyanide in the house, and if an accident *should* occur one fine day . . ."

"He'd get Daphne's money, Georgie's body—if I might put it coarsely but truthfully, and those two items, as we know from all the available evidence, were the only two things he wanted—wanted to the obsession limit, that is. The rest, social and professional advancement, would follow as day follows night."

Wilson sniffed. "We now have to find out who got ahead of him and turned the tables, and to do that . . ."

"We have to gen up on bee-keeping, finding out how the hive got in the garden, how the disease found its way into Maynard's apiary, and exactly how one uses calcium cyanide to kill bees."

"And that means a trip out to see Old Heatherington!"

"Yes, but first we must have a little talk with Mrs. Lanson."

Wilson glanced at the clock. "After lunch! We're late as it is."

CHAPTER VII
OLD HEATHERINGTON GIVES
A LESSON

MRS. BERNICE LANSON was idling in her garden, lolling negligently in a deck chair in a yellow summer frock, a sallow and discontented woman. She smiled sourly as the day-girl showed Knollis and Wilson through to her, greeted them with conventional civility, and then waited expectantly.

"I'm investigating the death of Gerald Batley," Knollis informed her, and waited in turn, watching her reaction.

"Oh, that!" she said. She sat down again, shaded the sun from her eyes with her hands, and looked up at him. "I hardly knew him, of course. It's my husband you'll be wanting to see, and, of course, he's down at the office in town."

"You've called at his flat several times since he disappeared," Knollis said, bluntly.

She gave a nervous laugh. "Me? There's some mistake, Inspector!"

"There's no mistake," said Knollis. "You were recognized by the caretaker."

He stood stiffly before her, his hands lightly clasped behind his back. "I wouldn't waste time, Mrs. Lanson. We found your photograph in his flat."

She smiled in a supercilious manner. "Is that so terrible, Inspector? I gave lots of them away at the same time."

"Your order at the Grecian Studios was for three copies; one copy of each pose," said Knollis. "It's your turn, Mrs. Lanson . . ."

She lowered her eyes, and plucked at a stray end of thread on the hem of the chair canvas. "I—er—gave him the photograph in a weak moment. We all get weak moments, don't we? When the rumour spread round town that something had happened to him I naturally wanted the photo back. My husband might have misunderstood if he'd learned of it."

"I think we should get down to brass tacks," said Knollis. "The inscription on the photo suggests something deeper than a platonic friendship. We have to clear these matters up, you know—and we keep going until we've done so."

She ran her tongue over her lips. "I went about with him at one time. The photo was just one of those relics of pre-marriage foolishness."

"You've been married three years and some months, Mrs. Lanson, and the photograph was taken last July!"

She said: "Oh!"

"You're wasting an awful lot of time!" said Knollis.

"People sometimes do silly things even after marriage," she said lamely. "I—er—well, I ran around with him for a short spell while my husband was down south on business. It was a purely innocent affair, but I made a mistake in giving him the photograph, and wanted it back."

"Why the sudden urgency?" asked Knollis.

She looked up, giving him a direct stare. "I didn't want his fiancée, Daphne Moreland, to find it. She'd have made a point of getting it to my husband. She's not . . . a very nice . . . person," she said, with great deliberation.

"That's all I need bother you about," said Knollis. "Thanks, Mrs. Lanson."

"The photograph!" she said, urgently. "I can have it back now?"

"Later," said Knollis. "Ready, Wilson?"

Wilson followed him from the house with a wondering expression on his face. "That was quick work and a sudden ending, wasn't it?"

"She was telling the truth, so why try to pull out more than the truth?" Knollis replied. "Suppose we go out to Mottingley now and have a word with the manager of Gregsons? I want to find out how Batley got round the regulations and hold of the cyanide. You know the regulations . . . !"

Wilson steered the car carefully through Clevely's crowded streets, hot in the summer sun. "The purchaser of cyanide has to be personally known to the pharmacist, or must be taken and introduced by a second person personally known to the pharmacist. The purpose for which the poison is required must be clearly stated, and the book signed. If Batley was known to Gregsons I'll eat my hat!"

The manager of Gregsons, a tall and slim man with an abnormally deep voice, was interested in the case, and only too willing to help in any way he could.

"I sold the first order myself," he informed them. "Old Mr. Heatherington came with Mr. Maynard in his car. He told me Mr. Maynard had foul brood in the apiary, and, of course, I knew that meant the destruction of the stocks, so I'd no hesitation in letting him have the stuff—although, quite frankly, I only keep it in stock for supplying to the municipal rodent officers. For anything but this particular purpose I'd have recommended potassium cyanide. It's a bit more difficult to handle, however, requiring the addition of dilute sulphuric acid to make it effective, and as Mr. Heatherington said, bees plus cyanide were enough to handle at one time without adding the complication! He was to be in charge of the operation, and he knew he wasn't playing with common salt!"

"And the second order?" Knollis murmured blandly.

"Mr. Maynard rang me. He said it looked as if the disease was spreading across the county. He'd now got it in his out-apiary at Wellow Lock, and would need more of the calcium cyanide. He wanted to know if he could have it without bothering Mr. Heatherington again. I told him that was quite all right since he was now known to me, and I understood the purpose for which he wanted it. He then wanted to know when he could come over the next day and be sure of finding me here. I told him when he *couldn't* find me here—I have to visit the sub-branches in town, you know! He hesitated then, and said it was most awkward, because the only time he could get over would be when I was out. I told him that would be all right; I'd leave word with my dispenser, and he would let him have the stuff. I added that

I'd prefer Mr. Heatherington to do the job for him, and he said he'd most certainly see to that, not caring to mess about with the jumping stuff!"

Knollis nodded slowly. "So that's how he worked it! Clever, and you can't be blamed in any way. I'd now like a word with the gentleman who served him."

The manager fetched a white-coated man with a fat face and large ears. "Mr. Fretwell."

"You served this second order of calcium cyanide," said Knollis, jabbing the poisons book with his finger.

"Oh, yes, sir! Mr. Johnson explained the circumstances to me, so, of course, I served Mr. Maynard without any hesitation."

"Now look," said Knollis chidingly, forcing a smile to his lips with the object of putting the dispenser at his ease; "didn't it strike you that there were obvious differences between the two signatures?"

"That was to be expected, sir," said the dispenser. "The man had three fingers in stalls, and a bandage round his right hand. He said he'd collected a packet—his own term, I assure you!— while inspecting the bees. He said the bee venom played—er— merry hell with him, and it was high time this much-boosted modern science found a cure for them instead of wasting its time on weapons of destruction. I told him we were recommending acidulated-chloro-iodine for external application, and benadryl for taking inwardly."

"So he signed the register under your nose, and walked out with the cyanide, just like that?" said Knollis, snapping his fingers with a loud crack.

"Right or wrong, that is the truth, Inspector."

"Can you describe him, Mr. Fretwell?"

Mr. Fretwell thumped his broad brow with a fist like a small ham. "I seem to remember him as a dark-complexioned gentleman, somewhat handsome in a flashy way, with dark wavy hair."

The manager started forward. "That isn't Maynard! He's fair and pale—sickly-looking!"

Wilson silently pushed photographs of Batley and Maynard under Mr. Fretwell's nose. The dispenser straightway jabbed a finger between Batley's eyes. "That's him!"

"And the other is Maynard," said Mr. Johnson. "We've unwittingly helped in a murder, Fretwell. I'm sorry, genuinely sorry. I wonder—are we still inside the law, Inspector?"

"I should say so," said Wilson.

Knollis narrowed his eyes and focussed them on the open poisons book. "That isn't the point. The vital fact emerging is that Batley didn't want anybody to know he'd acquired any cyanide. He didn't want it tracing back to him. If he'd had a legitimate use for it he could have found someone to introduce him to you, and then made the purchase in the normal manner. That is what I've been trying to establish—that the poison was to be used for an illegal and criminal purpose. You needn't reproach yourselves. Batley would have got the stuff somehow or other!"

On the way home, Knollis insisted on calling to see Old Heatherington. They found the old man in his apiary, sitting on the rustic seat in his white jacket, and with his panama tipped over his eyes as he watched the bees leaving and returning to the hives.

"We're safe down here?" Knollis asked anxiously.

"Safe as houses," replied the old man. He made room for them, and patted the seat in silent invitation.

"We've been to Mottingley, checking up on your purchase of cyanide," said Knollis.

"It was all right, wasn't it?"

"That was, but the second order wasn't."

Old Heatherington took his pipe from his mouth.

"There was no second order. There was enough of the stuff to kill half of the bees in the county. What's left is locked up in the house."

"A second lot was bought and signed for in Maynard's name, Mr. Heatherington."

The old man shook his head doubtfully. "Then something queer's been happening, sir."

"It was Batley," said Knollis. "We've established that." He explained the trick Batley had played.

"Now why did he want calcium cyanide?" the old man asked calmly. "He wasn't a bee-keeper!"

"That's the point," said Knollis. "Why did he want it? By the way, how do you use the stuff when killing bees?"

Old Heatherington fumbled in his pockets. "I want a piece of paper about two inches square—three inches will be better."

Knollis found a used envelope in his wallet, and handed it over. The old man folded it across the diagonals.

"You press up the sides, and get something like a little boat. You put a teaspoon of powder in it—and don't use the spoon for stirring your tea after! Then you fill a shallow saucer or a tin-lid with water, float the paper on it, push it in the entrance, and all but close the entrance slides. The water soaks the paper, gets at the cyanide, and the gas is set off. The bees are dead in seconds, and the flying bees that are out get it as soon as they stick their heads inside."

"Exactly as Batley was killed!" exclaimed Wilson, before Knollis had time to kick his ankle.

The old man shook his head. "There was some rum jiggery-pokery there. The stuff's too dangerous to sell in cardboard boxes like I'm told it was in. They put it in tin cylinders with screw-on caps that are sealed."

"But the label of the cardboard container was found in the well!" said Knollis, professing ignorance.

"Can't help it, sir," said Old Heatherington. "If that was so, then the label had been taken off the real tin and stuck on the cardboard box. That's why I knew something was wrong when I read about it in the papers the morning after I found him!"

"Then why the deuce didn't you let us know!" Wilson demanded, heatedly.

The old man smiled. "I'm a bee-keeper, and if anybody that doesn't keep bees tries to tell me my job I get mad!" he said in a mild voice.

"Batley wasn't a bee-keeper?" asked Knollis, although Daphne Moreland had already told him the truth.

"No, sir, but his father was," said Old Heatherington. "Teddy Batley was one of the best bee-masters in England in his day. I've worked alongside him, and I know. He always wanted young Gerald to take it up, but he was allergic to stings, and one or two of them would put him on his back for a fair time, so he couldn't go in for it. But he knew what to do, mind you! There was nothing wrong with his theory! No reason why there should be if it comes to that, since he was born and brought up in a house that was filled with talk of bees from morning to night!"

"How did the disease get into Maynard's apiary, Mr. Heatherington?" Knollis asked the old man directly.

Old Heatherington sighed, tapped his pipe on his heel, and felt for his pouch again. "It was put there, Inspector. I knew you'd ask me that sooner or later if you knew your job. I told Inspector Wilson here that he'd need me, and he has, you see, and he'll need me again before all's finished! But what made you ask, sir? How did you tumble to it?"

"Because the trouble that carried off his fruit was also put there."

The old man thumbed the tobacco into the bowl of his pipe. "I reckoned that as well, but couldn't prove it. I didn't mention it to him because I reckoned he'd got enough on board without knowing it was chemicals and not virus. You never saw rasps and currants and such go off that fast with disease! It wasn't natural. They were as right as rain one day, and the next night they were done for. Philip knows his theory, but he's no experience behind it, and it's that as makes the difference, sir!"

"That's true enough," said Knollis.

"What was it he used on the fruit, sir?" Old Heatherington asked casually.

Knollis flashed a quick glance at him from the corner of his eye. "Who used?" he asked sharply.

The old man didn't wink an eye or move a muscle as he replied: "Young Gerald."

"You knew that, Mr. Heatherington?"

"I twigged it when the bee trouble arrived. What did he use, sir?"

"Sodium chlorate. We had the soil analysed."

The old man sighed. "I reckoned that—or copper sulphate."

"He used copper sulphate on the hard fruit trees," Knollis told him, and immediately asked, as his part of the exchange of questions: "What did he use for introducing the disease?"

"Young Gerald was a nasty piece of work, and I'm glad his father never lived to see it," sighed the old man. "He took diseased brood and put it in healthy hives. Phil's own brood was all right, you know, but we couldn't allow it to live after that stuff had been with it a day or two. It might have been safe. It might—but you never know, and you've other beekeepers to think about."

"Then the bees themselves weren't affected?" asked Knollis.

"Oh, no, sir! It's a brood disease, and nobody knows much about it. The old hands have rare arguments in the bee papers, but nobody gets anywhere. You can save the flying bees if you want to, but I wouldn't do it on account of them carrying infection. You see," said Old Heatherington, "bees always fly back to the site of the hive, and not to the hive itself, so if you shift a hive without putting another on the site the bees coming back from the fields will just fly round that square yard until they drop from exhaustion. So if you take the diseased hive away, and put a clean one on the site the bees will fly into it and accept it as home, but as nobody knows how the disease is carried—well, that's why I destroyed Phil's."

"Why did he do it?" asked Knollis, curious about the old man's suspicions.

Old Heatherington struck a match on the sole of his boot, and, without looking up, said: "He wanted young Georgie, and couldn't get her."

"Spite, in other words?" suggested Knollis.

"I thought that at first until Mr. Moreland came to see me. Young Gerald was going to marry his daughter—they said. Now Mr. Moreland's a lawyer and a right smart man, a man I can take my hat off to . . ."

Knollis and Wilson glanced at each other, and waited while the old man puffed his pipe into life.

"Seems—that young Jerry—that's got it!—had said something to Miss Moreland, and her father, being smart as I've said, thought he might have said something his daughter didn't quite understand. It was something about Phil having no backbone, and a hint that as likely as not he'd stick his head in a gas oven if he got too much trouble round his neck—he didn't know Phil! Anyway, Mr. Moreland explained he'd heard about Phil's troubles from his brother-in-law, Mr. Lanson, and he'd put two and two together and wondered if he had what he called a case to put forward. I reckon he was trying to chuck young Jerry out, but he didn't say so in as many words."

"Moreland!" muttered Wilson. "The dark horse!"

"I told him what I suspected," said Old Heatherington, "but I told him I hadn't proved it, so didn't want my name mentioning. He asked me what it was worth to help him sort the job out, and I told him I was of the mind to work it out for my own satisfaction as well as his, and I didn't want anything for it. I did that, but Mr. Moreland didn't come back after Gerald cleared off, and so I didn't bother getting in touch with him. I was satisfied."

"You solved it?" Knollis asked eagerly.

"Look at my bees, sir," said the old man. "Dark with grey rings, aren't they, and just a bit of yellow on the thorax. A Caucasian strain with a bit of yellow in them, and Phil Maynard has—or had—the same strain since he got them from me. Now if you'll come indoors . . ."

He took them to the house, unlocked a drawer, and produced two test tubes in which dead bees were floating in a colourless liquid.

"Preserved in formalin," he explained. "Now, these in this tube are from Phil's hives. Same as mine, aren't they?"

Knollis examined them intently, and nodded.

"They look the same brand to me," said Wilson.

"Now see the others!"

"Almost a bright orange," said Wilson.

"As near a pure Italian as you'll get in England, sir," said the old man. "Now I'm not going to get too technical, but I tackled two angles when I started looking into this business. First, there are two sorts of frame you use in a hive, those with a solid top bar, and those with split top bars. You get a sheet of wax foundation with the pattern of the cells stamped on it, and with the split top bar type you prise open the slit and slide the wax sheet in between, and then nail up the slit like a clamp. In the others there's a rebate beneath the top bar, and you lay the edge of the foundation in it, and nail a strip of wood across to hold it. I use the solids because we're troubled with what's called a wax moth that lays eggs in hives, and the split bar makes a good place for them to lay in. I fitted Phil up with solids, and yet when I opened up after Phil found the foul brood I noticed frames with split bars among the others."

"Go on!" said Knollis, his lean features tense. "This is good detection!"

"This disease doesn't attack every cell on a comb at once, but spreads gradually," went on the old man. "Some of the grub or larvae had escaped infection and were emerging—hatching, you'd call it."

He held up the tube of bright yellow bees. "These came from the bars with the split tops."

"This is really something!" exclaimed Wilson. "We'll have to enrol him, Knollis!"

"And the final stage of your investigation?" asked Knollis, almost purring with satisfaction.

"Got an hour to run me out into the country, sir?"

"You can have a day or a week in such circumstances," Knollis assured him. "We're at your service."

The old man smiled and walked out of the house, jog-trotting down the yard to his honey-house while Knollis and Wilson watched him through the window. He returned with three veiled straw hats, a small roll of cotton wool, and a green poison bottle.

"You'll find this interesting," he smiled. "We're going to Jason's Knoll. You'll know the way, Inspector Wilson?"

As they drove the nine miles Old Heatherington explained the line of thought that had, in his opinion, and he wasn't dogmatic about it, solved the riddle of the diseased apiary.

"Teddy Batley was a good bee-keeper, and a keen experimenter," he said. "He was out for a good strain of the purest Italians he could get. He sent to Italy for queens, and started work. Now to get a strain and hold it pure you have to raise your bees miles from the next apiary, otherwise when your virgin queens go out on mating flights they might get mated by drones from another apiary. You understand that?"

"We've both read Maeterlinck," said Knollis.

"Aye, that's good enough. So Teddy Batley had two queen-rearing apiaries miles from anywhere."

"Where was the other?" asked Wilson.

"At Wellow Lock, where Phil Maynard's working now—or tried to work. Anyway, when Teddy died, and young Gerald couldn't take over on account of what they call this allergy of his to bee venom, all the stocks were sold. I had some of them. It suddenly struck me after this trouble came up that I couldn't remember hearing of anybody buying his near-pure Italian strain from Jason's Knoll, so I went out. I can drive a car, although I'm not keen at my age, so I borrowed Phil's with the story I wanted to look round Wellow Lock again, and took a run to where we're going now. The apiary, if you can call it that, is in a dell at the foot of the knoll, and hidden in the woods. It's a long way from any path, and the chances are you'd never find it if you didn't know it was there. I'll tell you the rest when we get there."

In due course he asked Wilson to pull up at the end of a cart-track leading from a side road, and they walked from there. A quarter of a mile further on the old man told them to put on the veiled hats. "Tuck the bottom of the veil well inside your jacket, and pull your socks over your trouser turn-ups. Then stuff your hands deep in your pockets as soon as you meet bees. These are wild bees now, not butterflies, and they'll be out as soon as the news gets round. I'll quieten 'em, of course, when we get there. We usually smoke them, but these are terrors, so I'm using this methylated ether stuff. That quietens 'em!"

He threw a long leg over a fence and led the way through the high bracken and fern that covered the floor of the wood. Below them in the hollow they saw three dirty hives which had once been white, and then the bees began to greet them, darting out like bullets to ping against their clothes and veils.

"Just keep going, and don't bash at any of them," the old man said quietly.

Wilson looked at Knollis through the veil. "If you know of a nice quiet riot conducted with broken bottles, lead me to it after this!"

Old Heatherington led them behind the hives. "Never walk across the line of flight from the hives. That's when they hit you and really start stinging."

"What are they doing now?" Wilson demanded. "I've at least a dozen in each sleeve now."

Old Heatherington tore the cotton wool into pads, poured about a teaspoonful of the anaesthetic on each pad, and pushed one into the entrance of each of the three hives. "We'll wait now," he said, happily.

He filled his pipe, threaded the stem through a hole in the veil, and lit up, while Knollis and Wilson watched him with mingled amusement and amazement. He stood with his head askew, listening to the disturbed roar within the hives. After a few minutes he raised the roof of the first one, and nodded.

"We can work now. See how the brood box is covered with a canvas quilt? That's an idea that's slowly going out. I use framed sheets of three-ply with a narrow glass panel let in so's I can see what they're doing without upsetting them."

With thumb and finger he slowly peeled back the canvas quilt. "They seal themselves in with propolis, the gummy stuff they get from chestnuts and sycamores and such like trees. Now this brood chamber should have ten frames of comb in it, and you'll see there's only six. They've filled the space with pieces of comb in a regular mix-up. Notice the difference in colour between the comb in the frame and this other stuff?"

"That in the frames is almost black, and the other white," said Knollis.

"The white is new comb, built only this summer," said Old Heatherington. "That tells me that the frames were taken out this year. See the idea?"

Knollis nodded. "You've worked this thing out very logically, Mr. Heatherington. You're to be congratulated."

"It's just knowing my bee-keeping," said the old man. He lifted a frame from the hive and held it up. "See how some of the cells are capped with a shallow dome? That's healthy brood, going through a metamorphosis—same as a caterpillar turning into a butterfly. Then you'll notice some of the cappings are sunken. The larvae are affected with foul brood disease. There are two sorts: what's known as American Foul Brood, and European. This stuff is the worst type. Then, to top up, look at the colour of the bees on the frame. See what I meant back there?"

Knollis watched the stupefied bees, some merely clinging to the comb, and others wandering about as if in a daze or a trance, but all of a bright yellow, almost orange, hue.

"What do we do now, Mr. Heatherington?" asked Knollis.

The old man returned the frame to the brood box, covered it down again with the quilt, and replaced the roof before answering.

"Either trust my judgment, or go round the county examining the stocks of all the bee-keepers," he said with a queer smile. "If you find another stock of that colour, and in a healthy condition, tell me, because I'd like to buy them for my own apiary—or a queen or two from them. But you won't, sir! You'll find some that look like them, but if you get an expert to check he'll find slight differences in colour, and banding, and size. No, this is Teddy Batley's forgotten apiary, and the bees are just about unique."

Knollis was looking round the site. "You always stand the hives on bricks or concrete, Mr. Heatherington?" he asked.

"Yes, sir, usually with a piece of slate between leg and brick. It stops damp from rotting the legs."

"I see," said Knollis. "Tell me, did Maynard suspect the cause of the trouble?"

The old man gave him a suspicious glance, and looked worried. "I don't know, sir, and that's the truth, but I've wondered. Yes, I've wondered!"

They ran him home after he had removed the wool pads from the hive entrances, and thanked him enthusiastically for his help and practical demonstrations. Then Wilson swung the car round in the village street and started back to town.

"We'll have to see Frank Moreland, Knollis," he said, softly, "and tomorrow's Sunday, and he's a keen church-goer."

"We'll still have to see him, Wilson."

After a long period of silence, Knollis said: "Notice anything at Jason's Knoll, Wilson?"

"Nearly all the bees in creation. I think I shall have a bash at bee-keeping. It looks an interesting hobby."

"The building bricks, I mean."

"There were four, one under each leg—twelve bricks in all for the three hives."

"And at the end of the row, almost hidden in the undergrowth, four bricks and no hive."

Wilson started. "I never saw them. Oh, I see what you're getting at! The hive at Mrs. Doughty's cottage!"

"That's it!" nodded Knollis.

CHAPTER VIII
MR. MAYNARD HIDES THE ACE

GORDON KNOLLIS intended to spend the Sunday morning in a deck-chair in the garden behind his hotel. It was a warm day, and such light breezes as tended to rise were shielded from the garden by the rose-covered stone walls.

He and Wilson had an appointment with Moreland for early afternoon. Until then he could relax. He collected the Sunday papers and settled down to skim them, his grey trilby pulled well down over his eyes.

He smiled cynically as he learned from one paper that Inspector Knollis of the Yard was in possession of startling new facts regarding the Clevely murder, and from another that the case was progressing satisfactorily and an arrest was imminent.

A third one, apparently not interested in venturing into the realms of prophecy, gave a full page to profile résumés of his previous cases, more or less accurately. It reviewed his first big case, the Lomas case in Burnham, his return to the same city to unravel the mystery of the Sable Messenger, the case of the Threefold Cord, and the murders of Richard Huntingdon and Dr. Hugh Challoner, concluding with the comforting remark that he was a force to be reckoned with, and the Clevely case could not be left in better hands.

> *This slim, lean-faced, keen-eyed man who rose from the ranks of a provincial police force is an investigator who knows his job, and is fully capable of utilizing his experience. Gordon Knollis, who once pounded a beat in the city of Burnham, can hardly be called a sociable man, but he is an acute observer who can add two and two together and make them add up to neither more nor less than four. A certain person in Clevely must be shaking in his shoes, and awaiting the inevitable end. . . .*

Knollis grinned boyishly. The praise tickled his vanity, but he doubted whether he was a force to be reckoned with, and was satisfied that up to now no one had any reason to shake in their shoes. It was one of those cases which needed wiggling out. His last murder investigation, into the death of Dr. Challoner of Sturton Lacey, was a different matter, one in which three people, all suspect, each tried their best to incriminate the other two. In this present case he seemed to be up against a conspiracy of silence, not because any suspect or witness was trying to shield anyone else, but because at least three people had been guilty—if that was the right word—of movements and actions which they feared might be misconstrued and render them liable to suspicion. Consequently, they all played the old Brer Rabbit game of laying low and saying 'nuffin.

There was Daphne Moreland, for instance. She'd made no bones about going to the cottage on the morning of the seventh of June when tackled directly and when bluffed into believing that Knollis knew far more about her than he did, but she would most certainly not have volunteered the information, and had indeed tried to make him believe she'd first gone on the ninth. Why the evasion?

Knollis scowled under the brim of his hat and threw his mind back to past cases in search of a similar instance. He tapped his fingers in a gentle tattoo on the open pages of the *Sunday Argosy*. It had happened in the Lomas case. On that occasion, when he got down to it, he found himself breaking down what should have been a first-class alibi. Was the same happening here? Was Daphne Moreland playing with him, allowing him to break down an apparent alibi with the intention of drawing attention to herself, knowing full well she could clear herself if it came to the pinch, and thus shielding someone by what might be called a negative method? The possibility was intriguing.

Then the Maynards. They also were playing the Brer Rabbit game. They were as silent about other people's movements as about their own—or about Philip Maynard's since Georgie was safely in hospital at the critical time. What was Philip Maynard doing throughout that day? The pile of copies of *The Reader* had given Knollis an idea, suggesting that Maynard had rigged himself an excellent alibi, one that could neither be proved nor disproved—in his own opinion. Knollis had different ideas on the subject, and intended to break him down before many hours had passed. Wilson had complained that he never went far enough with his interviews, Knollis replying that he went as far as was necessary, and that it did the potential witnesses no harm to wonder for a few hours exactly how much he did and did not know. The suspense was apt to give them the jitters, and loose the control which reason held over their tongues. By taking the available facts of evidence as a whole, the most interesting point in Knollis's view was Batley's so obvious sudden departure for the cottage. Three questions arose: why had he gone, who did he meet there, and who drove his car back to the Grafton Flats?

A light step sounded behind him, and, as he looked round, a hand fell on his shoulder. It was Wilson, in an open-necked tennis shirt, flannels, and a brightly-checked sports jacket.

"Hello!" Knollis greeted. "I wasn't expecting to see you before lunch. Can't you relax for an hour?" Wilson sprawled out on the grass at his feet, stretching his long legs with a sigh. "I know! I know! I fully intended laying off this morning, and doing; nothing more industrious than pulling up a few weeds in my garden, but I couldn't rest with this thing on my mind, so I ambled down to the office and then found Coxon's and Collier's reports on my desk. I thought maybe you'd like to see 'em."

"Tell me about 'em," Knollis suggested from under the hat. "I'm not in a reading mood this morning."

"It'll be quicker, anyway," Wilson agreed. "Coxon was left, you'll remember, to do the flats. He's collected loads of evidence about the fight in the early hours of the seventh, but it all boils down to this; somebody came in a car, there was a dickens of a fight, and then somebody left in a car. Those flat residents seem to be a most incurious set, and Coxon couldn't find one who'd admit to getting out of bed to scout round the place or even squint through the curtains. And the times vary between ten and twenty past three for the arrival of the car. Coxon reports that every clock in the place was right by the wireless—they always are. He suggests twenty past three would seem to be the correct time for the arrival."

"Giving Maynard time to come out here after dropping his wife off at home," said Knollis. "Premeditated assault, since if he hadn't wanted to come into town to beat up Batley, and hadn't wanted Old Heatherington to come with him he could have gone back by the main road."

Wilson nodded. "Hm!"

"I've an idea what they were up to," said Knollis, "but that can wait. Let's have the rest of the news."

"Collier's report," said Wilson, drawing a sheet of foolscap from his pocket. "He went to the nursing home. Maynard appears to have kept them busy with personal and telephone calls. They remember things like that in a nursing home. It isn't like a hospital. They accept the humbug and charge it on the bill."

Knollis, who appeared to be asleep, opened one eye. "Times of the telephone calls, Wilson? Collier get them?"

Wilson grunted. "Good job for us she was in a nursing home, and not in the district hospital. The wenches booked the calls. I had a word on the blower with Collier before I came along, and he says they emphasized the fact that they always book incoming calls. Idea is for the patient to have all inquiries from anxious friends relayed to them; it makes 'em feel important, and cools 'em down when they eventually meet the bill. This job cost Maynard a solid fifty quid. However, you impatient man," he said, as Knollis wriggled in his deck-chair, "the calls came through at one-thirty and four-forty-five. He'd been up at the home at ten past one, but they wouldn't let him see her because she was still under the influence."

"I remember him saying that," nodded Knollis. "It makes a rattling good alibi. I doubt if we can prove it, but I'll bet both calls were made from the foyer of the cinema—they do have a phone there?" he asked, anxiously.

"Penny in the slot job," said Wilson. "You think he skipped out between calls?"

"Some such notion is running round my head," Knollis admitted. "I don't think he saw the flick he said he saw."

"He seemed to know all about it," protested Wilson.

"That is the whole point," said Knollis.

"How are you going to prove it?"

"How did Collier make out at the cinema?" asked Knollis.

Wilson shrugged. "Couldn't get a line on him at the Rex, of course. Not surprising, considering it's over a month ago and they take in several thousand people a day, but still, it does show he didn't do the old trick of deliberately drawing attention to himself before slipping out by some back way to do the job. Er—you do think it's coming down to Maynard, don't you?"

"I think he's done something of a highly suspicious nature," said Knollis.

"Same thing," said Wilson.

He was silent for a minute while he tried to press the tag of a shoe-lace through an already occupied eyelet. "There's Mrs. Lanson," he said, casually.

Knollis turned his head sharply. "Oh? Why?"

"I—er—dropped across something at the club after I left you last night. Mrs. Lanson was trying to borrow money late in March—she wanted a hundred in a hurry."

Knollis raised his eyebrows, and waited until Wilson had wangled the tags of both laces into the eyelets to his satisfaction.

"Lanson isn't short of a hundred," said Wilson. "If she wanted it for legitimate purposes she could have asked her husband for it, surely? That's my angle on it."

"From where did she try to borrow it?"

"Bloke named Jephson. Money-lender, accountant, and book-debt collector. One of those 'erbs who advertise to lend any amount on note of hand. You know the stunt! All they want to do is look round the house and see if there's enough stuff to flog if they have to distrain. Mrs. L. couldn't allow that, and she'd no policies or anything she could use as security, so she didn't get the loan!"

"Who told you all this confidential stuff?" Knollis asked, curious.

"The Yard use informers and stool-pigeons," said Wilson, as if in defence of his methods. "It was Jephson's chief clerk. I've used him at various times—although this job was accidental. I was asking him if the Maynards had tried to tap his firm. Just an idea that came into my head, you know! He said they hadn't, but Maynard's sister had, and that was where I switched my ears at right angles to my head."

"I wonder why she wanted it?" muttered Knollis.

"Why should she hang around the flat?" Wilson said.

"Could be!" Knollis agreed. "It was a heck of a price to ask for a photograph. She could have got out of it cheaper than that!"

"How?"

"Buy a dozen or more and lash them round her friends, all signed, so that the one was lost among the many. She could have told him to go to blazes then. That's what I'd have done in the circumstances."

Wilson whistled softly. "That's definitely a notion, but she hadn't got your brains, old man. And how about the romantic inscription?"

Knollis waved the objection away as trivial. "Sign 'em all in extravagant terms."

"I see," said Wilson.

Knollis threw the papers aside and eased himself from the luxury of the chair to stretch his arms. "Got your car here?"

"I don't walk if I can help it. Against my principles. Where do you want to go?"

"Oh, Mansard House!"

"For what?"

"A talk with Maynard. It's time we shattered that alibi of his."

Wilson got up from the grass, looking hard at Knollis. "You can do that?"

"I think so," Knollis said with quiet modesty. "He's broken it himself. All we need do is make it obvious to him. He'll come clean this time, Wilson."

"It'll put us a long way forward if you can. How do you intend to work?"

"That depends on Maynard's attitude. You have to adjust your act to the mood of the audience."

"Okay," sighed Wilson, and led the way to the car. On drawing level with the apiary they saw Philip Maynard working at a hive. Knollis put a hand on Wilson's arm and asked him to stop. He then called over the hedge, asking if they could go and watch the work.

Philip Maynard waved. "Go and ask my wife for gloves and veils."

Ten minutes later, feeling like deep-sea divers for the second time in twenty-four hours, they watched Maynard going through his hives.

"I thought they'd all been destroyed," said Knollis.

"They were," Maynard replied. "Old Heatherington helped me to collect a dozen new stocks—one from here, and another from there, and so on. I'm making nuclei from them to build into new stocks for next season. That won't mean anything to you, of course. You don't happen to be interested in beekeeping by any chance?"

"Interested in everything," Knollis said briefly.

"I might have a smack at this some time," Wilson said, enthusiastically. "It's the sort of hobby you can do when you want to relax. I tried fishing once, but packed in when it came to ripping the hooks out."

"The humanitarian attitude, eh?" said Maynard. "I think I'd feel the same, Inspector. Taking life is pointless, mainly."

"Why the negative qualification?" asked Knollis.

"I'll take it back," Maynard smiled through his veil. "Taking life is pointless. By the way, you haven't come here on a Sunday morning to talk about bees and ethics, have you?"

"We came to talk about bees," said Knollis. "We want to know how this brood disease got into your hives."

Maynard replaced the roof of the hive on which he was working. "That's the lot for to-day. Get well away from the hives before removing your veil. They're a bit ratty—there's thunder about."

They followed him to the gate and then took off their gloves and veils.

"How does brood disease get into a hive?" said Maynard. "It's still a mystery to the scientists, but the boys of the old school say it's the result of bees using dirty drinking places."

"You misunderstood my question," said Knollis. "I want to know how it got into *your* hives!"

Maynard looked at him for a short space of time, and then nodded. "You wouldn't be in a position to ask that if you didn't know something. You've been to Newbourne to see the old man!"

"And to Jason's Knoll?"

"In which case your question was purely a rhetorical one, needing no answer," said Maynard.

Knollis watched his pale features closely, but Maynard was perfectly at his ease and in control of himself. He balanced his veil and gloves on the hedge and stuck his hands in the side pockets of his white overall suit. "You think it was me who did Batley in," he said, bluntly.

"There's no evidence to suggest that," said Knollis. "On the other hand I would like to know where you were from hour to hour on the seventh!"

Maynard gave a peculiar smile. *"And from hour to hour, we ripe and ripe, and then, from hour to hour we rot and rot, and thereby hangs a tale,"* he quoted.

"Another Shakespeare fan!" grunted Wilson.

"That isn't how *I* like it," said Knollis. "I've no time for philosophizing. I want facts!"

"I've already told you, Inspector!"

"In the morning you came home. In the afternoon you went to the nursing home, and then to the Rex Cinema to see the *Lady in the Lake* film. In the evening?"

"I stayed at home until seven, and then went to see my sister and her husband."

"You enjoyed the picture?" Knollis asked in a tone that invited a summary of the plot.

"It was excellently done," said Maynard in reply. "The camera represented the eyes of Marlowe, the detective, and you saw the whole story as he saw it. If he sat down, then the room as he saw it seemed to go up on the screen, and so on. One mistake, and the whole picture would have been ruined, but there wasn't a mistake, and it was a first-class and most enjoyable picture."

"And the shorts? You enjoyed them?"

Maynard laughed, somewhat uneasily. "Queerly enough, I can't remember anything of them."

"That doesn't surprise me at all," said Knollis. "I'd like to go to your house now if you can make it convenient. There's something I want to show you."

As soon as Knollis stepped inside the entrance hall of Mansard House he made for the copies of *The Reader*. He scanned the contents pages of several issues, and then folded back the cover of one of them and said: "Ah!"

"An article on new film techniques, Mr. Maynard! You'll allow me to read a paragraph to you? Listen to this!

The film of Raymond Chandler's, The Lady in the Lake, *is a case in point. Readers are conversant with the device of the Main-Character Angle, in which the story is told as seen through the mind and eyes of the main*

character, but in the third person, and usually in histor-
ical present. The device was transferred from the world
of literature to that of the silver screen in this film, the
camera representing the eyes of Marlowe, Chandler's
Private Eye. You saw the whole room as he saw it. If he
sat down, the room in which the action was taking place
seemed to move upwards on the screen. It was an auda-
cious experiment, since one mistake could have ruined
the picture. As it was . . ."

Knollis broke off and looked up at Maynard. "Need I go on,
Mr. Maynard?"

Maynard was staring at him as if he was a conjurer who had
just produced a rabbit from a fishing-net, while Wilson merely
stared.

"You didn't go to the Rex that afternoon," purred Knollis.
"You made two phone calls from there, at one-thirty and the
other at four-forty-five, but you did not see the picture, and
did not enter the auditorium. You can remember the film, or
pretend to do so, because you read this article which I myself
read some months ago. You can't remember the newsreel or the
short features. Your car was in the Rex park all afternoon, but
where were you? Did you take a bus to Mottingley, and then another back to the end of Windward Lane, thus not being seen in
Newbourne village? And what did you do during the morning,
Mr. Maynard?"

Philip Maynard tossed his lank hair back from his forehead.
"I spent the morning here at home, and the afternoon in the
cinema," he said, stubbornly.

Georgie Maynard came in from the garden, trim in a cream
blouse and short brown skirt. She was carrying a few sprigs of
mint in her hand. She stood in the doorway for a second, and
then walked slowly forward, looking from one to the other.
"What—what's wrong, Phil darling?"

"These two have made up their minds that I murdered
Jerry," he said, angrily.

"You couldn't have done!" she exclaimed, earnestly.

"Why not?" Knollis demanded quickly.

Philip Maynard signalled to her and she closed her pouted lips, a puzzled expression on her chubby face.

"So you do know something about Batley's murder!" snapped Knollis.

"Have you enough evidence to arrest me for his murder?" asked Maynard, tensely.

Knollis eyed him for a minute, and then slowly shook his head. "Mr. Maynard, I haven't," he said, frankly.

"That's a fair answer," said Maynard, "and I'll tell you one thing in return. I wasn't at the Rex that afternoon, except to phone the nursing home. You'll never find out where I was that afternoon! Only two people know—myself and my wife, and no one else will ever know!"

He turned his back on them and ran lightly up the stairs without looking back. Georgie Maynard tossed her chin, gave a superior little smile, and marched off to the kitchen, slamming the door behind her.

"We seem to be alone," said Wilson. "You won't be staying for lunch, Inspector Knollis?"

"I'm afraid not," Knollis replied with a wry smile. "I think we'll rake Frank Moreland out."

"The appointment's for this afternoon," Wilson complained. He glanced at the hall clock. "He'll only just be back from church."

"The right time to catch him," said Knollis. "I'll sort this thing out or resign!"

Frank Moreland, a broad and squat man with a square face, was not too pleased to see them, and complained about the intrusion on his Sunday privacy.

"The sand's running out of the glass," said Wilson. "We have to get moving before it's all gone."

Moreland filled them two fingers of whisky each, and pushed the siphon across. "Help yourselves. What do you want of me, Inspector Knollis?"

"Need I go round the bush?" asked Knollis.

Moreland shook his head. "Go straight ahead, sir! I'll give you fair answers. A client should always be frank with his lawyer, so I suppose the opposite should also obtain. What's wrong?"

"You went to see Mr. Heatherington at Newbourne some time ago?"

"Correct. He told you himself?"

"He did," said Knollis. "I'd like your version."

Moreland took a sip of his whisky before answering. "Batley was a rat," he said. "Unfortunately, my daughter was in love with him; if I'd opposed the marriage she'd have run away with him, so I agreed to it, hoping that once he was within the family I could tame and train him. We people are like you in some respects; we hear rumours and odd pieces of information, and I heard several about Batley, and didn't like them."

"Such as, sir?" asked Wilson.

"He'd tried to have an affair with Maynard's sister last year, and early this year tried to have one with his wife—and she's a nice little woman. I happened to hear about a remark he passed to Daphne, and, well, I'm a lawyer! I'm also a father, and I thought I saw a way of breaking the spell. I'm probably telling you a great deal you know already. . . ."

"Please go on," said Knollis.

"Batley told Daphne Maynard was the type to put himself away if he got too much trouble on board, and said how sorry he was for Georgie—Mrs. Maynard—having such a weak-kneed husband. Strictly speaking, it wasn't then, but later, when I stated my case to myself and saw a way of parting them. The Maynards had a spell of bad luck—"

"Yes, Mr. Moreland?"

"Taking each incident as a separate entity it was petty and insignificant, but when you began to add them together—"

"Yes?"

"Well, it struck me that Batley might have had a few fingers in the game for reasons of his own, and so I went to work."

"Yes?"

"I got a gardening expert to go round one day while the Maynards were out. That was easily arranged, because Lanson is a friend of mine, and discreet pumping from time to time led me to know when the place would be unguarded. The result? My expert reported that Maynard's troubles were not due to nature, but to dirty work. His plants had been ruined by chemicals. I next went to see the old gentleman at Newbourne, took him into my confidence, and asked him to delve into the bee trouble. You'll see what I was doing, of course—exactly what you're doing now, collecting evidence. I intended to push it all under Daphne's nose at the appropriate time, and then under Batley's, after which I intended to kick him across my lawns and through the gate. He vanished shortly after I went to see Mr. Heatherington, and I never knew the result of his researches."

"The results were as expected, Mr. Moreland," said Knollis. "He placed his evidence at our disposal. Batley was undoubtedly responsible for the Maynards' troubles."

"It's always nice to know one's been right," sighed Moreland, reaching for his glass.

Knollis and Wilson left him.

"It's tying up nicely, but it doesn't help us to find the culprit," said Wilson.

"Fetch Maynard in the car and meet me at Batley's flat," said Knollis. "A penny dropped while I was listening to Moreland's story. I fancy we've been gulled by either one or both of Batley's lady friends."

"How?" asked Wilson.

Knollis smiled. "Off you go, man, and don't be too long."

He watched Wilson walk away, and then turned in the opposite direction even before Wilson was in the car. He paced through the quiet and almost deserted streets to the flat. He examined the living-room carefully and then went to the corridor, closing the door behind him. There he waited, leaning against the wall with folded arms.

Maynard was surly and irritable, demanding to be left alone and in peace.

"If you're in a spot," said Knollis, "you've only yourself to blame for it. You can either help or hinder me, but I shall get what I want in the end. You came to this flat early on the morning of the seventh of June, and had a scrap with Batley!"

Maynard merely scowled at him.

"He had neighbours, you know," Knollis said with a subtle smile. "Unlike the normal householder he had them above and below him as well as on each side."

Maynard grunted. "I didn't think there were any witnesses."

Knollis didn't bother to tell him there weren't.

"Mr. Heatherington came with you."

"Yes."

"You searched the flat for gloves and a veil."

"Ye—es! How did you know!"

"Can you describe the state of the flat when you left it?"

Maynard grinned. "A bit rough, I suppose. We knocked Batley down after a tussle, and then I sat on him while the old chap searched the flat. The place did look a bit of a mess!"

"Tell me," said Knollis; "was he dressed?"

Maynard's eyes opened to their fullest extent. "You know that, too!"

"You answer the questions," snapped Knollis. "Was he up and dressed, or in bed and in pyjamas?"

"He was up and dressed," replied Maynard. "That was the whole point."

"He set fire to the honey-house at Wellow Lock?"

"Well, we think so," Maynard said hesitantly.

"So do we," said Knollis. "You came straight here to try and catch him before he could hop into bed? And then, once discovered in the state you expected, you decided to look for evidence pointing to his responsibility for the brood disease?"

"Yes, sir," said Maynard, in a respectful tone. "That was it."

"What made you think he was responsible for the fire?"

Maynard hesitated. "I'd been suspicious of him for some time, and just before we came away from the fire I saw the lights of a car go on about a quarter of a mile away, and then heard an engine starting up. The lights came towards Clevely, so once I'd dropped my wife at home I drove here instead of taking Mr. Heatherington straight home. I explained what I was going to do, and told him to wait in the car, but he came in with me. Batley said he'd just come from a dance, and I told him it was only just due to start, and hit him between the eyes. He would have been too strong for me alone, but I managed to trip him, and once we'd pinned his arms under his body I sat on him while the old chap searched until he found the gloves and veil."

"You'll agree the flat was somewhat disordered when you left?"

"Somewhat," smiled Maynard. "We had a good time!"

Knollis threw open the door. "Like this?"

Maynard stared. "Good heavens, no! The old chap went through the drawers and cupboards, but he closed them as he went on. Somebody else's been here since us!"

"That's all I wanted to know," said Knollis. "Did you come in Inspector Wilson's car, or your own?"

"Followed in my own."

"In that case you're free to return," said Knollis.

Maynard hesitated, as if loth to leave.

Knollis cocked an eyebrow at him. "Wanting to tell us where you were on the afternoon of the seventh?"

"No!" Maynard said sharply, and left them to it.

"What's the new notion?" asked Wilson.

"The missing key's worrying me," said Knollis. "The answer to the riddle lies with either Daphne Moreland or Bernice Lanson. One of them has the key and has been in here. By the way, can you turn two men loose on Maynard? I'd like to know what tradesmen call at the house on Tuesdays, whether they called on the seventh, and whether they found Maynard at home or not. Okay?"

"Pure routine," said Wilson. "Coxon and Collier can go to town on that assignment. But this key business?"

"One of them must, simply must, have it, Wilson!"

Wilson scratched the back of his neck and pulled a face. "Marston said they tried to egg him on to let them in."

Knollis perched himself on the edge of the table and looked down his long nose. "Suppose either of them were seen by Marston when about to let themselves in? Or suppose they were coming out when he appeared in the corridor? What better cover for their presence there than a request that they be let in?"

"That's something!" Wilson admitted. "We can cut out Mrs. Lanson, because her photo was still in the flat!"

"All the more reason why she wanted to get in, surely!" Knollis pointed out. "She may have been in several times, Wilson. You must remember that you and I are trained to look for unusual hiding places, and the average layman isn't."

"That's also true," grunted Wilson. "So one of them has the key!"

"Which means one of them got it from Batley, and since he wasn't likely to give it voluntarily while he was alive, we must assume that it was taken from him after he was dead!"

"Daphne Moreland could have been looking for evidence which would have justified her in giving him the chuck, and she could have saved her face at the same time," said Wilson.

"But Daphne Moreland told us she knew in her heart that he was dead, Wilson."

Wilson bit his lip. "Aye!"

He reflected for a few moments, and then said: "It means that the key was taken from him not after he died, but after he was coshed, and before he was pushed down the well."

"That's a fair conjecture," said Knollis. "I think we're getting somewhere at last."

Chapter IX
MR. BATLEY NEEDED MONEY

Gordon Knollis knew he had reached the point where he must get away from all human contacts and tumble the facts of the case over in his mind, uninfluenced and unprejudiced by either unreasoned beliefs or intuitive conclusions.

During the past few days he had wandered round with Wilson, interviewing witnesses and potential suspects; he had tossed ideas into the common pool for discussion, and in turn considered ideas thrown to him. Now he must get away, if only for an hour, and clear his mind.

After breakfast he wandered round to divisional headquarters for a car. He consulted the wall map of the district in the main office, left a message for Wilson to the effect that he would be back before lunch, and then drove out of Clevely along the Newbourne road, past Mansard House, through Newbourne, and so to the Doughty cottage in Windward Lane. He made his way to the far end of the orchard. The mouth of the well was still uncovered, the flagstones lying in the long grass, the hive standing under the lea of the hedge, unbalanced and awry.

It was here a man had met his death in an unnatural and bizarre fashion. To be knocked on the head was no uncommon fate among those who met their death by violence; to be poisoned was the lot of no small percentage of those who met their ends at the hands of their fellow-men; to suffer both was unusual, and suggested a rare combination of circumstances.

The coshing of Batley was no accident. The throwing of his body down the well was no accident. The presence of the calcium cyanide might be, but then again, if it was in Batley's possession without the knowledge of his assailant, why had Batley decanted it from the metal cylinder in which it must have been sold to him?

He squatted down and peered into the murky depths of the well. Sufficient to the moment were the problems thereof. The outstanding fact was that Gerald Batley was dead at the hands of a fellow creature. Motives were important, most certainly, but proof of commission doubly so; the why's and wherefore's could be sorted out later.

There were two main ways of conducting a murder investigation. One could either look for the person with the soundest motive, and then try to prove—fairly—that he did it, or prove that so-and-so was the only person who could have been at the scene of the tragedy at the stated time, and then prove his motive. The first was the theoretical and story-book method, and it was sometimes a sound angle of attack. In the present case Knollis was satisfied he would reach the murderer only by tracing the movements and alleged movements of the suspects, using the elimination principle.

In spite of this decision, he knew he must still consider motive. Knollis was no wearer of rose-tinted glasses, and no believer in the idealistic theory that human nature was altruistic in essence. Each man, consciously or unconsciously, had one primary question in mind when tackling the problems and difficulties of life: namely, *What can I get out of it?* It was a modification of the primal law of existence.

What then could any of Batley's associates get from his death? How could they benefit? Take them one by one, writing against their names all that was known of them and their connections with Batley . . .

Although Knollis's avowed aim was to rid himself of prejudice and intuitional belief, he was a human being, with all a human being's weaknesses and faults, and without realizing it he chose to start his mental inquisition with the person he believed to be the least likely to have been actively concerned with Batley's death. It may have been his experience as a gardener that was responsible, for, in effect, he was tackling an overgrown border, plucking out the weeds first in the knowledge that he must then get to the flowers.

Bernice Lanson. Who was she? A married woman who for a few short weeks had fallen under the spell of a reputed lady-killer. The fever, while it lasted, had been an intense one, as witnessed by the inscription on the photograph she'd given him, but having passed its crisis it faded rapidly away, leaving nothing behind but a dread fear of discovery. What then had Bernice Lanson to gain by Batley's death? A photograph, and a sense of relief—whether admitted to herself or not. A suspicion of her was too absurd for words. Even if her husband had learned of the short association the outcome could not be disastrous for her.

Knollis pondered on her attempt to borrow the hundred pounds. It was not necessarily significant—or was it? He would see her, and as far as his official regulations allowed, try to force an answer from her.

His legs began to ache, so he moved over and sat on one of the flagstones. He lit a cigarette and blew the smoke down his nostrils, two expanding columns of bluey-brown smoke.

Two people in the case could have murdered Batley; Daphne Moreland and Philip Maynard.

Daphne Moreland had nothing to gain from Batley's death but the saving of her face, and murder was a high price to pay for that, especially when her father was a lawyer, a man with a brain trained and accustomed to dealing with complex problems, and quite capable of handling Batley had Daphne desired it.

All through, or so it seemed to Knollis, Daphne Moreland had been playing to retrieve a lost position. Whether she had any knowledge of Batley's affair with Bernice Lanson was a moot point, but she certainly knew of his assault on his cousin Georgie's virtue, and in knowing that she knew of Batley's unworthiness.

How had she handled the resulting situation? By trying to rid herself of him? Certainly not. She'd tried to keep him, and had not refused to face the unpleasant consequences of finding him at the cottage with another girl. If that had happened, she would have had a hold over him for the rest of his life. That seemed to suggest that murder was not in her mind. The truth was that she was infatuated with him, and was trying to save him for herself, and save him alive. All the way through she'd tried to smother the evidence against him, but after his death her motive had changed, and she'd done so to save her face—always, always saving her face, actuated by the tenets of the code she'd expressed. Knollis realized it was no brilliant analysis he'd achieved, but at any rate it was a fair one. Daphne Moreland was not a satisfactory suspect, but she must remain one until further evidence cleared her. She'd been to the cottage on the morning of Batley's death, and that fact must be considered, and held in mind.

Philip Maynard was the obvious candidate for Teddy Jessop's rope, and while Knollis's intellect rejected the certainty his heart insisted that it would be Maynard who would take that grim and unethical nine o'clock walk later in the year. And the devil of it was that he liked young Maynard, liked him in spite of his evasions and his deliberate attempts to strew red herrings by the dozen across the path of investigation.

Maynard had presented an alibi, and that in itself did little to suggest innocence. The alibi had been burst wide open by a hunch and an odd fact filed away in the cabinet of memory—the remembrance of the article on the film which Maynard declared he had seen. Maynard had been elsewhere when he was supposed to be in the Rex Cinema. He had left his car in the park. He had finally admitted he was elsewhere—and then came the flaw in the theory that he had killed Batley. His wife had said only yesterday when he and Wilson visited the house: *But you couldn't have done!* And then, catching her husband's warning eye, had subsided. If Maynard had not been present, Knollis might well have learned the truth.

Knollis stroked his knee. Why couldn't Maynard have killed Batley? What did his wife know that would clear him of suspicion? Or had Maynard told some tale to cover *her* suspicions of him, and she, believing implicitly in her husband, had accepted the lie as truth? And had Maynard stopped her saying any more because he knew the story would sound so thin to anyone but an all-loving and all-believing wife?

If that was the case, it meant that Maynard was afraid of Knollis getting the story, working on the facts, and by disproving the truth of them reach conclusions that would lead him to the truth—a kind of exception that would tend to prove the truth.

That was the main difficulty of investigation. You could take fact A, and fact B, and say that A plus B added up to AB, and that AB equalled C, but you still could not read the *thoughts* of one's fellow-men. Maynard was sitting still, doing nothing, and saying nothing. Wasn't it Wilde who said silence was the unbearable repartee? And wasn't it a point of all the Eastern philosophies that with the weapon of silence one could triumph over all one's enemies. It was the philosophy of non-resistance, of course, and at the moment Maynard was leading on points in the conflict between himself and the Law represented by Knollis.

Knollis preferred a case where the suspect got windy and tried to cover his tracks when it was too late. It was then an open battle of wits, and the first man to anticipate the action of the other won hands down.

And then Knollis, lighting one cigarette from the remains of the other, wondered if it would be possible to panic Maynard, to make him move and betray himself. . . .

It was an idea worth thinking about. The case was static, and the effect was frustrating. Unless he did force action his reports were going to make dull reading when they got to the Chief Constable at Mottingley, and to his superiors at the Yard. His vanity was touched. He was proud of his reputation as an unraveller of problems—hadn't Aristotle himself said that many poets, meaning dramatists, tie the knot well, but unravel it ill? Knollis unravelled well, and he failed to see why his record should be broken because his suspect refused to help him by word or sign.

Maynard had good cause to remove Batley, and from a purely ethical if unsocial point of view it might be that he was justified, but the Law took a diametrically opposed view, and since Knollis served the Law it was his job to bring Maynard to book.

He rose and dusted his trouser seat. There were several jobs to be done; clear up the matter of the hundred pounds, find out from Georgie Maynard by hook or by crook why she believed her husband to be innocent, find out who took Batley's key, find out how the hive got from Jason's Knoll to Windward Lane, find out where Maynard went on the afternoon of the seventh, and finally, and most important, find out what brought Batley out to the cottage at so early an hour and in such a hurry. He threw his cigarette down the well and walked briskly to the gate and his car.

He found Bernice Lanson at home, a surly and discontented woman who looked as if life was no longer to her liking, and as if it had been that way for some considerable time. The corners of her mouth were turned down. Her welcoming smile was almost a sneer. "It's you again!" she said.

"May I come in?" Knollis asked.

She shrugged her narrow shoulders and stood aside for him to enter the mock-Tudor hall. She then closed the door firmly and folded her arms across her flat chest.

"Now what is it, Inspector?"

"Something delicate," said Knollis. He looked round the doors leading from the hall. "We're private?"

"The day-girl hasn't turned up," she said, sourly.

"The matter on which I've called probably has no bearing whatsoever on the case I'm investigating," said Knollis, "and I must admit frankly that you're not bound to answer my question, but I'm interested in a matter of a hundred pounds you tried to borrow late in March. Can you help me?"

She grimaced, wrinkling her nose in distaste. "Is nothing safe from the police? Are we being peered at and pried upon from one week to the next?"

"The information came to us accidentally," said Knollis. "We have to satisfy ourselves that it has no bearing on Batley's death."

"How much do you know?" she asked, quickly.

"That's quite a point," Knollis replied with a light smile. He tossed his hat on the oak chest beside him. "We're not getting anywhere, Mrs. Lanson. If you don't feel you can help me I must get my answers elsewhere."

"If you'll tell me why the matter looks suspicious I might feel more inclined to help you, Inspector!"

"You tried to borrow a hundred pounds from a man called Jephson. You had no security to offer, and consequently did not get the money. Tell me, Mrs. Lanson, why you couldn't ask your husband for it?" She nodded slowly several times. "I see your point. The answer is that he wouldn't have lent it to me."

She turned and tapped the barometer hanging over the chest. "Set fair!"

"But it might have been stormy?" suggested Knollis.

She gave an uncertain laugh. "The bottom would have dropped out, Inspector. You know why I wanted the money, of course?"

"I've a good idea," Knollis admitted. "Batley needed it."

"It was to be purely a business arrangement," Bernice Lanson said, tracing a circle round the dial of the barometer with a long finger. "Jerry was organizing his marriage for June, and he was flat broke. He wanted to borrow a hundred at ten per cent. I thought I could borrow at five, and make something on the side. He knew he was coming into his aunt's estate, but the legal arrangements were long-winded. He needed the money for the wedding."

"He could have borrowed on his anticipated legacy without borrowing from you," said Knollis.

"Jerry would never have exposed himself to anyone in this town, Inspector. That was his reason for tackling me. He knew I'd keep my mouth shut—for obvious reasons!"

"As long ago as last March," Knollis muttered.

"Jerry always thought a long way ahead. He knew I'd have to fish round for the money, and gave me time in which to find it."

"He didn't use any—er—persuasion?"

Her eyebrows rose in two steep arches. "Persuasion?"

"He didn't offer to return your photograph in return for your kindness in loaning the money?"

She stared down at her feet, and tapped the right one on the floor of the hall. "You know more than you've hinted, Inspector, although I don't know how you found out."

"It's my job," said Knollis, blandly.

"I suppose you could have called it something like black-mail," she said, slowly, "but he wasn't selling the photo back, you know! I was to have an I.O.U. before I handed over the money—if I got it."

"And if you didn't get it, Mrs. Lanson?"

"He would arrange that I could, and without his name being brought into it."

"O—oh!" Knollis exclaimed. He blinked and shook his head, two facts having suddenly amalgamated in his head to produce a third one, and a startling one at that.

"Look, Mrs. Lanson," he said, quickly. "After you failed to get the money from Jephson, did you try anywhere else?"

She shrugged her narrow shoulders again. "There was no-where else to try—nowhere I could think of. Jephson had made it abundantly clear that if I had no security, and no property in my own name which could be regarded as security, then I'd had it!"

"I see," said Knollis, knuckling his chin.

"It shook me somewhat," said Bernice Lanson, "because I'd always thought, judging by the adverts, that you could just walk in and borrow almost anything on your word of honour—signing a statement that you'd pay it back with interest. Well, it didn't work out that way!"

"It never does," said Knollis. "Long years ago Mr. Lloyd George pointed out that you never get ninepence for fourpence, and a lot of people in this country still don't believe it. It takes time to knock sense into a place where there's no feeling."

"Thank you, Inspector!" she said, gravely, and inclined her head in a mock bow.

Knollis smiled. "Sorry, Mrs. Lanson. That was a generalization, and not intended to apply to you. You were merely ignorant of the procedures of borrowing money."

He looked her up and down for a few moments, and then began to unfold his new idea, slowly and cautiously, and question by question.

"You know a fair amount about the lives of your brother and his wife, of course?"

"Why, yes, I suppose so," she agreed. "I was brought up with my brother, and we visit regularly."

"You know anything about bee-keeping?"

She shuddered. "Not a thing, and I don't want to know anything about the dirty stinging little things. I can't understand Philip keeping them—although the honey's pleasant enough, strangely."

"Honey and stings go together," said Knollis. "Even roses have thorns. You knew, of course, that your brother was opening an out-apiary at Wellow Lock?"

He flashed a glance at her, and knew on the instant that his supposition was correct.

"He was starting one this season, I believe."

"And had moved a quantity of equipment there in readiness?"

"Oh, yes, my sister-in-law was quite enthusiastic about the whole thing. She's that type, you know! Completely unsophisticated, and likely to rave about the smallest thing."

"They lost something over a hundred pounds' worth of equipment in the fire, or so I'm told," said Knollis.

Bernice Lanson nodded, and twisted her fingers together anxiously, meanwhile licking her lip with the tip of her tongue. "Ye—es, I suppose they did, judging by what Georgie said."

"Do you know whether the equipment was insured, Mrs. Lanson?"

She stared at him open-mouthed, but did not answer.

Knollis gave a grim smile. "Tell me, Mrs. Lanson, how soon after the fire at Wellow Lock did Batley get in touch with you?"

She still stared, and took half a step backward.

Knollis followed her. "You were to ask your brother to lend you the insurance money, Mrs. Lanson!"

"I—I don't understand what you're getting at, Inspector Knollis!" she protested.

Knollis brushed the denial aside. "You know the truth as well as I do, Mrs. Lanson. Batley burned down the honey-house at Wellow Lock. I'm suggesting it was insured for a hundred pounds or more, and that Batley told you to approach your brother for a loan—or get it promised to you for when the insurance company paid him!"

She looked away from him, flustered.

"Well, Mrs. Lanson!"

She suddenly gave way. Her hands fell to her sides as a token of surrender. "Yes, you're right. I didn't know he was responsible for the fire, but I guessed it."

"And he rang you . . . ?"

"Ten past eight that morning."

"How much did he tell you?"

"He merely said: *'Your brother's honey-house at Wellow was burned down in the night. Get cracking after the insurance money!'*"

"Your husband would be at home at that hour?"

She nodded. "Yes, and I had to use my wits or he'd have asked questions, so I called back: *'This is Mr. Lanson's residence. I'm afraid you have a wrong number.'* That satisfied my husband who was breakfasting in this room on the right. I heard Jerry laugh before he replaced the receiver. He knew my game. I rang him back about a quarter to nine, after my husband had gone to business, but I got no reply."

"One question," said Knollis. "How soon did you hear about the fire from your brother?"

"Oh, you know that as well," she said. "Half-past nine. He came to tell me about the fire and Georgie's collapse."

"And that would be when you told him the truth about Batley's racket?" asked Knollis, plunging into darkness in the hope of finding light.

Bernice Lanson now seemed to be under the impression that he knew the whole story and was merely seeking corroboration, so that she hesitated no longer in answering his probing questions.

"Ye—es, I knew he wouldn't let on to Rodney, my husband. I thought Jerry had had enough rope by then, that he'd gone far enough, so I told Phil he'd tried to blackmail me for a mild indiscretion he could prove against me."

Knollis considered the dial of the barometer, and threw his mind back to an interview at Mansard House, the one where the Maynards had played out the domestic drama without seeming to realize that he and Wilson were present.

Philip Maynard had then made it abundantly clear that he was aware of some lapse on his sister's part, but not the nature of it. And now Bernice Lanson was blackening Batley's character as fast as she could, not realizing that she was heaping evidence against her own brother.

Maynard was now shown to have a threefold motive for killing Batley. It was all very interesting. Maynard knew Batley had tried to steal his wife, had tried to ruin them both, had caused her illness through worry, and had blackmailed his sister—all of which boiled down to the fact that he wanted to avenge his wife and sister, and have his own revenge.

Knollis decided he had enough to think about for the present. He left the house, not failing to notice the expression of relief that crossed Bernice Lanson's sallow features as he picked up his hat and turned to the door.

He would see her again, later.

Chapter X
THE MAYNARDS MAKE A MOVE

As KNOLLIS DROVE slowly back to Clevely police station, the divisional headquarters, he once more worked over the known facts of Maynard's movements. He had been informed of the fire at one o'clock in the morning, the morning of the now significant seventh of June, and had taken his wife and Old Heatherington out there. Georgie Maynard said they left at a quarter past two. The distance from Wellow Lock to Mansard House was five miles. Maynard found his wife unconscious half an hour after he got back—but that meant back from Clevely, and not from Wellow Lock! Five miles from Wellow Lock to Mansard House, two-and-a-half miles from there to Clevely, three miles from there to Newbourne to drop the old man, and the half-mile back. So that, apart from the interlude at Batley's flat, Maynard had occupied the time necessary to drive eleven miles, and his wife had collapsed half an hour after that. But then he had contradicted himself, for he had also said he found her unconscious on returning from Newbourne. Knollis was not worried about the contradiction. The time of her collapse was unimportant, and if it became necessary to pin-point it then he could do so by checking the time at which the ambulance had been sent for. Maynard had travelled to the nursing home in the ambulance, and returned on a workman's bus at half-past seven. Bernice Lanson now said he called on her at nine-thirty, which was very obviously after he had been to the nursing home for the second time.

That was that! What followed? Maynard called at the nursing home for the third time at ten past one, and then phoned at half-past one, and later at a quarter to five. That left two gaps in his day; from half-past nine to ten past one, and from half-past one to a quarter to five.

Knollis shook his head as he steered carefully round a horse and dray. If only he dared let his imagination work! It would be a pretty story he could invent. He could imagine Maynard returning from the nursing home at half-past seven, and wandering round his home in a despondent mood until he got the car out an hour later and returned to the nursing home. They still wouldn't let him see his wife, so he went round to his sister. Query in passing; surely he'd already phoned her from his home? Check that. But having reached the Lanson home his sister told him of Batley's dirty work. Maynard, in Knollis's story, went straight round to the flat. Batley, judging by the evidential facts, was not there, so Maynard, still boiling with rage, went to look for him.

Knollis groaned. There were horrible holes in the story! If human nature was to remain constant, Maynard simply must have rung his sister after getting back from Clevely. He'd be so full, as the saying went, that he'd have to unload his troubles or burst. It was understandable that he'd made for home instead of going to see her when he first left the nursing home, since it was instinctive to return to the old cave when in trouble, but he must have rung her then. So that Bernice Lanson had lied when she said he called at half-past nine to give her the news. Note: see Rodney Lanson and trip him into telling the truth.

There was nothing wrong with the theory that Maynard went, fed up as he was, to see his sister after his second call at the nursing home; he needed comfort and sympathy, and his sister was the only person who could supply it. Lord, wouldn't Freud have gone to town on this affair!

The real hole in Knollis's imaginative reconstruction came when he reached the point at which Maynard went to Batley's flat for what was colloquially known as the pay-off and didn't find him there. Surely, surely he would have gone straight to Shipley's office to look for him there! That was a question that hadn't been asked of Shipley and his staff. Note: make inquiries.

And then, Batley not being there, how did Maynard know where to find him? *And that put paid to the notion that Maynard had lured Batley to the cottage!* How the deuce could he lure him there if he didn't know where to contact him? That was another theory washed out.

A sudden silence startled Knollis from his reverie. He blinked and looked round, to find himself outside the police station in Victoria Street with his brakes on and his engine switched off. He gave a faint smile and silently thanked his subconscious mind for bringing him safely through the Clevely traffic, since he was not conscious of having driven from the Lanson home on the outskirts of the town.

Wilson looked up with a cocked eyebrow as Knollis walked into the office. "The return of the prodigal!"

Knollis threw his grey trilby on the hat-stand and drew up a chair. In an earnest voice he said: "Listen, Wilson, old man . . ."

Wilson listened, nodding from time to time, and making notes as Knollis talked. At last Knollis concluded: "That's how I see it, Wilson. I know it isn't a good story, but it's the only one I can think up from the available facts."

"And what about Daphne Moreland?" asked Wilson. "Are we dropping her?"

"We can't," sighed Knollis, "but we have to fill the blanks in Maynard's day before we do anything else. I'd like to see Lanson and Shipley this morning."

Wilson glanced at the wall clock. "Five past eleven. Lanson will be round at the club until about twenty past. He takes his elevenses from a tankard. That gives us the chance of a drink ourselves."

"I don't usually drink during the day," said Knollis, "but perhaps you're right."

Wilson tapped his pencil on the desk. "There's a point, Knollis," he said, slowly. "We don't know the actual time at which

Batley's car left the garage. I've been thinking about that this morning, and have sent Coxon to check. Marston's statement says he went on duty at the flats at eight, and the car wasn't there when he got round to cleaning the garages. We took it for granted that the car was missing at eight, and that's wrong. The car was missing when Marston opened up—and that might have been half-past eight, nine, ten, or even later. We've boobed on that."

Knollis nodded his unwilling agreement. "Ye—es, it's bad thinking. Still, Coxon should clear up the point."

They went round to the Cavendish Club, two streets away, and Wilson pointed out Rodney Lanson almost as soon as they passed through the swing doors into the bar. He was a gingery-coloured fellow in a plus-four suit, a round-headed and full-faced man in the early thirties. Wilson went up to him and clapped him on the back familiarly. "Empty yet, Lanson? What's the poison?"

Lanson turned and grinned at him, looking at Knollis and nodding a welcome. "The sleuths taking to drink, eh?"

"We're always willing to suffer in the interests of duty," smiled Wilson. "By the way, this is my colleague, Gordon Knollis, of the Yard."

"Thought it must be you," said Lanson. "You called on my wife the other day, didn't you? She described you perfectly. I don't suppose she managed to tell you much about Batley's unsavoury past; she only played tennis with him long years ago, you know. Anyway, the drinks are on me, so what'll you take? Beer, or shorts?"

"Tankard of bitter for me, thanks," said Knollis.

"Mine's a mixed," said Lanson.

Lanson ordered and paid for the drinks. Wilson waited a few minutes, and then began leading the desultory conversation towards the real business of the meeting.

"Been out to Mansard House lately?" he asked, casually.

"Last night, as a matter of fact," said Lanson. "They seem to be getting over their troubles now."

"Must have been a dirty dose while it lasted," Wilson remarked. "Must have shook them properly on that last night when they got the fire and Mrs. Maynard's collapse within an hour or so of each other. I suppose you'd get to know about it almost as soon as it happened?"

"The fire, or Georgie's collapse?"

"Well, both," said Wilson.

Lanson paused in lifting his tankard to his mouth. He shut one eye and looked first at Wilson and then at Knollis. The tankard slowly descended to the counter. "Truthfully speaking, Wilson, is this a social trip or were you looking for me?"

"We were looking for you."

Lanson sniffed. "You might at least have paid for the refreshments!"

"I offered as soon as I came through the door!"

Lanson picked up his tankard. "There's nobody in the reading-room. Shall we adjourn?"

Knollis and Wilson followed him across the bar, through the billiards-room, and into a small room with a large bow window across one end. Lanson took a seat at a table beneath the window, and with his back to the light. "Now let's have it. What are you fishing for, and why?"

Wilson glanced at Knollis. "You take over?"

Knollis perched himself on the corner of the table, his favourite seat, and put his tankard down beside Lanson's. "It's a matter of this, Mr. Lanson. You must realize, strictly between ourselves, that your brother-in-law had the very best of reasons for wanting to—er—dispose of Batley. We don't think he did—do we, Wilson?"

"Good gracious, no!" exclaimed Wilson.

"We don't think he did," repeated Knollis, "but until we've proved that he couldn't possibly have done the job, well, we have to keep checking his movements. He's told us exactly what he did and did not do on that morning of the seventh of June, and we're looking for corroboration. Once the blanks are filled we can drop him and concentrate on—well, on another person."

Lanson gave a mysterious smile. "So you really know who the fellow is, and there is something in that guff in the papers about an arrest being imminent."

"Now come, Mr. Lanson," smiled Knollis; "you can't expect us to answer that!"

"I suppose not," said Lanson. "Anyway, what is it you want to know?"

"At exactly what time it was on the morning of the seventh of June when you got to know about Mrs. Maynard's collapse and admission to the nursing home?"

"Seven o'clock," Lanson said promptly.

Knollis and Wilson looked at each other. Both were registering surprise.

"Sure of that?" asked Knollis.

"He rang from the nursing home. They took her in somewhere between five and half-past, and put her straight on the table. She was in the theatre a heck of a long time, and Phil rang us while he was patrolling the place and waiting for news."

"Who took the call?"

"I did. I climb out of bed round about seven most mornings, brew tea, and take my wife a cup to bed. It's one of her luxuries. I was a bit early that morning, and had just switched on the electric kettle when the phone went. I was all for taking my wife round to the home, but Phil said it was no use, and he'd call round later in the morning and tell us what there was in the way of news."

"Did he?" asked Knollis.

"He rang again about ten to eight, from home. He said he'd seen her as they wheeled her from the theatre to the ward, and they'd told him she'd be all right. Then they bustled him out of the way. He came round after I went to business, and my wife phoned me after he left."

"Can you remember another phone call that morning, Mr. Lanson?"

Lanson scratched his head doubtfully.

"A wrong number," said Wilson.

"Ye—es, I've a vague remembrance of one. If it was that same morning I cursed it because I was trying to listen to the eight o'clock news, and my wife went to take the call. Yes, it must have been the same morning, because I remember saying the blinking bell was working overtime."

"Did you see Maynard that morning?" asked Knollis.

Lanson looked askance at him. "Where's all this leading to, Inspector?"

"Truth," Knollis said briefly.

"Don't you have to warn or caution me or something when asking these questions?"

Wilson laughed aloud and slapped Lanson on the back. "Funny, that! Don't be an ass, Lanson! That only has to be done when we've made up our minds to arrest you."

"Or Philip!" Lanson said quickly.

He took a drink and then traced a figure-eight in the spilt beer on the table. "You know," he said, cautiously. "I think you've deliberately misled me. You said you were trying to clear him, and you're trying to make out a case against him!"

"You're not bound to answer any of our questions," said Knollis. "You can leave our suspicions outstanding."

Lanson nodded several times. "That's a clever statement, Inspector. It's like me telling my wife I don't want to know where she's been. She immediately wants to tell me."

"Does she go out on mystery missions?" Knollis asked quietly.

"I can trust my wife to the ends of the earth!"

"We're lucky men," said Knollis. "There are men like Batley in every town and village in the country, and some men's wives fall!"

Lanson grimaced. "And some don't! Batley tried it on my wife while I was away last year. Lucky for him she made me promise not to do anything about it!"

"Tried it with your wife!" Knollis exclaimed in the most surprised voice on earth.

"Batley doesn't seem to have left many avenues unexplored," said Wilson.

"The swine actually wanted her to go away with him!" said Lanson, heatedly.

"Never!" Wilson exclaimed.

"It's true," said Lanson, shaking his head.

"So you've some idea how Maynard felt when he learned that Batley had tried the same game with wife," Knollis said, quickly.

Lanson blinked.

"And consequently you'll understand why we have to consider Maynard as a suspect—until his statements are confirmed," went on Knollis.

Lanson said: "I se—e!"

"Of course," said Wilson, "you're not going to pretend you didn't know Batley was responsible for Maynard's troubles, and that the shock and worry of them brought on Mrs. Maynard's miscarriage?"

"No," muttered Lanson. "I knew that."

"Wouldn't you have felt like murdering him?" said Wilson.

"I'd have wrung his blasted neck for him!"

"And that's how we think Maynard must have felt," said Wilson. "We're so sure he felt that way—knowing how we'd have felt if it had been us—that we're bound to pursue him until we've either got him or cleared him. Doesn't that make sense?"

"Okay," said Lanson, waving a hand. "I see your point. I apologize for accusing you of trying to trap me into letting him in for something. I saw him at a quarter to ten or thereabouts. He'd been round to Bailey's flat and couldn't find him, then on to Shipley's office and he hadn't turned up, so he came to see me—"

"He had his car with him?" asked Knollis.

"Yes. Why?"

Knollis shrugged. "That's all right. I just thought he was getting about pretty quickly. I take it he came to ask you where you thought he might find Batley?"

"Ye—es," Lanson said, reluctantly.

"Where did you tell him to go?"

"Didn't he tell you where he went?" countered Lanson.

He was met with a stony silence.

Lanson lolled back in his chair. "I was right first time, eh? So that's the stunt! You really want to know whether he went to—"

"Yes?" Knollis asked as Lanson broke off. "Whether he went—where?"

"Batley was murdered at his cottage at Newbourne, and you're not going to trap me into saying Phil went there, because he didn't!"

"In which case you can have no objection to telling us where he did go, Mr. Lanson," Knollis said in a bland tone.

"Oh, go to blazes!" Lanson exclaimed miserably. "I don't know where I stand now!"

"We seem to be empty," said Knollis. "You'd perhaps like a break while I fill them again."

"There's a bell," Lanson said, shortly.

"I prefer to fetch them," said Knollis.

Wilson flashed a glance of inquiry at him, but Knollis picked up the three tankards and went back to the bar.

"Is there a private telephone I can use?" he asked the barman.

"Public call-box in the cloak-room at the foot of the stairs, sir."

Knollis threw a ten-shilling note on the counter. "Fill these and one for yourself while I make a call."

He got through to headquarters and asked for Inspector Urban of the uniformed branch.

"Knollis here. Can you get Maynard's telephone line put out of order for an hour or so? Think the exchange will oblige?"

Inspector Urban thought that could be arranged, irregular though it might be. Knollis thanked him, collected the tankards and went back to the reading-room. He noted it was then five minutes to twelve.

"So you're not going to help us," murmured Knollis as he pushed Lanson's tankard across the table.

"No!" Lanson replied brusquely. "I've just told Wilson so, and that I take a poor view of the trick you've tried to play on me."

"There's gullery in every trade and profession but our own," smiled Knollis. "In our own jobs we're Galahads, *sans peur et sans reproche*. Ah well, here's long life and good health, Mr. Lanson!"

"Cheers," Lanson said sulkily.

Knollis broke off the interview as the clock struck twelve, and hustled Wilson back to headquarters and a car.

"We've to get out to Mansard House and complete an interview by one o'clock," he explained. "I've had Urban put Maynard's phone out of order."

"Blocking Lanson, eh?" said Wilson. "Smart move, that. He did go to the cottage, didn't he?"

"Don't we both think so?"

"We do," said Wilson. "There's one thing I can't grasp—why Shipley never told us Maynard called in search of Batley that morning. He readily tells us about Daphne Moreland, but not Maynard!"

"Let's call," said Knollis. "We needn't waste much time."

They came from Shipley's office at a quarter past twelve, puzzled men. Neither Shipley nor any of his staff could remember Maynard ever putting his head inside the premises since they negotiated his purchase of Mansard House. They were certain he had not called on the seventh of June, or any other morning within the past year, and yes, they all knew him by sight.

"Now blooming well what?" demanded Wilson, as he drove out to the Newbourne road.

"Put your foot down," said Knollis. "You know, Wilson, there's a catch in this business, and we haven't seen it yet."

He looked round at Wilson, and whistled softly. "It could be!"

"What could?"

"An idea that's just occurred to me."

Wilson groaned. "Not another! Please not that! It means another day and night of mental darkness for me. Have a heart, Knollis! Throw it away and let's just go on asking questions until something breaks."

"I've always had an objection to exhibiting my incompetence by revealing uncorroborated ideas," said Knollis.

"Them's big words where I come from," grinned Wilson. "Now what's the line we're playing to Maynard?"

"We've been to see his brother-in-law," said Knollis, with a deep sigh, "and please would he mind telling us whether he found Batley at the cottage."

"You're working some fast ones, old man," warned Wilson.

"The case demands it," replied Knollis. "Frankly, I don't like the method, and I've never done so much of it before, but the end must justify the means. This isn't a case you can investigate within the normal meaning of the word; you have to convince the interested parties that more is known than they imagine—and rub in the infallibility of the detective branch."

"The word bluff covers all that," said Wilson. "Any ideas to follow this third Maynard interview?"

"Yes. See Daphne Moreland this afternoon!"

"Why her? I thought we'd finished with her?"

"So does she," said Knollis, with a sniff. "I think she forgot to tell us something."

Wilson lapsed into a disgruntled silence, and then, as they neared Mansard House, he exclaimed. "Look ahead, Knollis. They've just driven off towards Newbourne!"

"I hope Urban didn't bungle that telephone job," snapped Knollis. "Yes, it looks like their car!"

"It came out of the drive, anyway," said Wilson.

"Follow 'em!"

"That, my friend, was my intention!"

They followed at a discreet distance. The Maynards' car went through the village, and along the Mottingley Road, then turned left down Windward Lane, vanishing round the bend in the wood-shrouded track.

"Now what, Knollis?"

"Drive into the lane, reverse out, and drive back towards Newbourne for fifty yards."

Wilson obliged without question, and drew up an inch from the grass verge. Knollis hopped out and lifted the bonnet of the car. "When we hear the car coming back, you stay put and watch through the mirror. I'm going to investigate plug trouble. They shouldn't recognize us at that."

Ten minutes crawled by, and then Wilson gave the signal. Knollis bent over the engine, and waited. Then he straightened his back as Wilson swore heartily. "They've gone on towards Mottingley!"

Knollis slammed down the bonnet and got into the car. "The road's clear, Wilson. Back up to the lane."

It took Wilson no more than four minutes to reach the cottage gate. Knollis was out of the car before the brakes were on. He pushed open the gate and ran round the end of the house, then through the rosery and the kitchen garden to the orchard. He was standing at the mouth of the well, when Wilson caught up with him.

"What's up, Knollis?"

"They've taken the hive!"

"Why on earth!"

Knollis shook his head.

"And where to?" demanded Wilson, as if Knollis should know all the answers.

Knollis again shook his head, and stood with his top lip between his teeth and his eyes near-closed.

"This is weird!" said Wilson.

"There's no point in taking it to Wellow Lock," said Knollis, "so they must be taking it back to where it came from."

"Jason's Knoll!"

"That gives me an idea!"

Wilson waved his hands. "Not that one, you don't! If you think I'm going into that dell without a diving suit, you've had me! Oh, no!"

"We'll follow them, and hide in the lane or somewhere. If we can see them coming back from the right direction we can use my idea."

"I'll go within four hundred yards," offered Wilson.

"That'll do," said Knollis. "I suggest you drive past the end of the track down which Old Heatherington took us. You can park there, and I'll go through the wood alone while you watch the road. That suit you?"

"And if you aren't back in ten minutes I'll ring the hospital to get a bed ready for you," chuckled Wilson.

"We'll see," Knollis said, grimly.

Wilson had the accelerator pedal almost flat to the floor most of the way. As they neared the end of the track they could see the roof of a black car showing above the hedge some distance down the lane. Wilson drove to the appointed spot, and bade Knollis a friendly good-bye. "It's been nice knowing you," he said.

Knollis vaulted the low fence, and made his way through the wood. He wasn't eager to meet the bees, but was fully prepared to take the risk. He climbed the knoll and started down the other side, moving cautiously until at last he caught glimpses of movement down in the dell. He got down on hands and knees, and crawled forward, the bracken making a safe and natural cover. There were now four hives where there had been three, and Philip and Georgie Maynard, dressed in white combination overalls, wire veils and gauntlet gloves, were working on the second hive, the second hive from the left as Knollis faced them through the screen of bracken.

The roof of the hive was lying some feet away from them, and Philip Maynard was apparently re-arranging the inside of the hive. He turned to his wife, and she handed him a small package wrapped in brown paper which he pushed well down inside the hive before replacing the quilt and roof.

Georgie Maynard clasped her gloved hands above her head in the boxers' sign of triumph. She picked up the smoker from behind the hive, and together they made their way back to their car.

Knollis hurried back to Wilson, running whenever the bracken thinned sufficiently to allow him to do so. He vaulted the fence and almost tumbled into the car in his haste.

"Drive off quickly!" he panted.

"Can't," said Wilson. "I haven't heard their car, and we mustn't risk running into them. What happened, anyway?"

"I'll tell you on the way back," said Knollis. "Meanwhile, can we get back to Mansard House before they do? Any short cuts?"

"If you don't mind a darned rough ride, yes," said Wilson. "I'm thinking they'll use the main road, Knollis. There's not so much chance of them being noticed as if they start wandering around country lanes. Now once they're away I'll give you the ride of your life, and you'll be thinking we're going over the fields!"

"Go to it," said Knollis.

Wilson went to it, and seemed to enjoy himself. Knollis told him what he had seen, and Wilson nodded from time to time, although keeping his eyes on the rough tracks.

Arriving at Mansard House he backed into the drive and pulled out again, making it look as if they had just driven from Clevely. Then he and Knollis lighted cigarettes, and waited.

CHAPTER XI
THE MASONS PRESENT A CLUE

PHILIP AND GEORGIE MAYNARD were almost cocky in their attitude towards Knollis and Wilson, and the two detectives smiled inward smiles, confident in their knowledge of the young couple's imagined secret.

"Any nearer arresting anybody?" Philip Maynard asked, perkily.

Knollis grimaced. "Yes and no, and that isn't a very satisfactory answer, is it?"

"It's ambiguous," said Maynard. He glanced at his wife, now dressed in a yellow blouse and fawn slacks. "Could you invite our visitors in for a drink, Georgie?"

Georgie smiled. "Why, yes! Do come in!"

"Nice of you," replied Knollis, "but we haven't time. We've just one question for your husband."

"Your speciality, Inspector!" said Maynard.

"My speciality," Knollis agreed. "You were in and out of Clevely quite a few times on the seventh, weren't you?"

Maynard nodded. "Yes, you know that!"

"I know that," said Knollis. "Can you remember seeing Miss Moreland that morning?"

Maynard gave him a suspicious glance. "You must know I saw her, otherwise you wouldn't have asked. I take it she's told you herself that we met?"

Knollis offered no reply.

"I saw her in Castle Street, Inspector."

"About what time?"

"Oh, between half-past nine and a quarter to ten as near as I can say. I wasn't watching clocks that morning." He looked hard at Knollis. "And what else?"

"That's all, Mr. Maynard. Does that surprise you?"

"There are usually so many supplementary questions, Inspector. I was waiting for them."

"Not this time," said Knollis. "It's lunch-time, and we mustn't keep you from your table. Good morning, and thanks."

He and Wilson returned to their car, leaving the Maynards standing in the doorway, hand in hand, looking after them curiously.

"That was short and sweet," commented Wilson. "What's the notion?"

"Think your bee-keeping friend, Normanton, can spare us an hour round three o'clock?"

"He'll jump at it. He fancies his chance as a detective."

"Ask him to bring gloves and veils for three."

"We're going to open the hive at Jason's Knoll, of course?"

"We must, Wilson, but before going out there I want to see Daphne Moreland. There's just one question—my speciality, as Mr. Maynard says."

"And any supplementary ones?" asked Wilson. "Maynard seems to have your style weighed up now."

"That's all right," said Knollis. "It's a fair exchange, because I've weighed up Maynard's own. There's a good story going to emerge from this case. I can smell it."

Wilson nodded as he drove through the suburbs of Clevely. "I've suspected that for some hours. You haven't said a great deal, but I know you've something up your sleeve."

"You can't say much when you only suspect, and don't really know," Knollis excused himself. "The picture's becoming clearer now, and I think the next few days will see the affair cleared up. These things are always like jig-saw puzzles. You pick up a piece that looks as if it might fit, and then it doesn't, and you have to start looking all over again until you get one that does fit.

When you get it, you've filled out the picture or pattern by just that much, but it's enough to suggest to a greater degree what the finished picture might be like; it suggests the pattern of the whole. Maynard's just supplied us with a piece I've been looking for—not that's it's important in itself, but it suggests something else, just as Lanson's evidence suggested the possibility of a chance meeting between Maynard and Daphne Moreland."

"Did it?" Wilson murmured vaguely. "I never noticed anything."

Knollis made no reply, not wanting to embarrass Wilson by making the deduction seem as simple to arrive at as he had found it.

After lunch they went to see Daphne Moreland, and eventually tracked her down at the Clevely Golf Club's course outside the town. She was sitting with friends outside the clubhouse when they arrived, and she came straight to them as they stepped from the car, lounging towards them with her hands on her hips, tweed-clad, and supercilious in manner.

"This must be important!" she smiled. "What has brought you all this way out of town?"

"You saw Philip Maynard on the morning of the seventh of June, Miss Moreland!" Knollis said directly.

She paused a moment, eyeing him speculatively. "Yes, I did," she answered, finally.

"When?" said Knollis.

"When I was leaving Shipley's after inquiring for Jerry."

"He was walking past—or going in the offices?"

"Going in as I was coming out, Inspector."

"Ah!" said Knollis in a satisfied tone. "Looking for Gerald Batley, wasn't he?"

"Yes, or so he said."

"He actually told you that?"

"He asked me if Jerry was in. He looked pretty grim, too. I told him Jerry hadn't turned up for work, and I was wondering if he was ill. That wasn't exactly the truth, of course."

"He had the car?"

"It was parked outside. He offered me a lift home, but I had my own car just down the street."

"You saw him drive away, Miss Moreland?"

"He went towards the Market Square."

"And the time?"

"Probably about half-nine."

"Thanks very much," said Knollis. He literally pushed Wilson into the car. Daphne Moreland watched them drive away, and not until they were back on the road did he say: "Get it now, Wilson?"

"He went to see Lanson next, to find out where Batley might be."

Knollis shook his head. "Daphne Moreland's time is a bit early, but we can't quibble with her. No, he went to see Lanson, but not to find where Batley might be. He knew where he'd be, or so I think."

"Me," said Wilson, hunching his shoulders, "I'm not clairvoyant, so I'll merely ask my own stock question; where do we go from here?"

"To see Mrs. Lanson—"

"I have one question to ask her," said Wilson, in a fair imitation of Knollis's manner.

Knollis ignored the impression. "One question there, and I've cracked Maynard's alibi completely—by which I mean we'll know where he wasn't. The next job will be to prove where he was!"

"Nice for Maynard," murmured Wilson. "He certainly knows more about the job than I do."

The sarcasm went over Knollis's head. His eyes were near-shut, and he was solely concerned with his mental reconstruction of the events at the cottage on the vital morning.

Bernice Lanson was no more pleased to see them than she had ever been, and she certainly didn't like the way in which Knollis gently closed the outer door after she invited them inside.

"I'm in possession of certain information, Mrs. Lanson," said Knollis, "and require your confirmation of it. At what time did you and your brother arrive at Gerald Batley's cottage on the morning of the seventh of June?"

Wilson took in a great breath, and let it escape in a long hiss.

Bernice Lanson looked at Knollis as if he was the Witch of Endor producing ghosts from the thin air.

"Why—" she began, and then broke off, hesitated a moment, and went on: "We didn't go to the cottage!"

"You did," contradicted Knollis. "Your brother called for you between a quarter to ten and ten o'clock. You drove out to the cottage to have a few quiet words with Gerald Batley."

Her hands fell to her sides in a gesture of resignation. "Oh, well, if Phil's told you, that's that!"

Wilson heaved another sigh. Knollis made no sign that his imagination, aided by bluff, had put another ace in his hands.

"It would be about—what? About twenty past ten when you got there?"

Bernice Lanson agreed with that. There was neither spirit nor strength left in her. She was sagging badly.

"Batley's car was there?"

"Parked outside the gate. Yes."

"Did you see him?"

"He wasn't there, Inspector. Philip must have told you that."

"The cottage was open, or locked?"

"The doors were closed, but unlocked. Phil went in and looked round."

"You saw nobody else?"

She hesitated for a fraction of a second. "No, but we heard someone, Inspector. The wood, as you know, comes up to the boundary fences on the north and east. There was someone moving in the wood. Phil shouted Jerry's name several times, and then the movement in the wood ceased."

"Yes?" Knollis asked as she paused uncertainly.

"We came away then. Phil said he'd catch him another time and have a show-down with him. He drove me to his house and told me to take the car into town and leave it at Bentley's garage, from where he'd pick it up later in the day—he was coming into town again, of course, to see his wife."

"Why that?" asked Knollis. A puzzled frown came to his forehead until he realized he was supposed to know all she was telling him, when he forced a bland expression to his lean features. "Why didn't he take you home, Mrs. Lanson. Or drop you at his house, from where you could have caught a bus?"

"I had to make sure of getting home by half-past eleven, Inspector. My husband knew nothing of Jerry's dirty work, and I didn't want him to see me with Phil or anyone else, or he might have started asking questions I couldn't answer. He was coming home before twelve to change for a Rotary luncheon."

"Tuesday noon. Yes, that's correct," said Knollis. "A satisfactory explanation, Mrs. Lanson. One other question. Can you remember seeing any other car going towards Windward Lane as you returned home—a car belonging to someone you know, I mean?" She shook her head doubtfully. "I can't remember. My head was too full of my own affairs to bother looking for cars—and I wasn't expecting to meet anyone I knew!"

"Understandably so," said Knollis. "Ah, well, this has been both interesting and useful, Mrs. Lanson. We must thank you for your frankness."

She stared at him, and bit her lip. When she released she asked: "But Phil had already told you all this!"

Knollis gave her a Sphinx-like smile. "No, Mrs. Lanson! Not a single word of it! We reached certain conclusions by the exercise of reason, and merely needed your evidence to substantiate them."

She continued to stare at him. Then she glared. Then she walked past him and Wilson and opened the door. She stood there with the knob in her hand, her head in the air, and her sallow cheeks chalky white.

"That was a strong invitation to get out," said Wilson, as he closed the front gate behind them. "She don't like us now!"

"She'll like us less after the next interview," Knollis said, tersely. "I'm playing the slow game with her."

"Anyway," Wilson said, in a cheerful voice, "even I can see something of the final pattern now, so we must be progressing!"

"There's an interesting feature that's puzzling me," frowned Knollis.

"No!" exclaimed Wilson, with mock incredulity.

"Why they didn't clash with Daphne Moreland!" said Knollis, as usual ignoring any remark not immediately—and seriously—relevant to the thought in his mind. "She also, you'll remember, got back into town about half-past eleven in time to call on the dentist. Now what happened, Wilson? Were all three there together, all highly surprised to see each other? Did Maynard get rid of Bernice Lanson and then slip back by bus, or on a bike, or walk across the fields, or what? We're slowly narrowing the focus. We've got all three of them at the cottage between nine-thirty and eleven-thirty, singly or together. A lovely situation for conjecture! Anyway, at what time do we meet Normanton?"

"Due to pick him up at the brewery at three o'clock," replied Wilson, "and it's now half-past two. Perhaps if we went along now they might offer us a few samples!"

"We'll have another word with Lanson instead," said Knollis, earnestly. "Whichever of our new friends may phone each other after we've left 'em, we're sure Lanson's wife won't phone him! That means we can pump him!"

"About Maynard's visit."

"Correct," said Knollis.

Lanson was wary after his experience in the previous interview. He hedged Knollis's few questions, and they eventually came away no better off than they had been when they entered his office.

"I see your point," said Wilson, as he drove round to the brewery, "but do you think Lanson would have realized that Maynard was only checking to make sure he would be out of the way while he took Bernice to the cottage?"

"No," said Knollis, "I agree with your unspoken estimate of Lanson—he's pretty dim. Maynard could pump him dry and he wouldn't know what was happening."

"He twigged us," grunted Wilson, "but still, even a bloke as dim as Lanson must be able to realize that two coppers aren't playing Twenty Questions with him for a bag of nuts!"

They collected Hedley Normanton and his equipment and went out to Jason's Knoll. Wilson was firmly insistent that he was putting on the protective clothing before he as much as set down one foot within the wood, so Normanton and Knollis decided they might as well do the same.

Normanton used the smoker to subdue the bees, explaining that the purpose of pumping smoke into the hive was not to stupefy them, but to give them the idea their home was on fire, whereupon they would gorge themselves with honey in readiness for a getaway.

"They're so busy eating they don't bother with us," he said. "It's also said that when gorged they can't bend their abdomens over to sting—but I wouldn't bet on that myself! All along the way, bee-keeping is mainly a matter of separating the scientific knowledge from the legendary. Now which hive do you want opening up. I've smoked them all, which isn't usually done, but I'll admit these girls are wild, wild women."

The second one was pointed out by Knollis. "Someone's using it as a safe."

"That's a neat idea," said Normanton. "'Struth, they are wild! Come down here in a brown suit and they'd eat you alive. That's another old wives' tale, but one with some truth in it. They say the brown bear is the bees' hereditary and worst enemy, and his fur so thick and close that the bees can't get down to his skin. Racial memory connects brown with bears, and there you are!"

"I still think I'll have a bash at keeping them," said Wilson. "They can't all be as bad as these."

"You can work mine without a veil if you want to," said Normanton, "although I think only a mug or a show-off would do it. The eyes and throat are vulnerable points, and there's nothing clever in getting stung."

He tried the smoker again, to make sure it was still working. "This whatever-it-is? Is it actually among the frames, or between the brood box and the lifts?"

"We don't know," said Knollis. He smiled, and added: "Any more than we know what you're talking about."

Normanton grinned at him. "The brood box is the lower one with the deep frames in it. The super is the top one with the shallow frames. The lifts are the individual sections of the outer wall. You say somebody put something in this hive?"

"I was lying among the bracken on the side of the Knoll."

Normanton removed the roof and peered down into the cavity between the lifts and the brood chamber. "Nothing in there," he reported.

He pulled back a corner of the quilt and puffed smoke liberally under it and across the tops of the frames. A half-minute wait, and he removed the quilt completely. He smiled, took out two frames, leaned them against the hive wall, and put his gloved hand into the super. He passed a small paper-wrapped packet to Knollis. "Anything else, or shall I pack them up?"

"Close the hive," said Knollis. "This is what we wanted."

He squinted at Wilson through the wire gauze panel in the front of his veil. "Think we owe him this?"

"I think so," said Wilson. "Open it up."

Knollis waited until Normanton was ready, and then moved a short distance from the hives and untied the packet. It contained a short metal cylinder, and a latch key.

Normanton said: "Oh!"

"What's wrong?" asked Wilson.

"That's a calcium cyanide container."

"And the other's a key," Knollis said, unnecessarily.

Normanton gave him a curious glance.

"The key to the mystery," said Wilson, "and Batley's flat."

"The two together, plus the bee we found in the flat, will hang someone sooner or later," said Knollis. "Tell me, Mr. Normanton; did you know of the existence of this apiary?"

"Not until you told me of it. I remember old Edward Batley dying, of course, and I was concerned in the disposal of his stocks since I did microscopical exams of samples of bees to declare them free of disease, but I never knew he kept this place."

"We're told he was attempting to produce a new, or pure, strain here," said Wilson. "I'm telling you this because I think we owe you something of an explanation. This is where the brood disease in Maynard's apiary came from. Batley took frames of diseased brood and put them in Maynard's hives—you haven't inspected the combs, of course. Old Heatherington investigated the matter, and proved it to his own and our satisfaction. He has specimens in test tubes. You'll know what I'm talking about even if I don't use the correct terms. Some of the larvae weren't affected, and when they hatched out they were bright yellow bees against Maynard's dark ones. . . ."

"Ye—es," murmured Normanton.

"The old gentleman searched his memory," went on Wilson, "and couldn't think of anybody who had any bees just like these yellowy-orange ones, and then he remembered Mr. Batley's experiments, and came out here to look round. It was really this that set the ball rolling and ended in Gerald Batley's death. You'll keep that under your hat, of course!"

"So that's who killed Batley!" exclaimed Normanton. "'Struth, yes, I'll keep quiet. Sort of poetic justice, wasn't it, being finished off in that way. And yet I'd never have thought it of *him* of all people!"

"You never really know anyone," said Knollis. "It's often been said there's a saint and a devil in each one of us, and my experience confirms it. You never know which of 'em will come out. It all depends on the claims of circumstance—and self-interest."

"True enough," mused Normanton. He stared at the ground for a moment, and slowly raised his head to look wonderingly at Knollis through his veil. "There's something puzzling me."

"Such as?"

"Well, if Batley put diseased frames in Maynard's hives, which is quite feasible, what did he do with the ones he took out?"

Knollis and Wilson looked at each other. "That's quite a point," said Knollis, "and proves the advantage of calling in expert advice. It hadn't occurred to me."

"It may mean nothing," said Normanton, "but I just wondered."

Chapter XII
MR. MAYNARD ATTEMPTS TO BLUFF

KNOLLIS DID the obvious thing now the cyanide container was in his hands; he went out to Mansard House and asked to see the container which had held the cyanide with which Maynard's bees had been destroyed. Wilson's men meanwhile went to work on the key, looking for prints.

Philip Maynard said he had never been in possession of the cyanide after leaving Gregsons' shop at Mottingley; Old Heatherington had taken charge of it, since when Maynard had not seen it.

It was a satisfactory answer, and Knollis went on to Newbourne to interview the old bee-keeper.

The old man nodded. "That's right, Inspector. I've had it all the time. Want to see it?"

"Please," said Knollis.

The old man turned and unlocked a corner cup-board. An array of bottles and tins met Knollis's roving eye: Death's Head weedkiller, a medicine bottle half-filled with crystals of permanganate of potash, a packet of compost accelerator, a phial of rooting hormone, a ten-ounce bottle of methyl salicylate, the bottle of ether meth. which Knollis had already seen in action as a bee anaesthetic, two pill boxes whose labels he could not see, and a metal cylinder round which the old man's gnarled hand closed as he took it from the shelf.

"That's it, Inspector," he said.

Knollis took from his pocket the one found at Jason's Knoll, and compared the two. "Identical."

"So you've found Batley's, eh?" said Old Heatherington.

"This is it, without a doubt," replied Knollis. He stared reflectively at the conglomeration in the cup-board, although not thinking about them.

"By the way, Mr. Heatherington, the hive has vanished from Mrs. Doughty's cottage," he said, casually.

The old man looked up quickly. "Vanished, sir? Where's it gone?"

"Back to Jason's Knoll."

The old man sought for his pipe and pouch. "Back to Jason's Knoll? Back, did you say?"

"Surely it came from there?" said Knollis.

"I hadn't thought about it, sir. What makes you think it came from there?"

"There were three hives, with a brick under each leg of each hive."

"Yes, that's right," the old man nodded.

"At the end of the row were four bricks, almost hidden in the long grass."

"Ah, I see now!"

Old Heatherington filled his pipe and puffed the tobacco into life, flicking the spent match into the hearth. "That makes quite a little mystery, doesn't it?"

"There's another mystery," said Knollis. "What happened to the healthy frames of comb Batley took from Maynard's hives?"

"I can think of something to explain that, Inspector. My guess is they went into the fire at Wellow Lock. It was the only safe place for them."

Knollis glanced at him with new respect. It was a feasible explanation.

"He'd get rid of the evidence that way," added the old man. "It might be worthwhile looking round the ruins. You see, all Phil's frames would be in brood boxes or supers, and perhaps a few spares in a wooden or cardboard box. Young Gerald wouldn't bother packing Phil's frames if he was going to burn the lot, so I reckon he must have just chucked them in the honey-house and shut the door."

Knollis closed one eye and regarded the old man with the other. "You mean you've been out there and satisfied yourself that it happened as you've suggested!"

The old man gave a grin. "Yes, that's true, but I didn't want to say anything in case you thought I'd been poking my nose into your job."

"Look," said Knollis. "Those frames are made of wood, and the combs are wax. How could you prove Maynard's frames went in the fire."

"Same as I've said. All Phil's stuff was packed in one corner."

He sniffed, and, as an afterthought, added: "Wax foundation is wired, you know, Inspector. That helps it to take the weight without breaking down. The method of wiring varies with the manufacturer. Some wire it horizontal, some vertical, and some like a series of V's."

"And you found the wires—which hadn't been destroyed in the fire?"

"That's it, sir," said Old Heatherington. "In the middle of what had been the floor."

Knollis smiled ruefully. "It's about time I handed the investigation over to you. You're smarter at it than I am."

Old Heatherington rubbed his cheek with the mouthpiece of his pipe. "Well, I'm an interested party in a way, aren't I? I mean, the thing concerns two good friends of mine. The time to help people's when they're in trouble. I never did think much of giving flowers to folk when they're dead."

"Batley gets no flowers," said Knollis.

"He wasn't a friend, sir, but then again I don't spit on the graves of enemies."

"You've thought about this affair. What do you think about it?"

The old man pulled a stool from under the table and sat on it. He waved to the fire-side chair. "Might as well rest your legs, sir."

Knollis took the seat. There was a quizzical expression on his lean face, and his grey eyes were nearly hidden behind his half-closed lids.

"This business of asking questions to find a murderer works two ways," said the old man. "You ask questions of my friends, and they come and tell me what you've asked, and what they've answered, and then I try to make out what you're after. You don't mind that?" he asked, with a sudden anxiety.

"I suppose it's a logical reaction," replied Knollis. "I must confess I hadn't thought of it working that way."

"You see," said Old Heatherington, "I know now why the honey-house was burned down. It was on account of young Gerald wanting money off Mrs. Lanson. . . ."

"Where's this getting us?" asked Knollis.

The old man rubbed his sparse white hair. "I haven't got it sorted out properly yet, but I think I see what it's going to boil down to in the end—a woman."

"Why that?"

"A woman's the only thing could have got young Gerald to the cottage at that time of the day. I reckon he was expecting to meet a woman there, and I won't alter."

"He also wanted money," Knollis said, quickly.

"Fair enough," said the old man, "but we can't reckon that in, because Mrs. Lanson was the only one who knew that then. No, he was expecting to find a woman waiting for him."

"Yes . . . ?"

"That's all there is to it," Old Heatherington said, with a vague gesture.

Knollis got up impatiently. The old man was either incapable of expressing his thoughts, or had no ideas to express and was trying to make out that he had. Lonely old men were notably garrulous, and liked to make out that their years of experience had given them an insight into life not enjoyed by younger people.

Time was valuable, and Knollis could not afford to waste it. He handed back the cylinder of cyanide, saw it safely locked up, and then left.

On the way back to Clevely he debated the old man's theory. If Batley had expected a woman to be at the cottage, then what woman? Georgie Maynard was in hospital. Bernice Lanson was undoubtedly at home until her brother called for her, when they both went out to the cottage—which suggested that she had no appointment with Batley. He couldn't have been expecting Daphne Moreland to be at the cottage, otherwise she wouldn't have wasted time looking for him at the flat and the office.

Suppose Batley had been lured to the cottage by a faked call? In that case it could only have been made by a man, and the only man to be considered was Maynard. If this had happened, then why had he later collected his sister Bernice and taken her out there?

It was possible, of course, that Maynard was trying to provide himself with an alibi that morning, an alibi that could only be established as a result of his movements being checked—a static alibi which would tend to impress any investigator of its verity against his will; i.e., an alibi discovered when he was trying to find *damaging* evidence.

It would be a neat trick if Maynard had tried this. He would act suspiciously, his manner indicating that he had no intention of giving an account of his movements, and then, when the police really got to work they would find he had been with his sister, and he was cleared.

Had he murdered Batley after coming home in the workmen's bus, and before going back into Clevely? Note that he rang his sister at ten past eight. If he had murdered Batley then, how had he known Batley would be at the cottage, or alternatively how had he got Batley to obligingly go there? He would have to use the name of one of the three women in whom Batley was interested.

It didn't seem likely that he would use his wife's name, since news travels fast, and it was quite on the cards that Batley already knew of her breakdown. He couldn't use Daphne Moreland's name, for Batley was likely to know more about her movements and possible movements than Maynard did. Then again, there was the difficulty of Maynard's voice being recognized on the telephone; the distance between the house and the flat was only three miles, and his voice would be clear, and difficult to disguise.

Bernice Lanson? Suppose Maynard had known of the pressure Batley was applying on her, and had known it before the morning of the seventh of June? Suppose she'd rung back after her husband had gone to business, arranging to meet him at the cottage, and then suppose she had rung her brother, acquainting him with the arrangement, so that he went instead?

Suppose Maynard murdered Batley, and then returned to town to tell her Batley's car was there, but that he couldn't be found? And then took her out to the cottage, knowing full well the man was dead and his body disposed of? That would remove any suspicion from his sister's mind, and provide Maynard with a link in his alibi!

Knollis glanced at the speedometer, and slowed the car as he entered the centre of Clevely. All these theories were pretty ones, but the evidence to support them circumstantial and intangible.

The hive was another puzzling feature of the case. Why had it been brought from Jason's Knoll? Had Batley brought it, or were the Maynards responsible? Why had the Maynards taken it back to Jason's Knoll?

He decided to have a chat with Hedley Normanton about the matter; Old Heatherington was out of the question considering his deep attachment to Philip and Georgie Maynard.

He drew in to the kerb outside divisional head-quarters.

Wilson was in his office, waiting for him. "Don't you eat these days, or have you eaten?"

Knollis glanced at the clock. "Seven, eh? I'd lost count of time—and I've gained no ground to balance it!"

"Neither have I," grumbled Wilson. "The key had been cleaned, and handled with gloves. There isn't a trace of a print on it. In short, we're getting nowhere fast!"

Knollis nodded wearily. His lean face was pale, and his grey eyes lacking lustre. He sagged in his chair, and Wilson marvelled to himself that the straight ramrod of a man who had literally marched off the train a few days ago should have so changed in so short a time. That was the result of working keyed-up instead of the Wilson way. Knollis was a thorough and near-brilliant investigator, but he'd have to learn to relax if he wasn't to be an old man by the time he was fifty, in another three years.

"We're getting nowhere fast," Wilson repeated moodily. "I've had the Old Man in from Mottingley while you've been on the trail. He's getting impatient."

"If he can do the job better himself, why did he send for the Yard," snapped Knollis. "I know of two people prepared to let him have a go. How's the County Super feeling about it?"

"Desmond? He's with us all the way. So are Rankin and Urban. The Old Man was a bit annoyed because you weren't present."

"He gets my reports, and I can tell him nothing more than's in 'em," said Knollis. "Oh, well, Wilson, grab your hat and we'll go and see the Maynards again. It's time we had a showdown. That young pup's played with us long enough, and I intend to break him before midnight—and if I haven't done it by then I'll stay up all night!"

"Why not get him down here?" suggested Wilson. "The official atmosphere might intimidate him. He's played on his own muck-heap up to now, you know—and that's a distinct psychological advantage."

Knollis reached for the telephone. "Get me Mr. Maynard at Mansard House, Newbourne, please."

He handed his cigarettes to Wilson as they waited. Both lit up and smoked in silence. Then the call was announced, and Knollis smiled a tired smile at Wilson.

"Mr. Maynard? Inspector Knollis here. Think you could drop in on us at the police station this evening? There are one or two points left which we feel you could clear up for us. Your wife? No, I don't think we need her, thanks. You'll drop her at your sister's and come on from there. Very decent of her, I'm sure. We're so overwhelmed with work we just can't spare the time to come to your place. Thanks a lot! 'Bye!"

Wilson smiled grimly as Knollis finished the call. "What they call laying on the old flannel. Devil, isn't it, when you have to kid a bloke like that when you're feeling like kicking his pants? Now I think a cup of tea wouldn't hurt you. I'll organize it—and a few ropy buns."

A minute later he opened the drawer in his desk and threw a small cardboard roll across the table. "That came in from the lab at Mottingley to-day, half an hour before the old man arrived. The boffins have put the original murder box together for you."

Knollis fingered it with interest. "Usual type of container. Made spirally, probably by the mile, and cut off in lengths. Top and bottom edges rolled in by machinery, and a tin floor clamped in. All kinds of powders are sold in these things: baking powder, cream of tartar, boracic powder, pepper, and a thousand and one other household commodities."

"Tracing its source would be like looking for the proverbial needle in the ditto haystack," remarked Wilson.

"Worse," said Knollis; "we'd use a mine detector, or electronic diviner these days, and the needle would give up the ghost. However, you'd better make room for me at your side of the desk, then we can do the accusing justices' act on Maynard. Oh, yes, and I'll slip the container in your drawer. Got the key?"

"It's in there already."

The stage was fully set by the time Philip Maynard arrived. Knollis and Wilson had thick sheaves of official-looking documents on the desk before them, and a detective-officer was placed in a convenient corner with instructions to make copious notes, and as ostentatiously as possible.

Maynard came in cautiously, one eye on the uniformed constable who had led him through the passages from the inquiries window, and the other on Knollis and Wilson.

"Ah, come in, Mr. Maynard!" Wilson greeted him. He pushed the cigarette-box across the table. "I believe you smoke occasionally?"

"Not now, thanks," Maynard replied, still regarding him with caution.

"I'll leave them there," smiled Wilson. "But do take a seat, please!"

The detective-officer flicked a switch. The neon strips flashed jerkily for a few seconds, and then settled down to shed their light on Maynard's pale and strained face. Knollis noted his fidgeting fingers, and nodded approvingly; his man was beginning to lose his confidence.

Knollis leaned across the desk with a paternal air. "We think it's time for you to make a fuller statement about your movements on the seventh of June," he said.

"You're in possession of the full story—as a result of bluffing my sister," Maynard retorted.

"I don't think we are," said Knollis. "What, for instance, did you do with yourself between half-past eleven, and, say, ten past one, when you arrived at the nursing home?"

Maynard smiled as if that was an easy one to deal with. "I got myself a meal, of course!"

"I thought you didn't feel like eating that day, Mr. Maynard, and couldn't stand the empty house?"

Maynard blinked. He paused for a moment, and then said: "I—well, I prepared a meal, and then couldn't eat it."

"You didn't go back to the cottage, by any chance?" asked Knollis.

"Why should I?" Maynard demanded.

"That's quite a point," Knollis smiled. He opened the drawer in the desk and threw the metal cylinder and Batley's key across the polished surface.

Maynard stared at them as if he did not believe what he was seeing. The tip of his tongue appeared, and ran along his upper lip. "What—what are those?"

Knollis gave a bland smile, and pointed first to the cylinder and then to the key. "That is a calcium cyanide container, and the other doesn't look unlike a key. You'll agree with me?"

"Yes. Yes, of course," Maynard said, lamely.

"We found them in a beehive at Jason's Knoll, Mr. Maynard."

"J—Jason's Knoll?"

"Jason's Knoll!"

"In a beehive," murmured Maynard. "How queer!"

Knollis removed his arms from the desk and sat back in his chair. "What do you think about the police force as a whole, Mr. Maynard?"

Maynard looked surprised at the question. "It's—why, it's an admirable institution. We—we couldn't manage without it, could we?"

"A conventional reply, Mr. Maynard, which boils down to the old one about our policemen being wonderful. Do you regard the force as an efficient institution?"

"None more so, I should imagine."

"I see," said Knollis. He wagged a finger at Maynard. "And yet you think you are cleverer than the Clevely Borough C.I.D. and Scotland Yard put together!"

"I'm sure I don't, Inspector," Maynard protested. "I haven't said anything to give you that impression, have I?"

"No, but you're acting as if you believe it," said Knollis. "Listen, Mr. Maynard; at something after twelve to-day Inspector Wilson and myself came to see you. You were just leaving home in your car, accompanied by your wife. We followed you—does that suggest anything? From your home to the cottage in Windward Lane, and thence to Jason's Knoll. . . ."

Maynard nodded, very slowly. "So that's it, Inspector!"

"That's it, Mr. Maynard. We now wish to learn how you came into possession of the calcium cyanide container and the key of Batley's flat. In brief, what happened when you and your sister went out to the cottage that morning. And why let your sister have the car when you could easily have run her home? That's another question. And what did you do between seeing her on her way, and setting out for the nursing home to visit your wife?"

Philip Maynard put his elbows on his knees and buried his face in his hands. Knollis waited impatiently, reining his impulse to hurry Maynard into an explanation. Wilson might have been carved from wood; he sat with his arms on the edge of the desk, watching the game being played between Knollis and Maynard as if it was of no more importance than a game of noughts and crosses.

Maynard lowered his hands after a minute and laced his fingers tightly together. "You won't believe me if I tell you the truth," he said.

"We'd like the chance," said Knollis.

"I found Batley, dead."

Wilson jerked his head up sharply. "You *found* him—dead!"

"You think I killed him," Maynard said, miserably. "I didn't. I swear I didn't! He was dead, and in the well when I found him!"

"Your sister was with you," said Knollis. It was impossible to tell by the tone of his voice whether he was asking a question or making a statement.

Maynard shook his head. "She didn't see him. We heard someone in the wood. I called out several times, thinking it might be Batley. I told my sister to stay by the house while I went to look round. It was then I found him . . ."

"And his key, and the cylinder?" asked Knollis.

"They were lying in the grass near the mouth of the well. It was seeing them that drew me to it—otherwise I might have gone away without knowing anything about him. I went back to my sister and told her we'd call and see Jerry another time. I sent her off in my car because the bus into Clevely wasn't due for another twenty minutes, and I wanted to get straight back to the cottage, and didn't want her either to see me go back, or hanging round to delay me."

"And you wanted to drive Batley's car back to his flat, out of the way?"

Maynard nodded. "Yes, that was my idea."

He paused for a few seconds, and then gave Knollis a direct glance. "You must realize, Inspector, that I was in a bad spot. I recognized the smell of cyanide, and I knew Jerry Batley wasn't the type to commit suicide . . ."

Knollis looked round at Wilson with a wry smile. How differently Batley and Maynard had summed up each other's character!

". . . so I quickly weighed up how suspicious it would look if it was proved that I'd been near the cottage," went on Maynard. "We were in low water financially, and we could have done with my wife's aunt's money—and still can do with it, and into the bargain it was beginning to get whispered round that Batley had tried to steal my wife away. So one way and another I'd plenty of reasons for wanting him out of the way."

"There was also the matter of the hundred pounds he tried to chisel out of your sister," Knollis reminded him.

"I didn't know about that until that same morning," said Maynard. "Batley had been flying his kite pretty high with Daphne Moreland, was flat broke, and needed money for the wedding. Judging by what he told Bern, he needed to match the style of the preparations being made by the Morelands. His actual phrase, according to my sister was: *'I can't go to a fashionable wedding looking like a pauper, and there's no more tick at the tailor's. I've simply got to have money to see me over the wedding and the honeymoon, after which I can start stinging Daph and the Moreland old oak chest.'*

"You'd have let your sister have the money paid to you by the insurance company?" asked Knollis.

"Oh, yes!" Maynard said, quickly. "I didn't suspect her, and never would have done, of anything like an affair with Batley—or anybody else if it comes to that! If she'd told me she needed the money desperately, and couldn't tell Rodney, her husband, I should have thought she'd overspent her allowance, and left it at that."

"So that, one way and another, you thought appearances were against you," said Knollis. "What did you do when you got back to the cottage—or, first, how did you get there?"

"There was a Newbourne-bound bus due five minutes after my sister left me. I caught that into the village. There's a stile a few yards below Mr. Heatherington's cottage, and on the opposite side of the road. It takes you on a footpath over the fields and comes out in the lane a bit higher up than Batley's cottage. I had to take the risk of being seen. It was I who took up the two flagstones. I wriggled and pushed them across to the well and laid them across the top of it."

"So that when Mr. Heatherington found the body you had to stand by and act as if you didn't know anything about it?"

"Yes," said Maynard. "It was my wife's idea to move the stones. She has the idea that wells are romantic—you know how women are!—and she wanted to see it. I tried to get her away, but she'd made up her mind, and Old Heatherington was encouraging her, so that was that! Officially, the old chap found the body."

"The hive? What was the purpose of that?" asked Knollis.

Maynard gave an uneasy laugh. "Perhaps you won't understand, but those flags looked odd to me with nothing standing on them. They didn't seem to have any purpose but to cover the mouth of the well, so I decided it would tend to disguise their real purpose if I put a hive on them."

"I see," said Knollis, "but why one all the way from Jason's Knoll? You'd plenty of spare ones both at home and out at Wellow Lock?"

"Not at Wellow," said Maynard. "They went up in the blaze. It was just one of those odd fancies. In the first place I could get to Jason's Knoll quicker than Farndon Howe, where I had six empty hives. And you'll have guessed I was pushed for time, because I had to be back at the nursing home by one o'clock if I was to stand a chance of seeing my wife before tea-time. Then again, it seemed appropriate to fetch one from Jason's Knoll. Perhaps you won't understand, but it seemed to me, judging by Old Heatherington's remarks, that Batley had ruined my apiary with diseased brood from the Knoll apiary, and I had a sort of vision of Batley dead but able to see what was going on, and realizing that he'd got a hive as a tombstone. I can't quite explain. I'm not good with words."

"You can explain," said Knollis. He was suddenly alive again, his weariness gone, his eyes bright. "You thought up this scheme before you got to the cottage, or when you got there, Mr. Maynard?"

"Oh, when I got there," Maynard said, airily, his confidence restored. "It was the inspiration of the moment."

"You went alone, and fetched a hive from Jason's Knoll?"

Wilson edged forward an inch on his chair.

"That's right," said Maynard.

"How many journeys from the apiary to the car?"

"Two, Inspector. I took the roof and one lift first, and then the porched lift and the floorboard."

"Tell me, Mr. Maynard," said Knollis; "am I right in saying you favour those box-like wire veils?"

"Oh, yes," said Maynard. "I've had them right from the day I began keeping bees."

"Stitched to old trilbys?"

"Yes—but why?"

"Tell me," said Knollis, leaning over the desk with narrowed eyes; "did you go into that dell without a veil and gloves?"

Maynard looked up in sudden alarm. "Why—no!"

"Then where did you get them from?" demanded Knollis. "They couldn't have been in Batley's car, because you and old Mr. Heatherington took possession of them when you raided his flat earlier that same morning! There couldn't have been any such equipment at the cottage since Mrs. Doughty hated bees and everything concerning them! If you'd thought up this scheme before going back to the cottage you'd have brought the stuff with you—but you've said you thought it up there; it was the inspiration of the moment!"

Maynard sat with puckered brows, looking down at his hands.

"Mr. Maynard," said Knollis, "you're a liar!"

He turned to Wilson. "Which sergeant's on duty?"

"Collier."

"I suggests he comes and keeps Mr. Maynard company for a while. He may remember something he hasn't told us. You and I will meanwhile take a walk."

Wilson looked across at the note-taking officer. "Transcribe your notes in duplicate, and don't leave the office until Sergeant Collier arrives."

Out in the corridor he blew a sigh. "What are we going to do with him, Knollis?"

"Leave him to cool off. While he's safe here we'll send a car for Bernice Lanson. I want a minute-by-minute commentary of Maynard's doings that morning—her version."

He laughed, and clapped Wilson on the back. "Maynard forgets he's up against two men who are interested in bees!"

"But not those so-and-so's at Jason's Knoll," said Wilson. "You know, it's a good job for us he doesn't use those old net veils, or he might have got away with his story."

CHAPTER XIII
KNOLLIS SQUARES THE TRIANGLE

As a result of a last minute inspiration Knollis now had Philip Maynard in Wilson's office, Bernice Lanson in Inspector Urban's office, and Daphne Moreland waiting impatiently in an ante-room, and none of them aware that the others were in the building. He intended to get Bernice Lanson's story, compare it with Maynard's, point out the discrepancies to Maynard, get a new story from him—he hoped, and repeat the process until the truth finally emerged. He had Daphne Moreland there for an entirely different reason.

Bernice Lanson faced them with calm features, sullen as ever, but outwardly calm. The last light of day was striving to compete with the neon strips on the ceiling, and the smoke from Wilson's cigarette, parked on the ash-tray, swirled and spiralled towards the open windows. Bernice Lanson accepted a cigarette from Knollis and tapped one end on the surface of the desk with steady fingers.

"You've told us practically everything we need to know, Mrs. Lanson," Knollis said, gently.

"Then why this?" she asked, looking at him over the top of Wilson's lighter.

"It's a more detailed account of your visit to the cottage we'd like," Knollis replied. "What did you do when you arrived there?"

"Walked through the gate, and up the path to the house, of course."

"Quite," said Knollis. "And next?"

"Knocked on the front door, received no reply, and went round to the back to repeat the process. Getting no reply, I tried the door. I pushed it open and called Jerry's name. Then we went in, called up the stairs, and, still getting no reply, looked round the house."

"Yes, and then?"

"We went outside. It was then we heard someone moving about in the wood. Phil called Jerry several times, and then told me to wait against the back door while he investigated."

"How did he investigate, Mrs. Lanson?"

"Well, he went up into the orchard and apparently along the boundary hedge. He was gone some minutes."

"You heard no sounds of, say, a fight, or people talking?"

"I heard nothing, Inspector."

"I see," said Knollis. "Tell me, Mrs. Lanson, did he look at all tired or ill that morning?"

"Well, he'd been up all night," she pointed out, "but it's queer you should mention that, because when he rejoined me I told him he needed a good sleep. He looked awfully pale, and it looked to me as if the reaction was setting in after his two shocks of the fire and Georgie's collapse. He said he'd have a nap later in the day when he'd seen Georgie. He then drove back to the house, and sent me on with the car."

"You got home before half-past eleven?"

"Yes, nicely," she replied. "I left the car at Bentley's garage, walked up home, and was there a good quarter of an hour before my husband arrived at twenty to twelve."

Knollis was silent for a time, and then said: "Mrs. Lanson, you're absolutely certain there were only two cars outside the cottage—your brother's, and Batley's?"

"I'm positive, Inspector."

"Thanks," said Knollis; "that will be all. I'll have a man run you home."

She rose slowly, the fingers of her left hand pressed hard on the edge of the desk. "My brother has gone home?"

"He's still here, Mrs. Lanson," Knollis said, flatly.

"He can run me back then. He brought the car."

"Your brother won't be leaving for some little time," said Knollis. "He's busy checking the statements he's made—we always insist on that before a witness signs the transcription of a statement, you know!"

Bernice Lanson nodded her head. "Sounds more to me as if you're regarding him as a suspect. I'm not satisfied. I was with him all the time he was at the cottage, and I know he didn't see Batley there."

She paused, and then added: "You've paid a lot of attention to my brother, and he seems to have been here a long while."

"His statement was taken down in shorthand, Mrs. Lanson," Knollis explained. "It had to be typed before he could sign it."

She was still not satisfied. She walked to the door, and then turned back again. "He'll be home to-night?"

"Of course he'll be home to-night, Mrs. Lanson."

"I wondered," she said, cautiously. "You sometimes keep people a long while for questioning, and then finish up with charging them."

"He'll be home to-night, Mrs. Lanson. Right on your heels most probably."

She accepted her dismissal, said good night, and closed the door behind her very gently.

Wilson, who had been mute throughout the interview, rang a bell and sent for Daphne Moreland. She was wearing a plain frock of delphinium blue, and swinging a wide-brimmed straw hat by its ribbon of the same colour.

"I feel as if I'm about to be put to the Question Extraordinary by the Inquisition," she said, with a light smile that deceived nobody.

"Nothing so bizarre, Miss Moreland," said Knollis, putting on his best smile for her. "We were grateful for your admission that you drove out to the cottage at Newbourne on the morning of the seventh, but we're somewhat puzzled."

"You, puzzled," she murmured, in an incredulous voice. She lowered herself into the chair recently occupied by Bernice Lanson, and toyed with the hat ribbon. "In what way, Inspector?"

"At the time you say you were at the cottage there were two cars standing outside the gate, and yet you insist Batley's car was there alone. Can you explain the discrepancy between the two statements?"

"Whose is the other statement, Inspector?" she parried.

"Another person," said Knollis. "Can you explain?"

She lowered long lashes over her china-blue eyes.

"I'm afraid I can't, Inspector. There must be a mistake some-where."

"It amounts to this," said Knollis. "Either you made a mis-take when giving us the time at which you arrived, or chose to ignore the presence of the second car, or were actually with the people who turned up in the second car, and don't wish to reveal the fact."

She studied her shoes for a long second.

"A man's neck hangs on your incomplete evidence, Miss Moreland. Mr. Maynard's, to be exact. You wouldn't like to see him hanged because you hadn't been completely frank with us, would you? You like Mr. Maynard!"

"I could do with my father's advice," she said, without look-ing up.

"He'd give the advice he gives to his clients, Miss Moreland; tell the truth, the whole truth, and nothing but the truth."

"Are we justified in letting people down?" she asked.

"Are we justified in letting a man hang when he might be innocent?" Knollis countered, keeping his eyes fixed on her bent head.

She looked up then, with troubled eyes. "That's what I don't know. Phil Maynard wasn't guilty of murdering Jerry—I don't think so, anyway."

"Will it help you if I say that the second car was Philip May-nard's, and that he and his sister were at the cottage, looking for Batley?"

"He's told you that?"

"He's probably signing a statement to that effect at this very minute," said Knollis. "He's in Inspector Wilson's office with Sergeant Collier."

She flourished her hat. "In that case . . ."

The clerk in the corner of the office bent over his desk.

"I followed them—but not by design," she said. "There was another car in front of me as I turned into the Newbourne Road. Half a mile further on I recognized it as Phil Maynard's. Natu-rally thinking he was taking his sister to his home, I slowed up. I didn't particularly want them to see me. The car didn't turn into the drive, however, but went straight on, and, of course, I followed. I thought he might be going to see his old friend at Newbourne—what's his name, the bee-keeper?"

"Mr. Heatherington?"

"Yes, that's right. He lives to the left as you enter the village, but Philip turned to the right, and it began to dawn on me that he was going to the cottage. I'd made up my mind to see Jerry that morning if he was at the cottage, so when I saw Philip's car turn down Windward Lane I pulled up and began to wonder what to do.

"I drove on again past the end of the lane, and parked the car into a field gateway on the right of the road. Then I walked back and down the lane. There's a gate half-way down the lane, and on the left, so I slipped through that and walked down the hedge-side until I reached the cottage. Peeping through the hedge I saw two cars there, exactly as you've said: Jerry's, and Phil's. I followed the hedge by the side of the garden, and saw Bernice standing on the path behind the house. Philip was walking through the rosery towards the orchard. I waited where I was, and eventually saw Philip coming back through the rosery. He looked as if he'd seen a ghost, or been taken ill. It was only a matter of minutes before the car went away. I picked my way through a thin part of the hedge, and went to the cottage. It was unlocked, exactly as I've told you earlier, and Jerry certainly wasn't there. I looked in the outhouse, and round the garden, and then went back up the lane to my car and went home."

Knollis grunted. "And that's the whole story, Miss Moreland?"

"That's all of it, Inspector."

"You're prepared to sign a typed transcript in the morning?"

"I'll call round at any time you name."

When she had gone, Wilson shuffled round in his chair, and frowned. "So we've got him tied up except for the Jason's Knoll episode! Plus the period between seven-thirty and nine-thirty. I wonder why he lied about fetching the hive?"

Knollis gave a slow smile. "Because he couldn't have done it, Wilson. The man simply hadn't time. You know your district better than I do, so look at your wall-map and see what mileage he had to do between his sister going home, and his own arrival at the nursing home at one o'clock!"

"Then what the heck—" demanded Wilson.

Knollis pushed his chair back and put his legs up on the desk. "That was where he went and what he did during the afternoon session when he was supposed to be at the cinema! It was all very neatly thought out! I think we'll go back and have a few words with Mr. Maynard. He seems to think someone round here can't think as fast as he can . . ."

They went back to Wilson's office, to find Maynard stalking about the room and casting ferocious glances at Collier, who was apparently reading the evening paper.

"Not gone home yet?" murmured Knollis.

Maynard turned on him, viciously. "Not gone home yet! He won't let me! Can I go now?"

"When your statement's complete," smiled Knollis. He picked up the typed sheets and pretended to scrutinize them. "I could write the story of your doings on that day better myself!"

"I'm not surprised at that!" said Maynard. "The only snag is that it wouldn't represent the truth."

"At one o'clock you called at the nursing home and were turned away. At ten past you parked your car in the Rex car-park, and then phoned the nursing home. You then took a bus out to Windward Lane, collected Batley's car, and went out to Jason's Knoll. You had gloves and a net veil with you, one that folds up into little more room than a handkerchief would take—"

"I don't possess a blessed net veil!" interrupted Maynard.

"Batley did," said Knollis. "When Batley was playing conjuring tricks with your bees and those at Jason's Knoll he wouldn't want to be seen carrying a rigid wire veil round with him, so it's obvious that he had a net one. Now you and Mr. Heatherington took his gloves and veil away from him when you raided his flat that morning—ergo, they were still in your car, and you pushed them in your pocket before leaving the Rex car-park. It was all to your benefit both to leave your car in the park, and to use Batley's for the journey out to Jason's Knoll and back. You may have thought out your plan—your inspiration of the moment—while at the cottage during the morning, but you didn't do the job until afternoon! You fetched the hive in Batley's car, left it at the cottage, and went back for it that night, driving it to the garage behind the Grafton Flats!"

Maynard seated himself on the edge of the table, and shook his head. "No, I did not drive that car back to Clevely. The rest of your story is accurate, although I don't know how you got at the truth, but I left the car at the cottage, and how it got back to town is a mystery I haven't solved. Truthfully, I wouldn't have dared to be seen in town with it after finding Batley in the well. Doesn't that make sense, Inspector?"

"It does," Knollis readily admitted. "Yes, it does. But what were you playing at?"

"Covering myself, of course. Haven't I already told you that all the evidence was against me? That I'd half a dozen reasons for wanting Batley out of the way? The cards were stacked against me, so I tried to play them to my own advantage. I'd seen Batley down the well. I'd put the flagstones over it. They didn't look right; they looked as if they were *covering* or *hiding something*, and I wanted to avoid that. It suddenly came to me that if they looked as if they were *supporting* something instead of covering something nobody would get suspicious—and the obvious thing to my mind was a hive. Doesn't that make sense?" he asked, for the second time.

Knollis nodded. "Go on!"

"Old Heatherington's apiary was the nearest, but I couldn't borrow one of his, because it meant either taking him into my confidence, or stealing one, and in any case it would put suspicion on him if ever the body was discovered. I didn't want to use one of my own for the same reason, and then it struck me it would be grimly appropriate if I fetched one from Jason's Knoll—which I did."

"Why couldn't you have been as frank as this earlier in the case?" asked Knollis.

Maynard gave a wan smile. "I suppose I was afraid. I tried to cover myself and confuse you as much as I could. I didn't want you to know that I'd seen Batley after his death—it all looked so horribly black against me!"

"So now we've only one period to clear up and you will be off our hands," said Knollis. "Tell me, Mr. Maynard, what did you do between seven-thirty and nine-thirty?"

Maynard slid from the edge of the table. His jaw clamped tightly, his eyes mutinous, he stood glaring at Knollis and Wilson without speaking.

"We shall find out, you know," Knollis said, gently. "It's only a matter of time. By the way, did you know you were watched the whole time you were at the cottage with your sister?"

"Who by?" Maynard demanded.

"An old friend of yours," smiled Knollis.

"Not—not Old Heatherington!"

"A lady," said Knollis.

Maynard searched Knollis's features for a full minute. "A lady? An old friend? You mean Daphne Moreland was there!"

"I mentioned no names," said Knollis.

Maynard stared at him. "Then—then—"

"Then what, Mr. Maynard?"

"Then she watched us," he said, lamely, "and—and confirmed what I've told you!"

"And what your sister told us to-night," said Knollis.

"My sister? Has she been here?"

Knollis nodded. "Oh, yes, we had a chat with her while you were cooling your heels and waiting for your statement to be typed!"

"You go about things in a rotten underhanded way!" exclaimed Maynard, angrily.

"So do murderers," said Knollis.

"Can I go now?" Maynard demanded.

Knollis stood aside to clear the way to the door. "Why, yes! You could have gone any time you wished! Why didn't you say you wanted to go?"

Maynard muttered something beneath his breath and made for the door, not even bothering to bid them a good night.

"After him, Collier," said Knollis. "Give us a ring when he arrives!"

Knollis and Wilson took seats at opposite sides of the desk and sat looking at each other, Knollis keeping one eye on the wall clock. Ten minutes elapsed, and then the telephone bell rang. Wilson took the call. "He's at the Moreland house," he said, as he replaced the receiver. "What's the next move?"

"Let's put the cat among the pigeons," said Knollis. "Ring Lanson and ask to speak to his brother-in-law. When he says he hasn't landed back at the house just say that's queer because he left here half an hour ago. If Lanson gives you the chance, just say he's perhaps gone to see Miss Moreland! You see, Wilson, I'm convinced his wife knows only about half of the story, and it's time she knew the rest!"

Wilson turned to the telephone again.

Knollis waited until the call was finished, and went on: "You see, Wilson, I'm convinced that while his wife only knows half of the story she knows where he was between seven-thirty and nine-thirty, and we've to get it out of her."

"There's Maynard, and Daphne Moreland, and Bernice Lanson," said Wilson. "That makes a triangle."

"Add Georgie Maynard and make it into a square."

"That'll be funny—in the non-humorous sense," said Wilson. "The only person who was in hospital at the time of the murder, and she proves to be the star witness!"

"Maynard knows who killed Batley, of course," Knollis said, quietly.

"Ye—es," said Wilson, uncertainly.

"If you wanted to send a phone message that would bring a man to his death, where would you send it from?" asked Knollis.

"A public call-box, of course!"

"Suppose we have a handful of men busy round Newbourne in the morning, asking if Maynard has been seen using the call-box outside the post office?"

"We should have done that before," grunted Wilson. "Yes, I'll organize that."

Knollis put his knees against the edge of the desk and pushed his chair up on its two back legs. "That label's worrying me, you know! If the cyanide was decanted for the sole purpose of killing Batley, then why was it necessary to transfer the label? It was a warning, surely?"

"It means that it wasn't intended to be used against Batley," said Wilson. "Didn't you say Batley himself had concocted a murder plot against Maynard and Daphne Moreland? Wouldn't the label be more likely concerned with that side of the case?"

"Yes, it would," said Knollis, readily. "Tomorrow morning we'll give the cottage a good going-over, and then have yet another chat with Miss Moreland. An idea's beginning to stir in my mind—one that hasn't occurred to her!"

CHAPTER XIV
WILSON PRODUCES A NEW SUSPECT

BY NINE the next morning Knollis and Wilson were out at the cottage, playing at what Wilson called Sherlock Holmes. "I've been a copper heaven knows how many years now," he said, "but I honestly think this is the first time I've gone sleuthing on my knees!"

Knollis replied, from the opposite end of the kitchen: "If more people would spend more time on their knees there wouldn't be so much work for you and I! Well, there doesn't appear to be anything here. Tell me, Wilson, where would you decant cyanide if you found it necessary?"

Wilson sat back on his haunches. "I'll tell you. I'd have told you before, but I don't like interfering with your bright ideas. I'd have gone to work in the out-house."

Knollis looked round with surprise. "Why that?"

"Fresh air and no wind," said Wilson. "You've casement windows in this room, and can't open 'em without getting a draught through. In the outhouse you've only one window, a sash type, and you can open the top sash and still work with the light from the bottom one on your stuff without having to cope with the wind. And that's where I reckon Batley did his substitution trick!"

"I'll give you best," said Knollis. "Let's go."

It was Wilson, bending over an old copper set in a corner of the outhouse with a magnifying glass, who proved his own point.

"Knollis!" he said, in a low and yet tense whisper. Knollis walked over to him, and looked over his shoulder.

"There's something here," said Wilson. "Looks like a mixture of white grains and purplish crystals, and here, three inches away, is a dark brown stain. Got your tweezers. It's going to be a faddy job collecting the stuff, but it'll have to be done."

Knollis rubbed his chin thoughtfully. "There's a vacuum cleaner in the house. I've done the trick once before—cutting the bag from its supporting ring and tying a clean white handkerchief over it."

He looked through the open doorway to the house. "The flex might just reach to the point in the kitchen if we take it through the window. If not we'll have to ring for equipment." He gave a short laugh. "We're going to feel silly if it turns out to be soap powder!"

"Put your nose down and take a sniff," suggested Wilson. "There's no mistaking the smell, Knollis. This is where Batley switched the containers. Now I wonder what was in the cardboard one?"

Knollis turned and propped himself against the sink built under the window, looking at a shelf high up on the opposite wall. "Mrs. Doughty was evidently a scientific gardener. Look at the selection! Weedkillers, insecticides, soil fertilisers . . ."

His voice trailed away into silence, so that Wilson turned away from the copper to glance at him. "What is it?"

"I think I know how Batley meant to dispose of Daphne Moreland, Wilson," Knollis said. "Ring for your blokes to come and collect this stuff—they can bring the proper tackle as well. We'll go back into town. There's work to be done!"

Wilson rang from the house. They met the team of Collier and two detective-officers on the way back to Clevely, and

Wilson pulled up and told Collier for the second time what he wanted. "And get the stuff into Mottingley as soon as you can!"

He got the car under way again and then asked Knollis where the first call was to be.

"Charles' and Anderson's place," said Knollis. "I think we've missed something—and only by not asking the right questions."

The assistant was questioned in Mr. Charles' office again, and it was soon evident to Knollis that he was of the type who answer questions but never push themselves or offer suggestions unless they are asked for.

"When you discussed weedkillers with Mr. Batley," said Knollis; "did the conversation range over chemicals generally used in a garden, or was it restricted to the killing of weeds in paths?"

"Oh, well, it was a general conversation," said the assistant. "Mr. Batley was talking about the difficulty of keeping a garden in order when you had little time to spare for it, and I seem to remember telling him that spraying at defined times cut out a lot of trouble caused by pests and diseases. I mentioned blights, and cankers, and wire-worm and leather-jackets—"

"And—" began Knollis. He paused, and then went on: "I'm trying not to put any ideas into your head, trying not to put leading questions, and yet I feel I can't get the answer I want without asking you a certain question, so when I've asked it I do want you to say *No* if that is the correct answer. The question is this: were soil fumigants mentioned?"

The assistant answered straight away without any hesitation. "Oh, yes, sir! I told him that well-sterilized soil was half the battle."

"And you recommended . . . ?"

"Condy's Fluid, or, alternatively, pot. permanganate."

Knollis breathed a great sigh. "Thanks. That's the answer."

He pushed Wilson from the shop. "Daphne Moreland, Wilson, and now for the most careful and tactful approach I've yet had to make." He patted him on the back. "The case is nearly finished, old man! We've got it in the bag."

Wilson said nothing. He slid under the wheel, waited until Knollis had joined him from the other side, and started the engine. Five minutes later he pulled up outside the Moreland house. As they reached the front door it opened, and Daphne Moreland's father came out on his way to business.

"Oh, hello!" he greeted them. "Who are you after this time? Me, or Daphne?"

"We've really come to see your daughter," said Knollis, "but I think it might be as well if you were present at the interview."

"Why me?" Moreland asked, curiously.

"We've a theory," said Knollis, waving a hand that embraced Wilson. "If we're correct, the proof will emerge during our interview with your daughter. I'd be interested to see whether you reach the same conclusion as ourselves."

"Oh, well," said Moreland, and led the way back into the house. He found his daughter, and then ushered them all into the drawing-room. "Now then," he said. "What is it you want to know?"

Knollis addressed himself to Daphne Moreland. "We've been out to the cottage at Newbourne this morning, just looking round in a general way, and we wondered if Gerald Batley had any ideas about altering the lay-out of the gardens?"

Daphne Moreland scowled. "It's a silly sort of question to waste my time with, isn't it?"

Her father turned immediately. "Detectives don't usually ask stupid questions, Daphne. Did Batley intend altering the gardens, or didn't he?"

"He didn't—as far as I know."

"Was he in any way concerned about the state the gardens were getting into?" asked Knollis.

"Well, he did curse the weeds a few times when I was out there with him."

"Did he suggest anything in the way of a mass attack on them?" Knollis asked next.

Daphne Moreland hesitated. "Well, he had the bright idea that we might spend part of our honeymoon tidying the place up."

"I see," said Knollis, "and the idea of wielding a fork and trowel on your honeymoon didn't appeal to you?"

"Can you imagine it?" she countered.

"It's hardly a romantic notion," Knollis admitted dryly. "I take it he was a keen gardener?"

"About as keen as myself," she replied, cynically. "He loathed it, but said we ought to keep the place tidy until we could find some big buck navvy or horny-handed son of the soil to do it for us."

"That sounds like Batley all right!" commented Moreland.

"He was going to use chemicals to clear the paths, I believe," said Knollis. "He inquired at Charles' and Anderson's about the best stuff to use. They suggested sodium chlorate."

Moreland looked up quickly, but said nothing. Daphne Moreland nodded. "That was the scheme for the paths. He didn't see why we should tear our finger-nails to pieces coaxing dandelions from between the stones. The only snag was that the stuff might seep into the borders and damage them as well, so the whole idea was left over until we were living there."

"I see," Knollis said, heavily. "I'm a bit of a gardener myself, and I noticed the soil was a bit rank—there was a thin film of moss under the rose bushes. He'd noticed that, of course?"

"He'd noticed everything," Daphne Moreland replied. "It looked to me as if there was too much work to be done."

"Look, Miss Moreland," said Knollis, "can I suggest that he persuaded you into spending the honeymoon at the cottage, and that against your inclinations?"

She glanced at her father, and then answered: "Yes, that is so, Inspector."

Moreland returned her glance. "Then why the dickens did you fall for the notion?"

"Oh, well," she said, lamely, "he seemed so set on it, and I didn't like to disappoint him. He so passionately wanted us to be away from everyone for the beginning of our married life."

Moreland turned to Knollis. In a slow manner he said: "I think I'm beginning to understand!"

"Wasn't there any suggestion of starting the garden before you were married, Miss Moreland?" asked Knollis. "You'd surely expect a few visitors?"

"No. Jerry said we'd remain townees until we were married, and then go straight over to rural life."

Knollis turned to Moreland again. "I don't like asking this question, but would you mind telling me something of the financial arrangements? I mean, your daughter was to marry a man earning a comparatively small salary. I know you were to buy him partnership with Shipley, but did he stand to gain in any other way—in the matter of money, of course."

"I'd promised to continue Daphne's allowance for one year," replied Moreland. "Apart from that they were to be on their own feet. If Batley couldn't make a success of the partnership—well, he could, and I had confidence in him to that extent. Daphne knows I didn't like the fellow, but he was her choice, and I believe in people making their own decisions."

"Back to gardening," said Knollis. "If Batley had no knowledge of gardening, how did he intend to run the rosery and the orchard? Are you a gardener by any chance?"

Moreland answered the question. "Daphne is good at cutting flowers for the house. Beyond that she's as useful as a brown bear with a pack of playing cards! Daphne's talents are all mental ones—or perhaps I should say intellectual ones."

"He was trying," said Daphne. "He got no end of books from the library and swotted them up. Oh, yes, and he'd ordered gardening tools from Empton!"

"Such as?"

"Oh, a hoe, and a spade, and a fork, and a new lawn mower, and two watering cans. They were to be delivered after we got in the house. They'd have to be kept in the old outhouse, and it needed a new door and lock."

"Two watering-cans?" murmured Knollis. "Why two? One for each hand? Was he getting so ambitious?"

"He said one was for water and liquid manures, and the other for chemicals like the chlorate stuff you mentioned."

"I see," said Knollis. "You seem to have talked your plans over very thoroughly!"

"Oh, but we did, of course!"

"Did he mention using Condy's Fluid or permanganate of potash in the garden?"

"No—o, I don't think so, Inspector."

"Oh!" exclaimed Knollis, and sat back with a puzzled frown.

Moreland leaned forward. "Inspector Knollis, I think we should have all the cards on the table now. My daughter isn't a child, and I think you should tell her the truth. She might be able to fill in the blanks."

Wilson blinked at him from the opposite side of the hearth. "You mean you know what's in our minds? What was in Batley's mind?"

"My dear man, I suspected it as soon as Batley insisted on the romantic rustic honeymoon—and I didn't intend him to get away with it; that's why I got Holsen to vet Maynard's garden, and old Mr. Heatherington to go into the bee disease."

Daphne Moreland laid her hand on her father's arm. "What—what is all this?"

"You'd better brace yourself for a shock," he replied. "Jerry intended to murder you. Ask the Inspector if you don't believe me."

Then he sprang forward and caught her as she slid from the chair.

Five minutes later, white and shaken, she sat back in the chair, sipping a glass of weak brandy. "I'm better now," she said. "You'd better tell me all of it, please."

"We think," said Knollis, "that he was trying to drive Philip Maynard to suicide. That would leave Georgie Maynard a widow and free to marry. Then you would have met with an accident *after* your marriage, and he would have tried to marry her with your money. I wouldn't have told you this myself, but since your father has chosen to let you know the worst I can do no more than confirm it."

"So that was it!" she sighed. "That was why he said Phil was short of guts and would kill himself if the load got too heavy. Oh, Jerry! Jerry!"

Knollis waited for the bout of weeping to subside. He then said: "We now want to know who killed him, who got there first."

"I've told you all I know, Inspector," she said, earnestly. "I'm certain it wasn't Phil Maynard, because when he came back through the rosery he looked as if he'd met death himself. . . ."

"He had," said Knollis, "since he'd just found Batley in the well. But what we want to know is this: had Philip Maynard put him there earlier in the day? We've got every minute of his day checked but for the period between half-past seven and half-past nine in the morning. Did he kill Gerald Batley between those times? We've no means of knowing. But that is beside the point. What I want to know immediately is how Batley intended to murder you! And here is the question I'm bound to ask you since the answer hasn't emerged from the answers you've given me. Had Batley at any time shown you how to mix up any chemicals to be used on the garden? Had he given you any directions for mixing up any chemical mixtures?"

She held his gaze without faltering. "No, Inspector! The matter was never mentioned between us."

Knollis rose and walked to the window with his hands in his pockets. "The theory's fallen flat, Wilson. We're back at the beginning again."

He stood with his back to the room, speaking his thoughts aloud. "Bernice Lanson couldn't have been out there between half-past seven and half-past nine. She was at home, preparing breakfast, eating breakfast, answering phone calls, waiting for her brother. Mrs. Maynard couldn't have been out there; she was still under the anaesthetic. You weren't out there, Miss Moreland—were you?"

"You know my movements for that day as well as you know your own," she replied.

Knollis turned back into the room. "There's only Philip Maynard for it. His wife says he couldn't possibly have done it, but he stopped her explaining why—and that's a mystery on its own account. Why should a man stop his wife from clearing him of suspicion of murder? It doesn't make sense! It doesn't make sense, I say!"

"It does if he knows he can clear himself, and if he's *shielding someone else*," said Moreland.

"That's a possibility, I admit," said Knollis, "but shielding whom? His sister has a first-class alibi. His wife has a first-class alibi. There's only your own daughter left for him to cover!"

"It would seem so," murmured Moreland.

Determined to solve at least part of the mystery, Knollis turned his attention to Daphne Moreland again.

"You were going to spend some time at the cottage after your marriage," he said. "The kitchen cabinet was clean but empty apart from the parcel of food. What arrangements had you made for stocking the cabinet and pantry?"

"My mother's grocer was going to send up all I'd need two days before the wedding. Baking tins and so on were coming from the ironmongers. Oh, all that was fixed!"

"Among the stuff ordered from the grocer," said Knollis, "was there anything like baking powder, or cream of tartar, or pepper, or anything if it comes to that, packed in a thing like this?"

He drew the cardboard container from his pocket.

Daphne Moreland looked at it and then shook her head. "That would be no use. It wouldn't hold enough. My mother ordered a quarter of a pound of everything of that kind."

Knollis muttered something beneath his breath, and slipped the container back into his pocket.

Moreland rose as a sign that he thought the interview should finish. "It seems you're in a tough spot, gentlemen. I'm sorry about it, but I'm afraid we can do no more for you. My daughter's been perfectly frank, and I think she's ready for a rest."

He escorted them to the car and closed the door very firmly after Knollis had got inside. "I'm on the side of the law, naturally," he said, with a wry smile, "but you'll perhaps forgive me if I say I hope the case goes into the unsolved file. Whoever murdered Jerry Batley did the world a good turn. 'Bye!"

Wilson threaded the car through Clevely's traffic to the police station again, drew up at the kerb, and walked to his office with Knollis at his heels. There he flung his hat on the book-case of volumes on criminal law and criminal procedure, and flopped into his chair, drawing the bulky dossier of the Batley case towards him.

"Knollis," he said, with a twisted smile, "you can do what the devil you like, but I'm going through and through and through this evidence until I find what I want. This time I have an idea!"

"Good luck to it," said Knollis, "and I mean that. Before you settle down . . ."

"Yes?"

"Who was with you when you went out to Newbourne to take the body off Old Heatherington's hands?"

"Why—see, it was Sergeant Coxon."

"He took notes."

"Coxon would take the lot, commas and everything; he always does!"

"Is the transcript of the report you have there a verbatim one?"

Wilson bridled. "Lord, no! The old man rambled on and rambled on, all about bees and Shakespeare, and heaven knows what. I was fed up to the back teeth with him, but had to let him tell the story his own way or I'd never have got the vital bits."

"Old people are like that," said Knollis. He bent over the desk, pressed a switch, and spoke into the speaker of the inter-office communication telephone. "Please ask Sergeant Coxon to come in—and send me a copy of *Henry the Fifth*. Yes, *Henry the Fifth*, by William Shakespeare. That's right!"

Coxon arrived first.

"You were with Inspector Wilson when he went to the cottage at Newbourne to find Batley, Sergeant. The Inspector tells me you take the fullest possible notes, and then sort out the relevant from the irrelevant. That correct?"

"Correct, sir."

"You have notes—the original ones you took?"

"Here, sir," said Coxon, producing a bulky notebook. "They're in shorthand—I think you'll be able to read them."

"You can stick around in case I can't," said Knollis. "Help yourself to a chair. This is going to be a long session! Can you rustle up a pot of tea?"

Coxon could, and did, and then made himself comfortable in a corner. Knollis settled down with the report of the first interview with Mr. Samuel Heatherington, retired carpenter and wheelwright, resident at Number Eighteen, High Street, in the village of Newbourne.

After a time he remarked: "A garrulous old man!"

"Yes, sir," Coxon said, dutifully.

Wilson said nothing. It was doubtful if he'd heard the remark.

A little later the copy of *Henry the Fifth* was brought in. Knollis laid aside Coxon's note-book and turned to Act One, Scene Two of the play. He read the whole scene and then laid the book on his knees and stared up at the ceiling.

"So that was it!" he mumbled to himself.

Coxon raised his eyebrows. Wilson took no notice.

"You know, Wilson," said Knollis, "you were too impatient, old man!"

"Hm?" murmured Wilson, absently.

"I said you were too impatient with the old man. You should have let him recite his favourite passage from Shakespeare, the passage in Canterbury's speech which deals with the old boy's beloved bees. Listen to this:

> *For so work the honey-bees;*
> *Creatures that, by a rule in nature, teach*
> *The act of order to a peopled kingdom.*
> *They have a king, and officers of sorts:*
> *Where some, like magistrates, correct at home;*
> *Others, like merchants, venture trade abroad;*
> *Others, like soldiers, armed in their stings,*
> *Make boot upon the summer's velvet buds;*
> *Which pillage they with merry march bring home*
> *To the tent-royal of their emperor:*
> *Who, busied in his majesty, surveys*
> *The singing masons building roofs of gold;*
> *The civil citizens kneading up the honey;*
> *The poor mechanic porters crowding in*
> *Their heavy burdens at his narrow gate;*
> *The sad-ey'd justice, with his surly hum*

Delivering o'er to executors pale
The lazy yawning drone."

There was silence in the room for some seconds after Knollis's softly modulated voice had died away. Outside, beneath the window, the traffic passed and re-passed; a motor-horn sounded, a dog yelped and sped away from its four-wheeled and unnatural enemies, an ambulance cleared a path for itself with much clanging of its brassy bell, but in the room all was silence. Knollis stared at the printed page. Wilson stared down at the documents on his desk. Coxon stared at Knollis.

"The sad-ey'd justice, Wilson, delivering o'er to executors pale the lazy yawning drone!"

"That fits," said Wilson, stirring from his reverie.

"The only person we haven't suspected, and the one person with a fully adequate motive! He admits he'd rumbled Batley's plan to bump off Maynard and Daphne Moreland. What more do we want? All we have to do is prove that he was neither at his home nor his office between half-seven and half-nine!"

Knollis looked up and blinked. "Hm? What's this?"

"Moreland, of course! Frank Moreland! He bumped off Batley, and he's all but got away with it for one simple, so simple, reason! He knows the law, he knows how we work, he knows how our minds work—and consequently he's been able to keep in front of us all the time, priming Daphne with the wrong answers, and—oh, the thing sticks out a mile!"

Knollis passed no comment. He closed the copy of the play and laid it on the desk. He put Coxon's notebook in his pocket. He nodded to Wilson and Coxon and walked out of the office, closing the door behind him.

Chapter XV
OLD HEATHERINGTON TELLS THE BEES

On leaving divisional headquarters, Knollis went to his hotel, refused lunch, ordered a pot of coffee, and retired to his room with his own note-book and Coxon's. From his suit-case he took a large writing pad, and settled down at the small table under the window. He read carefully and diligently through his own notes, scribbling a comment from time to time on the pad. He next turned to Coxon's verbatim report of the first official meeting with Old Heatherington, and again wrote down his opinions as he went along.

An hour and a half passed in the silent room, and then he was disturbed by a gentle tap on the door. "Come in," he called, absently, and glanced over his shoulder to see Wilson standing in the doorway with a sheet of paper in his hand.

"I've got the result of the check on the call-box at Newbourne," Wilson said, solemnly.

"Yes, I know," Knollis nodded gravely.

"What are you talking about?" demanded Wilson. "You can't know!"

"It was Old Heatherington," said Knollis. He smiled with his lips, but his eyes remained grave.

Wilson stared at him. "Yes, that's right! He was the only person to use the box before eleven o'clock. The old girl at the post office heard the door of the box slam—there's something wrong with the check device, and got out of bed to see what was what. It was the old boy."

He then paused. "How the deuce did you arrive at that conclusion without having the report?"

"I haven't much use for writers of detective fiction as a rule," said Knollis, "but I happen to have a deal of respect for the father of them all—Edgar Allen Poe and his Dupin. He laid down the axiom that when the impossible has been removed from a problem, whatever remains, however improbable, must be the solution. Nobody else but Old Heatherington could have used the box—nobody concerned with the case, I mean."

"Ye—es," Wilson said, uncertainly.

Knollis gathered his notes together and swept them into his pocket. "Let's go and see Philip Maynard, shall we? The case is completed."

Wilson looked at him, shook his head, and then looked in the coffee pot. "You haven't touched your coffee, and it's stone cold now. Eh! Haven't you had lunch, either?"

"I didn't feel like it," said Knollis. "Let's go, Wilson. The sooner this job is over the better I'll like it."

Wilson walked from the room without asking any questions. By now he knew that Knollis would demonstrate rather than explain, and he was content to let him go his own way. He did voice one grumble as he switched on the engine and set the car in motion. "I still think I've a good case against Moreland!"

"I wouldn't contradict you," said Knollis.

Arriving at Mansard House, Knollis stepped from the car and strode to the open front door of the house to press the bell-push.

Georgie Maynard came from the kitchen, and stood in the doorway with one hand pressed to her heart. Knollis was standing like a statue, his jaw tight, his eyes near-hidden. "Your husband, Mrs. Maynard."

"He's—he's down the garden."

"Can you fetch him—please? It's important."

She turned away, leaving Knollis and Wilson on the step. When she returned, she was holding her husband's hand, exactly as she had done when Knollis first called at the house. Maynard took one look at Knollis's tense face, and his mouth tightened. For a brief second he swayed, and then appeared to have control of himself. "You'll come inside, won't you?" he asked, unsmilingly.

Knollis and Wilson followed the Maynards to the garden-room. Georgie Maynard, overpowered by the strained atmosphere, neglected to ask them to be seated, and the four people stood in a circle in the middle of the room.

Knollis took his scribbled notes from his pocket and consulted them. "Mr. Maynard," he said, "on returning from the nursing home at half-past seven on the morning of the seventh of June, you got out your car and went into Newbourne village, calling at Mr. Heatherington's cottage. You were there but a few minutes, and then left the car standing outside the gate, and walked a few yards up the road to the stile that leads to the footpath over the fields to the gate leading into Windward Lane a short distance beyond Mrs. Doughty's cottage. You did not go as far as the gate, but—"

"Then you know," interrupted Maynard. He threw the lank brown hair back from his forehead with his free hand. He looked at his wife. "It's all up, Georgie!"

She moved nearer to him, until her shoulder was pressing into his arm.

"One thing I don't know," said Knollis. "It's a trivial point, and insignificant, but why did you take the hive back to Jason's Knoll?"

"I suddenly realized that it came from a diseased apiary, and that even an odd investigating bee from Old Heatherington's apiary might carry back the infection. That's all there was to it. It was afterwards I thought up the idea of hiding the key and the canister in it. It seemed a safe way of disposing of them. I knew you suspected me, and thought that if you got a search warrant you might find them in the house."

"One other point," said Knollis. "Did you inform anybody—anybody at all—of your wife's collapse before you came back from the nursing home?"

"No!" said Maynard. "Only my sister."

"On your return from your raid on Batley's flat, did Mr. Heatherington come into the house with you?"

"No, Inspector. I drove him straight to his home, turned round in the street, and drove back home."

"So that the first person to know of her collapse was—"

"My sister, when I phoned her from the nursing home."

"Thank you," said Knollis. "We'll be back later. Please don't leave the house."

He strode from the house to the car with Wilson beside him. "Newbourne, Wilson, please."

"Old Heatherington's?"

"Yes," said Knollis.

The old man was resting on the couch when they arrived, and called to them to let themselves in.

"I'm not feeling too good," he said, as they entered his living-room. "I've been worried to death about Philip and Georgie, and I haven't been sleeping well, and one way or another I seem to have put a few years on my own back. Any news yet?"

"Plenty," said Knollis. He pulled up a chair so that he was facing the old man. Wilson propped himself against the mantelpiece.

"I've been wondering about bees," said Knollis. "Philip Maynard admits that he brought the hive from Jason's Knoll and stood it over the well. . . ."

"Yes, he told me," said Old Heatherington.

"Where would your bees have parked themselves if that hive had not been there?" asked Knollis.

"Probably in the woods, in a hollow tree, or some such place. On the other hand, if the hive hadn't been there, with its smell of bees, and wax, and honey, they might well have stayed up the tree in my garden long enough for me to collect and hive 'em!"

"Why didn't they go into an empty hive in your own apiary, Mr. Heatherington?"

The old man smiled. "It's one of those things that aren't done, Inspector, like potting your opponent's white in billiards. You never leave an empty hive with the entrance open; it might attract a swarm from somebody else's hive."

"So that if Maynard hadn't left the hive entrance open your bees wouldn't have gone to it, you wouldn't have followed them, and Batley might be lying down the well to this day!"

"That's it, Inspector," nodded the old man. "I told Inspector Wilson that morning there was a fate in it. I tried to tell him what Shakespeare said about bees—"

"And the lazy yawning drone," interrupted Knollis.

"Aye," said the old man, "in another few weeks when there's no more need for the drones in the hive you'll find the workers turning them out to starve to death or die of the night cold."

"Like Batley!"

"Like Batley, sir!"

"On that same morning, Mr. Heatherington, you used the telephone call-box outside the post office?"

The old man looked deep into his eyes. "Yes, I rang Philip's sister to tell her about Georgie's trouble."

"That checks," said Wilson, with an authoritative nod. "Sometime after half-past seven it was."

"That's right, Inspector."

Knollis gave Wilson a flashing glance that might have meant anything, and turned back to the old man.

"You'll have guessed from that how we've traced Philip Maynard's movements on that morning? He drove out here to give you the news, and then took a walk over the fields to Mrs. Doughty's cottage. He entered the garden through a thin part of the hedge. Later in the morning he returned with his sister, found—we'll say—Batley's body in the well, and after taking his sister out of the way he set to work to disguise the fact that Batley was in the well. He walked the two flagstones across the garden and placed them over the mouth of the well. Later in the day he used Batley's car to fetch the hive from Jason's Knoll. What we don't know is how he got the car back to the garage at Clevely! Now there's a mysterious point!"

Old Heatherington reared up on the couch. "You—you aren't going to arrest Philip, are you?"

"That depends," Knollis said, smoothly.

"On—what?"

"Whether you have any evidence that can clear him."

"But you can't arrest him, Inspector! He's got a wife!"

"Batley nearly had one," said Knollis, "but nobody considered him. One person is as good as another in the eyes of the law. Anyway," he said, with an airy gesture, "you've helped me a great deal with this case, and you were quite right when you originally told Inspector Wilson that we'd have to come to see you again."

The old man fumbled for his pipe. "I'm pleased if I have helped you, but sorry if I've done anything to hurt Philip!"

Knollis watched him silently until he had charged his pipe, and then said: "You helped me when you gave your opinion that nothing but a woman could have got Batley out to the cottage at that hour of the morning. You helped me again when you showed me how to use cyanide for killing off no-good bees— and drones! You helped me still further when you opened that corner cupboard and showed me the cylinder of calcium cyanide. You helped me when you said you could drive a car. You helped me when Inspector Wilson offered to have a man run you home in the car from the cottage, and you said there was a track through the wood and over the fields. You helped me when you left a dark-coloured bee behind in Batley's flat—"

He leaned forward, and added: "Tell me, Mr. Heatherington, had Georgie written letters to Batley in the past? Is that what you were looking for? Or were you looking for the photograph which you didn't find?"

The old man grimaced. "You're a clever man, Inspector. Georgie once told me she'd written some pretty passionate letters to him when she went out with him in the early days of the war. I found them, and burned them in my own grate."

"And now tell me how you killed Gerald Batley!"

Wilson jerked into life. "You mean—!"

"I mean that our good old friend here may be a nice man and a good bee-keeper, but he most certainly murdered Gerald Batley!"

He paused to listen as a car pulled up outside.

"That's the Maynards, Wilson. You might as well fetch them in."

They filed in before Wilson when he returned and stood hand in hand, looking and waiting. Knollis ignored them.

"You see, Mr. Heatherington, you couldn't have known about Mrs. Maynard's illness when you made that phone call. It was impossible. Your call was to Gerald Batley. Shall I tell you what happened?"

The old man sat silent, staring into the bowl of his pipe.

"All the way through it was the bee trouble that actuated you. First the brood disease, and secondly the burning-down of the honey-house and equipment at Wellow Lock. Oh, yes, you love human beings, and think a great deal of these young people, but you have lived your life with bees, and have the mind of a bee. Batley to you was a lazy yawning drone, of no use to anybody, and so you decided to eliminate him. You rang him and told him that Mrs. Maynard had left her husband and had gone to his cottage in Windward Lane. You told him you were sorry for her and thought he might be able to help—that, or some such story. Then you walked across the fields, and waited for him in the garden. You felled him . . ."

Knollis paused, and waited, looking from Old Heatherington to Maynard and his wife.

Old Heatherington sighed. "A horrible mistake's been made, Inspector. I think we'd better tell you the truth—don't you, Philip?"

Philip Maynard nodded. "The mistake was mine—I thought he was dead."

"You see," said Old Heatherington. "I knocked him down and began to go through his pockets. I'd only found the key and the cylinder when I heard somebody moving about in the wood, so I ducked through the hedge into the field. I saw Philip force a way through the opposite hedge . . ."

"I'd followed Mr. Heatherington," said Maynard, taking up the tale. "I lost him in the wood, and it must have been while I was crawling through the undergrowth to the fence that he heard me. The first thing I saw was Batley lying beside the mouth of the well. I thought he was dead, and that my friend had killed him, so I pushed him down the well and got away as quickly as I could."

"So you didn't find the key and the cylinder by his side as you said?" Knollis accused him.

"Not then," said Maynard.

"And you?" asked Knollis, turning to the old man.

"When Philip left I went back to the well," he said. "Batley wasn't dead when Phil pushed him down. I'd intended strangling him after I'd searched him, and then I should have pushed him down the well. He was a bad lot, but I didn't want him to recover consciousness and die slowly of starvation, so I hunted round for some means of either getting down the well to him, or for something to drop on his head. I went into the outhouse among other places, and found something that told me a story. There was a heap—"

"Of permanganate of potash crystals on the copper," interrupted Knollis.

"That's right, sir, and it was then I examined the cylinder, and it was filled with the crystals—"

"Which are now in the medicine bottle in your corner cupboard," Knollis interrupted again.

"Yes, sir. There was also a trace of white powder on the copper, and that was calcium cyanide. So I started to put two and two together . . ."

"Reaching what conclusion, Mr. Heatherington?"

"That Batley was planning some further dirty work, otherwise why should he put permanganate crystals in a cyanide container, and what had he done with the cyanide? I went back to the well, and realized that the other container was in his pocket, and that it could only be a matter of minutes at the most before he'd be poisoned, because I use permanganate in the garden and I buy it in a little cardboard tube. . . ."

"So you went home, Mr. Heatherington, and didn't return until next day, when the flagstones and hive had been placed over the mouth of the well! That was when Mr. Maynard found the keys. Now, Mr. Maynard, you can tell the rest of the story— or shall I tell you? Your sister told you of Batley's attempt to force her into borrowing from you, and you had no other course open to you than to pretend to be righteously indignant—and so, of course, you also had to pretend to race out with your sister to Newbourne to tax him with his rottenness. It was then you got the shock of your life. Candidly, I don't think there was anyone moving about in the wood that morning. I think you convinced your sister that there was, and her imagination did the rest, giving you the opportunity of looking down the well to make sure that Batley was still there. That was where you got the shock, because you saw that Batley had changed position, and that radically, since you pushed him down. You realized then that he was not dead when you pushed him down. Your immediate impulse was to get rid of your sister, and that done you returned to the cottage, put the stones over the mouth of the well, and thought up the scheme with the hive."

He looked at Maynard. "Any objections?"

Maynard did not answer.

"You moved the hive the next afternoon—that afternoon, I should say, and came back the next day to make sure that all was in order. That was when you clashed with Mr. Heatherington again, and found the key and the cylinder. Mr. Heatherington, having done what he wanted with the key, now wanted to dispose of it, and his shock must have come when he found two heavy stones and the hive over the well!"

"Yes," sighed the old man. "I was trying to lever one of the stones up so's I could drop the things down the well. Then I heard Phil's car draw up, and I panicked. I dropped them and hurried through the hedge. From there I saw Phil pick them up and put them in his pocket. He had a good look round, and went away again. There was nothing more I could do, so I went home and tried to forget the whole thing. It was sheer fate that brought the affair to light. If Phil hadn't brought the hive and left the entrances open the bees wouldn't have swarmed in it. I couldn't face having the bees back after they'd settled over Batley's body, so I sent for Phil. I wasn't allowing for Georgie coming, as I'd intended to have a quiet talk with Phil about what we'd both done, and agree on a story we could both stick to if Batley was ever found. But Georgie turned up, as she always does, and, woman-like, she couldn't keep her nose out. She wanted to see if there really was a well under the hive, and she wouldn't be said no, so Phil and me looked at each other, knew each other's thoughts, and decided to find the body. I reckon that's the end of the story."

"That is the end of the story," said Knollis.

"There's one thing," said Old Heatherington with a smile. "I'm giving the bees to Philip, and an old superstition says I must say good-bye to them and tell them they've a new master. You'll allow that, sir?"

"I'll allow that," said Knollis, softly. "I'm going to hate taking you away, Mr. Heatherington. You're nearer to nature and the things that matter than anybody I've known."

"Aye, perhaps so," said the old man, "but the laws of nature aren't the laws of man. Nature always wins, of course, in the long run. Ah, well, let's get down the garden!"

It was a solemn procession. Old Heatherington leading the way in his once-white linen jacket. Knollis next, his face an expressionless mask. Then Philip and Georgie Maynard holding each other's hands so tightly that their knuckles showed white. Wilson brought up the rear, watching for any attempt to escape on the part of either Old Heatherington or Philip Maynard—for Maynard was now to be regarded as an accessory after the fact.

Arriving at the first row of hives the old man turned with an apologetic smile. "This'll sound silly to you, sir," he said to Knollis, "but I'll feel more comfortable in my mind if it's done."

He tapped on the wall of the first hive, and announced in a loud voice: "You have a new master. Work well for him as you have for me!"

Then on to the second hive, the third, the fourth, the fifth, and the sixth, while four white-faced people watched him solemnly. He returned to the first hive, moved to the beginning of the second row, and moved along that in the same way. Having handed over the twelve hives to Philip Maynard in the manner dictated by an age-old superstition he stood looking at Knollis.

"That's that," he said. He felt in his pocket. "I keep two pipes, you know, Inspector! One to smoke when watching my bees—Phil's bees, and one for last thing at night, or just last thing!"

"What do you mean?" asked Knollis, suddenly alert and alarmed.

The old man knocked his pipe out into his palm. "As you give, so you should receive," he said. "Goodbye, all!"

With a sudden movement he tossed the contents of his palm into his mouth, and three seconds later was writhing on the floor.

Knollis and Wilson began to move forward, and then paused as they realized they would have to run the gauntlet of the hives. Philip Maynard had no such qualms. Loosing his wife's hand he dashed between the rows of hives to his old friend. Old Heatherington was lying with arched back, his long arms thrashing like flails. Maynard tried to kneel beside him and put his arm under his head, but with one wild sweep the dying man knocked him aside. Maynard tried to recover his balance, but fell over the old man's body, lurched forward, and fell head first against the twelfth hive with a resounding crash.

"Phil!" shouted Georgie.

She started forward, but Wilson grabbed her arm and dragged her back, struggling furiously, along the garden path to the house. He forced her inside and quickly changed the key from inside to outside, locking the door on her. Then, his lip tight between his teeth, he ran back to the apiary. Knollis was on his hands and knees, crawling between the hives, trying to keep below the line of the flight as the bees from the first five hives flew in and out, undisturbed by the raving madness of their sisters at the end of the row.

"What can I do?" bawled Wilson. "In God's name what can I do?"

"Get veils from the honey-house, and the bottle of anaesthetic from the house!" shouted Knollis.

He reached Maynard, grabbed at his foot, and began to drag him backwards between the hives. Maynard had both hands clapped tight over his face and was moaning. Knollis gritted his teeth as the assault was turned on himself and the bees in dozens attacked his hands, his neck, and his face. At last he got Maynard back to the main path. He got to his feet, heaved Maynard over his shoulder, and ran towards the house. Georgie Maynard came running round the house from the front door, flourishing the green bottle of methylated ether.

"Give me those veils!" she demanded, as Wilson returned from the honey-house.

She snatched them from him, pulled one over her head and ran down the garden to the twelfth hive, opening the bottle and spilling its contents across the alighting-board.

Knollis and Wilson were in the house when she got back. Maynard was stretched across the hearth, still holding his face in his hands and moaning. Knollis was bending over him, while Wilson was bending over Knollis in turn, busily picking the dozens of stings and dying bees from his flesh.

"They're damned hot," said Knollis, "but leave me alone for now. We must get Maynard to hospital."

Georgie Maynard pushed them both aside and knelt beside her husband. She literally tore his hands from his face, and then screeched and tumbled across his body in a dead faint.

* * *

Wilson was the only good man of the party that night. The stings he had received had caused him no trouble beyond an intense surface itch for the first half-hour. Knollis was not so lucky, and Wilson was worried about him, for two hours after they got back to Clevely he had collapsed, and was now in the Clevely and District Hospital, feeling distinctly groggy.

Wilson walked to his bed at the far end of the ward and shook his head sadly as he looked at him. "If your name wasn't on the chart I wouldn't know it was you, old man," he said. "You look like a grotesque balloon. How you feeling?"

"Better, but still deadly," Knollis muttered, through swollen lips. "You still mug enough to start keeping bees?"

"Normanton says I'm apparently immune, so the answer's yes. I think they've got something!"

"So do I!" said Knollis. "Maynard? How is he?"

Wilson was about to answer when he saw Georgie Maynard being ushered into the ward by a nurse. "Mrs. Maynard's here now, Knollis. By the expression on her face, things ain't too good. Oh, Lord!"

Georgie Maynard walked slowly to the foot of the bed and stared solemnly into his unrecognizable features. "I want to thank you for what you did for Phil, Inspector. It was too late, of course, but you weren't to know that. It was very brave of you."

"How is he, Mrs. Maynard?"

Wilson, watching her closely, noticed the quavering lip and her effort to brace herself. He slid a long arm and a great comforting paw across her shoulders.

"He—he tried to help a friend, Inspector," she said, slowly.

"Yes, Mrs. Maynard," said Knollis. "All things must be judged by the motive—they are in heaven, if not on earth."

"I'll—I'll have to work the bees myself from now on," she said, quickly, and then caught her lip between her teeth.

Knollis reared up in bed, staring with incredulous eyes through the swollen mess of his face. "Not that!"

It was then she collapsed in Wilson's arms, all the strength gone from her body. "Phil's blind! Oh, God, he's blind! He's blind!"

Wilson caught her and laid her across the foot of Knollis's bed as a nurse came swiftly and lightly down the long ward.

"Can't we do *something*, Knollis?"

Knollis looked at him, and looked through him, with eyes that searched the whole of infinity and eternity for an answer.

"Can't you think of *something*, Knollis!"

Knollis answered grimly: "Wilson, I'm not God!"

THE END

Lightning Source UK Ltd.
Milton Keynes UK
UKHW021843120921
390455UK00007B/899